WILLIAM FOLLETT

World War Dragons

Contents

Acknowledgments   v

Introduction   1

I   Part One

Chapter 1   5

Chapter 2   15

Chapter 3   20

Chapter 4   26

Chapter 5   29

Chapter 6   33

Chapter 7   42

Chapter 8   48

Chapter 9   54

Chapter 10   62

Chapter 11   67

Chapter 12   71

Chapter 13   78

Chapter 14   100

Chapter 15   106

Chapter 16   112

Chapter 17   115

Chapter 18   121

Chapter 19   126

Chapter 20	129
Chapter 21	136
Chapter 22	142
Chapter 23	146
Chapter 24	152
Chapter 25	164
Chapter 26	184
Chapter 27	187
Chapter 28	192
Chapter 29	198
Chapter 30	202
Chapter 31	208
Chapter 32	215
Chapter 33	219
Chapter 34	223
Chapter 35	232
Chapter 36	242
Chapter 37	258
Chapter 38	262
Chapter 39	267
Epilogue	275
Lost City of Man Preview	278
Preview Chapter 1	279
Preview Chapter 2	285
Preview Chapter 3	296
About the Author	314

Acknowledgments

To my parents, who never once rolled their eyes at my strangest imaginings, but instead cheered them on. Your unwavering support and limitless patience turned my wild ideas into something I could share with the world. Thank you for believing in my creative nonsense, for nurturing it, and for loving me all the more for it. This is for you.

Introduction

July 1944. A month has passed since the world watched with bated breath as Allied soldiers stormed the beaches of Normandy, securing a vital foothold on mainland Europe and forever changing the course of World War II. The French coastline remains scarred from the D-Day invasion of June 6th, in which thousands of soldiers, ships, and aircraft converged in a massive assault against Nazi-occupied France. Now, a month later, buoyed by their initial success, Allied forces advance deeper into French territory. Every town liberated and every inch of soil claimed brings them closer to the heart of Germany, the stronghold of the Nazi regime led by Adolf Hitler. However, German resistance remains fierce. Desperate battles rage across the countryside, each side striving to vanquish their enemies. Though the tide has turned in favor of the Allies, victory is far from certain. It is within this crucible of conflict that this story unfolds.

I

Part One

Chapter 1

Sunlight struggled through the dense canopy of leaves that shrouded an ancient castle, casting an unsettling mosaic of light and shadow over the overgrown grounds. The castle, with its weathered stones and crumbling towers, seemed almost a part of the landscape, as if it had grown from the very earth itself.

The site on which it stood was far older and more enigmatic than the castle. Ancient rites and forgotten magic clung to the soil, and the forest floor was strewn with remnants of a time before recorded history. Stone markers, half-buried and carved with cryptic runes, hinted at long-lost rituals.

Nestled deep within the heart of Germany, the once-grand structure bore the scars of neglect. Yet recent signs of activity—churned earth near the crumbling gatehouse, power lines, and fresh tire tracks—hinted at a functional transformation.

A sleek black Mercedes-Benz 770 stood parked in the clearing before the ruined entrance, its polished chrome accents gleaming under the dappled sunlight—an automobile favored by German officers to project authority and dominance.

Two figures emerged from the car. One was a tall, imposing

man with a shaved head and a face etched with arrogance. A recent cut marred his lip and chin, starkly visible now that his cap was removed. He wore the unmistakable black uniform of an SS-Obergruppenführer, his name tag glinting coldly in the filtered light: Rupel. His uniform was crisp and immaculate, every detail perfect and precise, projecting an air of relentless authority. For Rupel, this meticulously maintained appearance was not a facade; it was a mantle of control.

The other was a young soldier whose youthful face contrasted sharply with Rupel's. He followed his superior attentively, posture rigid, eyes fixed forward—a picture of disciplined obedience. His uniform was equally pristine, every button and crease in place, reflecting the standard demanded of him.

The young soldier stiffened as his gaze swept the castle's looming, shadowed entrance. He swallowed hard, eyes shifting before he forced them still. Rupel observed the reaction with faint satisfaction. There it was—the subtle crack in resolve.

"Remember," Rupel said, his voice a menacing whisper. "The man we're meeting, this… scientist—he is as disturbing as you've heard. Keep your wits about you."

The young man swallowed again, his mouth dry as he nodded, the weight of his superior's words settling in his stomach like a cold stone. Rupel's gaze lingered on him, his next words carrying a sharp edge of warning.

Rupel's eyes bore into him. "Remain sharp. We must keep control at all times," he said, each word precise, like the cut of a blade. "So then, I ask you, soldier—do us both a favor. Do not let him see your fear."

Rupel turned sharply on his heel, his boots crunching against the gravel as he strode purposefully toward the castle.

Behind him, the young soldier followed, his jaw clenched, forcing himself to match Rupel's pace, determined not to show any sign of hesitation. But as they approached the arched doorway, his heart pounded harder, and he silently prayed that he would be able to mask the chill crawling up his spine.

Rupel's presence at the castle signaled the gravity of the situation; the Reich had grown impatient with the delays and failures reported from the hidden laboratory within. As he approached the meeting, Rupel dismissed the nagging doubt about whether his authority would hold sway over the man in charge. The eccentric scientist often displayed a blatant disregard for authority.

But Rupel had no intention of ceding control. Straightening his uniform and steeling his resolve, this meeting would proceed on his terms.

The interior of the castle offered a chilling contrast to the lushness outside. Dust motes danced in the faint light filtering through narrow slits in the walls. The air hung heavy with the smell of damp stone and decay, and cobwebs draped the corners like spectral tapestries. The pair moved with purpose, their synchronized steps creating a rhythm that Rupel found oddly reassuring in the disordered environment.

A gaunt lab technician appeared and silently led the two men further into a dimly lit interior. The technician's clothes hung loosely on his willowy frame, frayed at the edges and stained with indeterminate substances. His hair, a greasy tangle of unkempt strands, clung to his scalp in uneven patches. A faint sweet odor mingled with sweat emanated from him. His lips were curved into a perpetual smile, yet his eyes betrayed a cold menace, akin to a predator eyeing its prey.

He moved with a peculiar gait, each step deliberate and measured, as if he were barely conscious of the floor beneath him. His bony fingers twitched occasionally, hinting at a nervous energy barely contained beneath his composed exterior.

Rupel cast a sidelong glance at the technician, suppressing a shudder at the unsettling grin that stretched his lips past his gums.

The soldier following shifted uncomfortably as well, his hand subtly tightening around his rifle.

They followed the technician deeper into the bowels of the castle, passing through corridors that seemed to absorb sound and light alike. Wires hung loosely along the stone walls, supporting electric bulbs that flickered intermittently, casting erratic shadows. The air grew colder and heavier as they descended further.

Finally, they arrived at a heavy wooden door, its surface marred with age.

As the technician pushed it open, the door emitted a deep, resonant groan that echoed through the corridor, revealing a laboratory filled with harsh shadows. Strange contraptions and arcane apparatuses filled the space, their surfaces dulled by use and time. Glass vials containing mysterious liquids bubbled and hissed, emitting faint wisps of colored smoke that twisted and danced in the air.

A massive chalkboard dominated one wall, filled with an impenetrable tangle of equations, arcane symbols, and hastily sketched diagrams.

In a corner, a machine hummed ominously, its many gears

turning with deliberate precision, while its brass dials glowed faintly. Cables connected it to a central table bearing a stone slab marked with intricate carvings that seemed to pulse faintly.

The faint scent of burning herbs mixed with ozone and machine oil permeated the air, and faint whispers seemed to emanate from weathered artifacts: an ornamented dagger, a golden amulet, and a black mirror mounted in a frame of twisted silver.

As Rupel and the soldier entered, they felt the technician's eyes bore into them. His unsettling grin widened imperceptibly as he observed them, his gaze leaving each of them with an uneasy sensation.

A short, elderly man emerged from the shadows, his face obscured in the dim light which cast grotesque shadows across his wrinkled skin.

This was Herr Krammer, an enigmatic visionary whose mind teemed with fantastical ideas and innovations which pushed the boundaries of science and engineering—beyond what could be considered natural.

Whispers of his unconventional methods and eerie experiments echoed through the corridors of Reich command, painting him as both revered and feared.

Little was known of Krammer's origins, his past veiled in shadow like the enigmatic experiments he conducted. Stories circulated that he had emerged from a dark corner of Hessen, a region of Germany steeped in old traditions, dotted with medieval towns and dense fairy tale forests.

Krammer's unnaturally short stature and large nose lent him a distinctly gnome-like appearance. Despite his age and diminutive size, the man radiated an uncanny energy—

a palpable aura that seemed to hum with the intensity of his intellect. His sharp, penetrating eyes seemed to bore into Rupel, leaving him with the unsettling impression that Krammer knew more than anyone else in the room—perhaps even more than anyone ought to know.

Rupel couldn't help but judge Krammer's height with disdain, his mind fixating on the Nazi regime's policies on eugenics. If he had the authority, Rupel would have had Krammer sterilized or worse, to cleanse the Reich of imperfections.

Yet, maddeningly, Krammer seemed untouchable.

His sudden emergence meant there was no trail of information or background that could be used against him. This lack of tangible history rendered him immune to the usual investigations and accusations that plagued others within the Reich.

Moreover, Krammer possessed a keen ability to forge alliances with those in influential positions within the Reich. His words carried an unsettling weight, his gestures calculated to disarm and impress. Even skeptics and adversaries often found themselves drawn to him, swayed by the aura of certainty and brilliance he projected. It was as though he had a sixth sense for pinpointing the vulnerabilities of those around him, exploiting their ambitions, fears, or insecurities to bend them to his will.

Krammer's ability to manipulate perceptions and control narratives within the corridors of power rendered him more than just a scientist—he was a political force unto himself. His elusive origins and deft maneuvering created an unassailable shield, insulating him from both legal and moral accountability. Instead of the revulsion his actions warranted, he garnered respect, even awe, from his peers. To them, he was an innovator whose genius transcended conventional morality—a perception Krammer skillfully cultivated and ruthlessly exploited.

Those who fell under Krammer's sway became his staunchest defenders, accomplices in his agenda. Questions about his unorthodox methods or dubious origins faded under the spell of his persuasive charm. They shielded him from scrutiny, championed his projects, and upheld his reputation as a visionary, even when the truth of his monstrous experiments, including human ones, began to circulate.

"Obergruppenführer Rupel, welcome!" Krammer's voice rasped from the shadows. "I trust you are here to tell me the traitor has been dealt with and you've returned with my missing component!"

Rupel stood rigid, his icy blue gaze sweeping across the chamber, taking in the strange contraptions and arcane apparatuses. The young soldier remained frozen at attention behind him, his eyes locked straight ahead. He resisted the temptation to let his eyes wander over the unsettling curiosities scattered around the room or to look at Krammer, fearing he might fall under a spell.

"You were supplied with a substantial amount of uranium, Herr Krammer," Rupel began, his voice dripping with disdain, still not looking at the old man. "Enough to construct for us a fission bomb. Command requests that the weapon be delivered as promised." Finally, he allowed his gaze settled on the old man.

A humorless chuckle echoed from the darkness. "Pah! One bomb?" Krammer scoffed. "It is, how do you say, a Tropfen auf den heißen Stein - a drop on the hot stone. You have many enemies, and only one bomb? Where would Germany deliver such a thing decisively, I ask?"

"And once deployed, the allies will know that the atom can be split and create their own. I promise you, if you use such a bomb against any of them, they will have no qualms about eradicating Germany ten times over with their own."

He emerged further from the shadows, his face now fully illuminated by the flickering light, revealing a twisted smile. "I gave you something better!" he declared, his voice gaining a manic edge. "Something that will make projecting German control of the battlefields child's play! That's how Germany will win the war! And when I can create more, the world!"

Rupel's face flushed with anger. "I am NOT here to discuss tactics, Herr Krammer!" he spat. "The fate of your 'projects' will be decided." With a hiss, he continued, "NOW, explain the absence of the bomb! If you won't account for it, I'm to deliver you to face the consequences!"

He stepped closer, projecting menace. "Berlin wants no more excuses. The Reich can't afford delays or failures. Your work is critical, and they demand results, not theoretical scenarios."

Krammer remained unbothered, a hint of a smirk playing on his lips. He theatrically sighed. "Very well," he began, his voice dripping with false sincerity. "The object that the traitor—" he paused for a beat, something unreadable crossing his features— "absconded with… that IS the bomb. All one needs to do is crack its shell, and a devastation beyond imagination will be unleashed."

Rupel visibly relaxed, a smug expression crossing his face. He mistook Krammer's calm demeanor for submission, convinced that his intimidation had worked. "Excellent!" he exclaimed. "I'm relieved you saw reason, Herr Krammer. It's a shame you lost control of such a potent weapon." His tone shifted back to one of smug authority. "Your 'traitor' was reported fleeing west. The Luftwaffe is mobilized to intercept him." Internally, Rupel thought, *Once it's recovered, it will be out of Krammer's control.* "As they say, 'a wounded hare cannot outrun a wolf.'"

Pausing dramatically, he added, "And, Herr Krammer, for you, this is far from over. There are those who would see you stand trial for your negligence. We shall speak again, and soon."

With that, Rupel turned and strode out of the chamber, his entourage following close behind. Krammer watched them go, a wry glint in his eyes.

Alone with his assistant now, Krammer approached a large map of Europe that hung on the stone wall, its corners curling slightly from the cool, earthy atmosphere within the castle. He traced a winding route with his gnarled finger.

"Hmm," he muttered, eyes narrowing with focus, "he will seek refuge far from Reich territory... far from my reach... seeking anyone with the power to aid him, beyond the continent with allies he believes might thwart my designs."

He turned towards his assistant, who had the same manic grin as before plastered across his face. Krammer pointed a bony finger at the English coast on the map. "Here is where he will go," he said, his voice a gravelly hiss. "I think it's time you had something fresh, my friend. Find a pilot and get across the channel. You know what you're looking for."

"Take this," Krammer said, holding up a flat granite stone. Its surface was marked by symbols, three intricate grooves and several shallow cup marks.

Krammer reached for a matching granite stone on a nearby shelf, its surface worn smooth by years of use. Before handing over the stone to his assistant, he carefully aligned it with its twin. With deliberate, ritualistic motions, he pressed the two stones together, grinding one against the other. The faint rasp of stone on stone filled the chamber, growing louder as his movements intensified.

Then, a sharp spark leapt from the contact point. A delicate wisp of blue smoke curled into the air, its ethereal glow briefly illuminating Krammer's sharp features. He paused for a moment, observing the reaction with quiet satisfaction, before extending the stone toward his assistant.

"Make contact as I showed you once you've found it," Krammer instructed as he handed over the stone.

"If you can retrieve it, find someone useful to ensure your return." Krammer's voice dropped lower, filled with malice. "But if retrieval proves impossible... if they hinder you... break the shell." With a sinister glare, he added, "Make sure you're somewhere densely populated."

Chapter 2

As the sun dipped towards the horizon, painting the sky in hues of orange and purple, a cool evening breeze swept across the windswept cliffs of Dover, England, carrying the salty tang of the sea. Two members of the Home Guard, Orville and Thomas, stood watch, their faces etched with the weariness of a day spent gazing over the seemingly endless stretch of ocean.

The Home Guard was a force of civilian volunteers, many too young, too old, or otherwise unfit for regular military service. Dismissed by some as little more than a "dad's army," its ranks were drawn from every walk of life—farmers, factory workers, shopkeepers, and retired soldiers—men united by a shared resolve to defend their country in its hour of need. Whatever others thought of them, the Home Guard served as a vital secondary line of defense against invasion and enemy air raids.

Orville, a wiry man with a prominent mustache and thin mutton chops, peered intently through his binoculars. His weathered face reflected a time when bold styles were the norm, now revealing an indifference to changing fashions. The worn brown tweed jacket draped over his frame had become a second skin, a familiar comfort in a world moving forward without him. On his head sat a slightly oversized Brody helmet, tilting at a precarious angle that made him look perpetually startled. Despite its awkward fit, Orville wore it with pride, a small badge of honor that transformed him, in his own mind, into a soldier defending his nation.

At sixty-two, he harbored a constant yearning to contribute more to the war effort. Memories of serving in a Casualty Clearing Station during the Great War never left his thoughts—the sight of blood, the cries of the wounded, etched into his memory. His age now relegated him to watch duty, a role he embraced with resignation.

Nearby, Thomas sat comfortably on a weathered stone wall, puffing casually on a cigarette. The fading glow of the sunset briefly illuminated the network of wrinkles etched around his eyes, each line a testament to a life lived through hardship and resilience. A well-maintained mustache added a touch of distinction to his rugged features, a point of pride that he believed elevated his otherwise unassuming presence. His worn flat cap, slightly askew, cast a shadow across his thick, bushy eyebrows.

He and Orville had been inseparable in their youth, their bond forged through a shared childhood of mischief and adventure. The two musketeers, they had called themselves, a title that seemed grand and heroic in their boyhood imaginations. Now, even though the years in their lives had accumulated, their camaraderie endured.

Despite the monotony of their current duty, Thomas found solace in the quiet time they spent watching the ocean together. It was a calming contrast to the chaos and horror he had endured as a machine gunner in the trenches of World War I.

In his youth, Thomas had witnessed the brutality of war firsthand—the deafening roar of gunfire, the pervasive filth, and the comrades lost in the brutality. Those memories never left him, lingering like shadows. Yet here, on the cliffs, there was a sense of peace. The steady rhythm of the waves, rolling endlessly and indifferent to human struggles, offered him a small reprieve. Their constancy provided a comforting contrast to the uncertainty of wartime.

After returning from the war, Thomas had wielded the tools of a butcher, deftly carving through meat with the precision of someone born to the trade. He had learned from his father and, upon marrying soon after his return, ran the butcher shop alongside his wife. Together, they worked tirelessly, their shared effort bringing them brief happiness in the post-war years.

However, the loss of his wife, taken too soon by illness, left him and his son with the butcher shop and the poignant memories of how much she had filled their lives. Despite their grief, Thomas and his son continued to run the shop, with his son growing up learning the trade. Eventually, Thomas passed down the family's butcher shop to his son, who now carried on the tradition amidst the challenges of wartime rationing. This continuity was reassuring to Thomas, anchoring him in the lands his family had inhabited for generations.

"Think we'll be doing this much longer?" Thomas asked, exhaling a plume of smoke.

Orville peered intently through the binoculars, "Nah," he replied, his voice carrying a hint of wistfulness. "We're pushing the Huns back proper. The war'll be over by Christmas, mark my words."

Thomas chuckled. "That's the spirit! Ye know why they

keep sending us up 'ere, though?"

Orville started to reply, but a sudden shift in his gaze caused him to cut himself short. He peered intensely through the binoculars, his brow furrowing in concentration.

"Of course," he stammered, his voice laced with a hint of confusion. "To keep us out of the…" His words trailed off as his attention was focused through the lenses. "…way…"

His eyes focused on the sky, his hands trembling slightly. He adjusted the binoculars for a clearer view.

Orville remained fixated on the sky, "Thomas!" he exclaimed, his voice frantic, his hands trembling as he clumsily pushed the binoculars at Thomas. "It's heading West!! Towards Wooten!"

Thomas took the binoculars, squinting through the lenses. He scanned the darkening sky, searching for whatever had startled Orville.

"Do ye see it?" Orville urged, his voice rising.

"Whatever it was, I don't see it, mate." Thomas grunted, still searching.

Orville went to his bicycle leaning against the wall. "We need to get after it!" he cried.

"Hold on, Orville!" Thomas protested, lowering the binoculars. "After what? Ye haven't told me what you saw!"

Orville ignored him, pushing the bicycle towards Thomas. "Collect yer coat! We have to hurry!"

"Hurry where?" Thomas said, exasperation creeping into his voice. "We can't abandon our post, and anyway, how do you propose to catch something flying while on a bicycle! Tell me, what did ye see?"

Orville stopped, his face pale and drawn. He looked at Thomas, his eyes wide with a combination of fear and desperation.

"Ye'll think I'm daft," he said in a thin, shaky voice barely audible over the distant crashing waves. "I swear to ye, it was a..."

Chapter 3

Morning broke gently over the farm, its first light casting long shadows across the yard as Sarah emerged from the cottage, sleep clinging to her eyelids. The sky above hinted at a day of unbroken sunshine.

Sarah, a slender 12-year-old with curly chestnut hair that fell in waves around her shoulders, rubbed her eyes wearily. She wore a faded floral dress and a sweater with stitched elbows, typical for a chilly morning.

In the drive, her mother readied to leave on her bicycle, a basket sitting on the handlebars with her lunch. Her mother, in her late thirties and still a bombshell, wore her few crooked teeth and sharp English nose as part of her character. She was determined to support the war effort and sustain the farm, so she had taken a job at a nearby factory, and though the work was tiring and the hours long, it was a sacrifice she made willingly.

"Morning, sleepyhead," her mother greeted warmly. "Running terribly late, dear. You can see to your breakfast and the chickens, can't you?"

Sarah mumbled a sleepy affirmation, her mind drifting to the empty chair at the kitchen table, the place where her father used to sit. A wave of sadness passed over her face, the kind that appeared in quiet moments when she thought no one noticed.

She shuffled over to her mother, her gaze drawn to the basket teetering precariously on the handlebars.

"Oh, darling," her mother said, pausing to smooth Sarah's hair. "Look at that face!"

"It's nothing, Mum," Sarah mumbled, trying to stifle a yawn.

Her mother's face softened with a touch of sadness. "I know, sweetheart. I wish your father was here as well."

Like many, Sarah's father was conscripted early in the war, leaving the farm and his family behind to serve his country. His absence was a gaping hole in their lives, filled only partially by letters that arrived sporadically, often weeks late. They both missed him terribly, a constant ache in their hearts that never quite went away.

With a quick embrace and a whispered "Love you, see you this evening," her mother pushed off and pedaled away, the crunch of gravel fading into the distance as she rode off.

Sarah lingered in the drive, watching her mother disappear down the lane, the silence pressing in as the bicycle vanished from sight. She wrapped her arms around herself and sighed, turning back toward the house.

At twelve years old, the isolation of farm life weighed heavily on her. Tending the farm without her father had been hard for them. The days stretched into an endless cycle of chores and responsibilities, a relentless grind that Sarah found tedious. She and her mother did their best, but every task seemed all the more difficult without her father's steady presence and strong hands. They made do, scraping by as best they could, but the farm was emptier, lonelier, without him.

School had been a lifeline during the term, a chance to hear voices other than her own and find small moments of comfort in the familiar hum of lessons and chatter. But now, with school on summer break, those fleeting connections were gone, leaving her days even quieter and lonelier. Even when school was in session, Sarah had felt isolated from the other children. They rode their pushbikes through the village square and gathered at each other's homes, always together, their laughter and easy camaraderie a constant reminder of the distance between them and her.

Truth be told, Sarah wasn't sure she could be friends with them even if she tried. It wasn't simply shyness—it was the constant fear of saying the wrong thing, of being laughed at, of standing out in ways she couldn't control. The confidence to step into their world felt like something other children were born with, while she stood outside it, watching.

So Sarah stayed on the sidelines, watching but never joining, feeling out of place—like she was standing on the edge of something she couldn't quite reach. By the time the school day ended, the others scattered off together, their voices fading into the distance. And as always, Sarah trudged home alone down the dirt lane, her footsteps the only sound in the stillness of the countryside.

She loved her mother and knew how much she was needed here. The war had taken her father, and the farm relied on the two of them to keep it running. But sometimes, in the quiet hours, Sarah felt invisible. She was part of the farm, part of the fields, which she loved—but not part of the world where the other children lived, where friendship and fun and adventure weren't a distant dream.

She glanced toward the road, half-hoping to see someone— anyone—coming up the lane. Visits from neighbors were rare, and friends even rarer, especially with the war. Most of the time, it was just her, her mother, and the chickens. Not exactly the company she dreamed of. She wished for something to happen—something big and exciting to shake up the farm's never-changing rhythm.

Sarah sighed and pushed the loneliness aside. She had chores. The weight of responsibility rested firmly on her young shoulders. Yawning again, she grabbed the basket for the eggs from the stoop, the practiced routine offering some comfort in the dawning day. As Sarah moved about the yard, her footsteps echoed against the quiet backdrop of the farm buildings.

The chickens greeted her with their usual flurry of clucks and flapping wings. It was a sound she'd heard a thousand times, but today, it felt louder, sharper, as if trying to make up for the silence everywhere else.

Sarah worked quickly, her small hands scooping up warm eggs and settling them into the basket. The routine was familiar, so her mind wandered as it often did. Beyond the coop lay the fields, stretching endlessly under the pale morning sun. Sometimes, she thought of them as a prison, hemming her in with chores and rules. Other times, she imagined them as the edge of an unexplored map, the start of an adventure waiting for her to find it.

Basket in hand, Sarah made her way back toward the house, her steps slow as the morning sun climbed higher into the sky. The air was cool, though the stillness hinted at the promise of a warm day. As she glanced back towards the barn—more a workshop her father used for his projects—something made her pause.

Her eyes were drawn upward to the roof, where a dark

spot stood out against the weathered shingles. She squinted, straining her eyes to see more clearly. It wasn't just a shadow. It was a hole. A hole with edges that were jagged and splintered, as though something had smashed through from above.

Sarah stopped short. "Something went straight through!" she mumbled, clutching the basket tightly as her gaze remained fixed on the gaping hole.

Curiosity stirred, and with a glance toward the empty lane where her mother had disappeared, Sarah set the basket down carefully by the cottage door.

Sarah was acutely aware of the ongoing air war over England. The ever-present threat of an air raid was woven into wartime life. Though rare in the countryside, she had heard distant drones of planes and was certain she had once heard the muffled thud of an explosion.

Curiosity wrestled with unease as her mind raced with possibilities. *Could something have fallen from an airplane? A bomb? No, why would someone target their quiet farm? Could an airplane have crashed? No, the damage would be more extensive. Perhaps a pilot, forced to bail out?*

"Oh dear!" she thought, her hand nervously playing with a strand of hair. *What if a "Jerry" pilot had bailed out here?* The very idea gave her a chill, imagining the potential danger of an enemy soldier so close, perhaps part of a larger invasion force with others nearby.

Fear tightened her throat, but a new thought pushed through the disquiet. *What if the pilot, or whoever it was, were injured? They might need medical assistance.* The conflicting emotions of fear and concern wrestled within her as she considered the implications. Curiosity urged her forward.

24

The familiar creaking sounds of the barn, usually comforting, now seemed strangely absent. Sarah's imagination conjured up a myriad of scenarios lurking within its dark interior. Taking a deep breath to calm herself, she cautiously approached the barn, the silence pierced only by the soft padding of her own footsteps.

Drawing nearer, she peered toward the barn doors as she navigated around a low awning sheltering her father's car beneath a canvas tarp. She noticed the doors were ajar, the closer door was angled enough to hide whatever might lay within.

As Sarah paused to ponder her next move, the barn doors both slammed shut with a deafening crash, shattering the fragile silence. The sound jolted her. She froze. Her heart pounded in her chest, a frantic drumbeat in the sudden stillness. *Someone was inside!* Panic seized her.

Thoughts of a German hiding in the barn raced through her mind, urging her to escape. Without hesitation, Sarah spun on her heel and bolted. Her scream—a primal shriek of terror—tore through the air as she raced down the lane. The sudden clucking and fluttering of startled chickens erupted from the coop, adding a chaotic cacophony that drove her fear. Loose stones skittered beneath her feet, each echoing her frantic heartbeat. The image of an enemy lurking in the barn fueled her desperate flight. Sarah's fading scream lingered in the air. A gentle breeze rustled through the surrounding fields, carrying the distant chirping of birds.

Through a dusty windowpane, a fleeting shadow moved within the dim interior of the barn.

Chapter 4

A gentle breeze rustled through the fields near the village of Whitfield, some 30 kilometers away, carrying the sweet scent of honeysuckle. Paddie Bird, a woman whose face bore the sun-kissed marks of a life spent outdoors, hummed a cheerful tune as she set off. Today, her mission was a simple one: collect some plump berries from a patch nearby for a batch of summer jam.

As she reached the clearing, a frown creased her brow. Her blackberry patch, usually a vibrant tapestry of greens and purples, was obscured by a tangled mess of thick vines. Unlike the familiar, delicate branches of her blackberry bushes, these vines seemed an unnatural green.

Intrigued, Paddie entered the patch. A faint, sweet scent hung in the air, almost sickly, yet strangely alluring.

"That's might strange," she muttered, leaning down and feeling a stray vine with her calloused hand. The vine seemed to recoil. Curiosity overcoming her caution, Paddie moved in to examine the vines more closely.

Nestled amidst the mass of vines, a flash of orange caught her eye. Unlike the perfect, round gourds displayed in shops come autumn, this pumpkin was a misshapen thing, no bigger than a child's head. Its surface was bumpy and uneven, but what truly sent a shiver down Paddie's spine were the dark gouges and ridges that seemed to form a grotesque, grinning face.

"Dear Lord..." Paddie whispered, her voice barely a breath against the summer breeze.

Paddie reached out a tentative hand to touch the pumpkin. A jolt of revulsion shot through her as the fingers of her other hand brushed something cold and solid beneath the vines. She carefully pulled away a section of the green tendrils, revealing a horrifying sight. The lifeless face of a man stared back at her, his skin a sickly pale, eyes vacant, a deathly grin on his lips.

Panic surged through her. As she took a tentative step back, her foot was caught in something. Glancing down, she saw that thick vines had tangled around her ankles. These felt slick and cold to the touch, sending a wave of nausea through her.

Before she could call out, the ground beneath her feet seemed to shift. With a desperate jerk, she managed to pull one leg free, but the vines tightened their grip on the other, digging into her flesh and drawing a sharp cry of pain. Suddenly, they gave a violent tug, yanking her off her feet and sending her sprawling to the ground.

Scrambling to get back to her feet, Paddie fought back tears of pain and panic. The world tilted precariously, the wind whipping her hair into a frenzy. She strained to reach the basket, desperately searching for something, anything, she could use to get free.

But before she could reach it, a single vine, thick and cold, had snaked out from the writhing mass. It coiled around her neck with a sickening, constricting pressure. The air left her lungs in a strangled gasp. With a final, desperate look towards the endless blue sky, a tunnel of blackness consumed Paddie's vision. The pressure on her throat remained.

A sharp pinch pricked the back of her neck, then chilling laughter echoed in her mind, a sound devoid of humor, filled with malice. Images flashed before her eyes – grotesque vines bursting from the earth, consuming everything in their path.

Chapter 5

The afternoon sun cast long shadows across the winding country road as Peter, a thirteen-year-old clad in a crisp Boy Scout uniform, marched purposefully down the lane. His sandy brown hair ruffled in the breeze, and his clear hazel eyes scanned the path ahead. With his brow furrowed in concentration, he set a brisk pace, occasionally glancing back at his younger sister, Olivia, trailing behind him. Seven years old, Olivia struggled to keep up, her tongue peeking out in a determined effort. Her vibrant red hair, stark against the lush green countryside, was topped whimsically with Peter's Boy Scout hat, which she had claimed for their adventures.

Peter inhaled deeply, savoring the scent of the outdoors that filled him with a familiar thrill. There was nothing quite like being out in nature, a feeling only amplified by the crisp uniform on his back.

"Do we have to march so fast, Peter?" she panted, raising her voice over the rhythmic crunch of their footsteps on the gravel road.

Peter, ever the proper older brother, replied with a hint of annoyance, "You wanted to tag along," maintaining his steady pace. There was a subtle satisfaction in his voice, a sense that imbued the moment with an air of formality—as if he were an officer commanding a soldier.

Their mother's long hours at the factory, contributing to the war effort alongside Sarah's mother, meant Peter was needed to look after Olivia, and he accepted this responsibility, taking his role as her guardian seriously. Olivia, in turn, adored her brother and wanted to be wherever he was, no matter the pace or task.

Together, Peter and Olivia shared a deep bond forged through their adventures exploring the English countryside. They would roam together, discovering hidden paths through lush green meadows, investigating crumbling castle ruins, and unearthing artifacts that whispered tales of England's rich history. Olivia's eyes would sparkle as she and Peter acted out stories of knights and dragons, turning each outing into a thrilling escapade.

From a distance, a frantic figure came into view from behind them. Sarah, her face flushed and hair windblown, waving her arms in the air with an urgency that made Peter stop short, eyebrows raised in surprise.

"Wait!" she cried, desperate to be heard, her voice hoarse with exertion. "Oh please, stop!"

Olivia, momentarily forgetting her fatigue, turned to see who was approaching. She paused, recognizing the girl as being from one of the farms nearby.

Sarah stumbled towards them, collapsing dramatically against Peter in a fit of breathlessness. Her chest heaved with exertion, and her eyes held a wild look.

Peter, ever the Boy Scout, reacted quickly and took control of the situation. "Cripes! Did you run all the way from your place?" he exclaimed, concern in his voice. He squinted at her for a moment, finally recognizing her. "Olivia, she needs water—hand her the canteen, will you?"

Eager to assist, Olivia unstrapped the canteen from her shoulder and held it out to Sarah. Sarah took the canteen gratefully, gulping down several large swallows before collapsing back against Peter, her breaths coming in ragged gasps.

Sarah continued to cling to Peter, gulping down water from the canteen as if it were the elixir of life. Her chest heaved with each ragged breath, and her eyes, wide and terrified, darted between Peter and Olivia.

Peter and Olivia exchanged glances. Clearly, something had spooked Sarah considerably.

"Alright. Sarah, isn't it?" Peter said gently. "Take a moment. Catch your breath and then tell us what got you in such a state."

Sarah took a shuddering breath, her body slowly calming. "Our barn," she gasped, her voice trembling. "There was a hole in the barn roof. I looked … and there was someone there! A Jerry pilot! He slammed the door shut the moment he saw me, so I ran! I ran to get help, but the neighbors were out. I was on my way to the village when I saw you."

Peter's brow furrowed deeply as he took a moment to digest what Sarah had just told them. "A German pilot in your barn?", his voice tinged with disbelief and concern as he struggled to grasp the situation.

"Yes!" Sarah exclaimed urgently, her voice trembling with fear. "That's what I've been trying to tell you! There's a gaping hole in the roof where he fell through! He's hiding in there! We need to get the army!"

Peter chewed his lip, his mind grappling with the weight of Sarah's words. The idea of an enemy pilot lurking nearby was daunting. If the homeland was being invaded, they would need the army.

"Olivia, you and Sarah, head on to the village for rein-forcement," he said finally, his voice firm despite the nervous tremor in his stomach. "Someone needs to go back."

Sarah's eyes widened in protest as she realized what Peter was planning. "You can't go back," she blurted out, her voice desperate. "He might get you…"

Peter met Sarah's gaze, his jaw set in a determined line. "I need to go back and get eyes on him," he explained firmly. "We can't risk him scarpering into the countryside."

As Peter spoke, a sense of duty surged within him. He felt it was his responsibility to go back, his duty ingrained from years of Boy Scout service. People relied on Scouts like him to take care of things, he was entrusted with this role and he couldn't bear the thought of failing in his duty.

Chapter 6

The split-rail fence divided the fields from the farmyard. Anxious, Sarah crouched low in the tall grass, peering through a gap, watching Peter on the other side. The grass made her legs itch, and flies buzzed around her, occasionally landing on her arms and legs, prompting her to brush them away in frustration.

Peter had told her and Olivia to leg it to town for help while he went back to the farm alone. But Sarah couldn't bring herself to abandon him, so she'd followed him, determined to talk him out of his daft plan, insisting that the safest choice was for all three of them to go to town together.

As they approached the farm, Peter instructed Sarah to keep an eye on the cottage and Olivia to watch the road while he had a look at the barn. Olivia stayed put as he'd told her, but Sarah wasn't about to be told what to do on her own farm. Besides, she didn't like the thought of being alone with the enemy running loose.

Her stomach twisted in knots as she kept at him, trying to talk him out of his plan to go to the barn alone.

"Peter!" she hissed, her voice laced with worry. "This is a terrible idea!"

From the other side of the fence, Peter shot Sarah a glare,

his voice a harsh whisper. "I told you to keep an eye on the cottage!" He was doing his best to move silently through the grass, each step careful and deliberate, keeping even the crunch of the grass barely audible.

"And I told you," Sarah retorted, scrambling through the fence and making her way towards him, "we should have gone for help!"

The farm was isolated and filled with perfect hiding spots for an enemy soldier. Sticking around like Peter was doing was simply reckless.

Peter stopped momentarily, dropping to one knee as frustration rose in him. Sarah's noisy scrambling through the grass was anything but subtle. He couldn't help but think, *As bossy as the girls at school. Properly fits in, this one.*

Their wills silently fought, each sure that they were right, each trying to will the other to understand. A shared breath eased the tension between them slightly. Then, Peter began to explain their situation. Again.

"We had a plan," Peter hissed, his frustration still simmering. He had carefully laid out their roles. Sarah had thrown a wrench into the well-oiled machine. "Olivia watches the road for any sign of him there. You were supposed to keep an eye on the cottage. While I reconnoiter the barn. If any of us saw anything, we signal and scarper."

"But why…?" Sarah began, her voice barely a murmur.

Peter cut her off with a shake of his head. "For goodness sake! So we have the whole place covered," he finished.

"This whole thing is ridiculous," Sarah argued. "We shouldn't be playing soldiers."

Peter clenched his jaw. Playing soldiers? This was serious, and time was of the essence. His gut instinct told him that they needed to identify where the German spy was so he couldn't lose himself in the countryside to do who knows what. It was so sensible. Why wasn't she getting it?

Deciding he was finished discussing the matter, Peter pointed towards a nearby cluster of trees, a silent instruction for Sarah to stay put. "The barn is just ahead," he whispered urgently. "Just stay here while I check it out. If anything seems wrong, run and get help, alright?"

Sarah tried to argue further, but Peter ignored her and turned to crawl towards the barn, keeping low to the ground. Sarah crouched behind a large tree, her eyes fixed on Peter, her fingers caught a strand of hair that she anxiously twirled between her fingers.

Peter pressed himself against the rough bark of a tree and slowly peered around it, his eyes scanning the barn for any sign of movement, straining to see every detail. *No movement. Wait. The doors... what did that mean?*

Peter looked back at Sarah and gestured for her to come closer, using hand signals. When she didn't understand, he finally whispered harshly, "Sarah, come here!"

Sarah moved up carefully and crouched behind him, her eyes darting nervously around.

"You said the Jerry slammed the doors shut, right?" Peter whispered urgently.

"Yes," Sarah quietly confirmed. Confusion danced across her face as she leaned to look past Peter towards the barn. Her brow furrowed in thought, trying to understand what Peter was seeing. Then, realization dawned on Sarah's face. "Oh!" she squeaked.

The barn doors hung wide open, like a gaping maw ready to swallow them whole. A prickle of unease crawled up her.

"I'm going to get a closer look," Peter whispered, his voice tense. "Don't move."

Sarah remained frozen, her breath caught in her throat, eyes fixed on the gaping open doors of the barn. Each second felt like an eternity as Peter crept slowly towards the barn, acutely aware of the risk of being spotted from inside.

After an exhausting slow approach Peter reached the weathered, rough wooden wall and pressed himself tightly against it. He took a deep breath, willing his heartbeat to slow. His fingers gripped the uneven surface of the wood as he inched his way along, muscles tense with anticipation. The adrenaline coursing through him made it difficult to keep his movements deliberate and cautious.

With painstaking care, Peter finally positioned himself beside the open doorway, obscured from the view of anyone inside. He hesitated, his mind racing with the possibilities of who lay in wait. *What if the German was just inside, ready to pounce?*

Gathering his resolve, Peter cautiously, slowly, leaned forward, straining to peer into the dim interior of the barn. Shadows danced ominously on the walls, the musty scent of the barn mingling with the creaks and groans of the old wood. His eyes scanned as far as the gloom allowed, searching for any sign of movement, any hint of danger.

Then, as his gaze swept over the rough surface of one of the open doors, Peter froze. There, scratched into the wood in uneven letters, was something unexpected. His brow furrowed in confusion. "What the…?" His voice barely a whisper against the backdrop of his racing thoughts. "A message?"

Back by the tree, Sarah watched Peter in rapt anticipation.

A figure slowly emerged from the trees behind her.

Olivia hesitatingly approached, "Sarah—" Olivia began in a whisper as she reached out to touch Sarah's shoulder.

The quiet of the farm was shattered. A bloodcurdling scream ripped through the air. Peter's face contorted in shock and fear, his heart pounding in his chest. Panic surged through him like an electric shock. He froze. *"Run!"* his mind screamed to his body, *"RUN!"*

Peter burst away from the barn, his legs pumping in a desperate bid for escape. The ground blurred beneath him as he sprinted past the spot where he had left Sarah. His breath coming in ragged gasps, adrenaline fueling his every stride.

Sarah and Olivia stood rooted to the spot, watching his retreating form. Only when Peter realized that the girls weren't running did he skid to a halt. His chest heaved, his body shaking, sweat trickling down his face, and his eyes expressed confusion as he turned and walked back towards them.

"What happened?" Peter barked, his voice laced with exasperation. The rush of adrenaline had stripped away his earlier caution. "W-what'd you scream for?"

Disbelief washed over him as Sarah blurted out, "It was Olivia! She surprised me!"

Peter turned sharply towards Olivia. Olivia, tears filling her eyes, in a sniffling whimper. "You two were gone for ages, and... I got scared."

Peter's anger melted away as he took in Olivia's trembling form. Guilt gnawed at him; She was only seven and he had left her all alone to watch the house for all this time. He sighed and reached out instinctively, his hand resting gently on Olivia's shoulder. "I'm sorry, Liv," he said softly, his voice filled with regret.

Olivia, despite her tears, managed a small, trembling smile.

Peter knelt down to her level, wrapping her in a warm embrace. "You're okay" he promised. Olivia buried her face in his shoulder, hugging him back.

Turning back to Sarah, Peter's mind was filled with thoughts about the message scrawled on the barn door. He turned towards the barn, it seemed more mysterious and less ominous now.

"There was something written on the door," he said. "I ought'a check it out."

"Stay here," he instructed, his voice firm despite the tremor in his hands. "Both of you. And this time, be quiet, alright."

With a deep breath, Peter crept back towards the barn. The message on the door was still there, scratched, in broken English, into the weathered wood: "**NO HARM HURT HELP**" Confusion clawed at him. *Was this a plea? A warning?* He took another deep breath for courage and leaned in through the gaping doorway. A wave of stale air, thick with the scent of dust, washed over him. The harsh midday sun cast long, dramatic shadows across the interior through the hole in the roof and the open doors.

The barn wasn't empty; it was more of a workshop than a traditional barn, with a sturdy wooden floor worn smooth from years of use. Stacks of rough-cut wood, weathered crates, and old barrels were scattered throughout, creating deep pockets of shadow where someone—or something— could easily hide. Near the back, an old Fordson tractor sat hitched to an ancient horse wagon loaded with boxes, casting long, heavy shadows across the floor. Along the opposite wall, shelves and tools leaned haphazardly, their outlines softened by dust and cobwebs that clung like veils.

Peter called out tentatively, his voice echoing strangely in the stillness, "Hello?"

His heart pounded a frantic beat as he listened for a reply. Carefully, Peter crept into the barn, his eyes continually scanning the shadows. He stepped over a pile of wood planks, careful not to dislodge any loose boards. He squeezed between a stack of dusty crates and an overturned wheelbarrow, his hand brushing away cobwebs as thick as fishing nets. The air grew thicker with dust, threatening to make him cough.

He reached the tractor without any sign of an intruder. Disappointment that should have been relief gnawed at him. *Did they get away? Who wrote the message?* There was no sign of anyone, no sign of a Jerry pilot, nothing out of the ordinary besides the cryptic plea itself.

Just as he was about to turn back satisfied that the barn was empty, a hint of movement caught his eye in the dim light. Something seemed to shift. He squinted, his pulse quickening. There, nestled among a pile of old rags and farm equipment in the back corner, was something large and living. Its form, obscured in the shadows, defied identification. A quiver of fear ran through his legs. Peter's mind fought against what he was seeing, his breaths began coming in short, shallow gasps.

Peter scrambled back the way he came. Every creak of the floorboards, every sound seemed amplified as he knocked into the crates and barrels, shelves and tools, snagging his clothes. Vaulting over and tipping a barrel, his foot caught, sending him sprawling.

He hit the floor hard, the air knocked from his lungs. Pain shot into his ankle, but adrenaline shoved it aside. He scrambled to his feet, ignoring the throbbing, and lurched towards the barn entrance. Just as he reached the doorway, his foot caught the frame.

With a surprised yelp, Peter went sprawling again, landing face-first in the dirt with a muffled "whooommfff!" For a terrifying moment he couldn't breathe and the world seemed to spin. He lay there, gasping for breath, his heart beating in his chest.

The sounds he had made echoed in the stillness. Was it coming after him—? Frozen, Peter squeezed his eyes shut, waiting for it to pounce and tear him apart... anything. But there was only silence. A tense, heavy silence that pressed down on him like a physical weight.

Slowly, ever so slowly, Peter rolled over and peeked open one eye. The barn entrance gaped before him, bathed in the harsh midday sun. Stillness. No movement. Taking a shuddering breath, Peter pushed himself to his hands and knees. He winced as his ankle protested, but the throbbing was duller now.

Trying to ignore the pain, he scrambled to his feet and quickly limped away from the barn, nearly colliding with Olivia. Sarah followed a beat behind, both their eyes wide with alarm. The two girls had seen his tumble and rushed to his side, their faces etched with concern.

"Peter! Are you alright?" Olivia gasped, her voice trembling slightly.

"What did you see?" Sarah chimed in, her eyes directed nervously towards the barn.

Peter knelt to check his ankle, his heart still a frantic drum solo against his ribs. Then he struggled to stand, wincing as he put weight on his throbbing ankle, the memory of his clumsy escape flashing before his eyes. Looking back at the barn, he felt cold fear despite the midday heat. The dark maw seemed ominous again, the silence inside thicker and heavier than before.

He opened his mouth to speak, but the words wouldn't come. How could he explain what he saw? How could he describe the form in the shadows, its nature defying any explanation? They'd think him a fool spooked by his own imagination.

"I saw..." he began, uncertain how to continue, "a big..." He trailed off, searching for the right word, the right way to explain what he saw without sounding ridiculous. "You'll think I'm daft! It was a—-"

Chapter 7

Sarah's jaw dropped, disbelief etched across her features. "A dinosaur?!" she exclaimed, her voice a mix of amusement and exasperation. Olivia, standing behind Peter, peeked nervously at Sarah.

Peter fidgeted. "Honestly, Sarah," he pleaded, desperation creeping into his voice, "I wouldn't lie about something like this. I swear on my honor, that's what I saw!"

Sarah scoffed. "It's the silliest thing I've ever heard!" she declared, already marching toward the weathered barn door. The inscription scratched upon the wood—a message that moments ago seemed ominous—now seemed to her nonsensical in light of Peter's frantic claim.

Peter's hand shot out, grabbing Sarah's arm. "You can't go in there!" he blurted, his voice filled with worry.

Sarah, momentarily startled, pulled her arm free. Ignoring Peter's protests, she approached the barn and peered into the dark interior.

Peter couldn't believe what she was doing. Sarah's reckless-ness bewildered him. *Earlier, she had chastised him for being foolhardy, and now here she was.*

Sarah's heart thudding in her chest. *What am I doing?* she thought, surprised at her own boldness. Just minutes ago, she'd been terrified at the idea of going back to her own farm. Now she was charging ahead, as though she weren't afraid at all. She felt Peter and Olivia's eyes on her, and a strange warmth surged in her chest.

I'm showing off, she realized, the thought both startling and oddly thrilling. She wanted them both to like her, to see her as brave, wanted Peter's wide-eyed disbelief to turn to respect. For once, she wanted to be the one others looked to, the one who stepped forward instead of standing on the sidelines.

Her thoughts spiraled as she hesitated. *Does she seem foolish to them?* She felt a hot flush of embarrassment mix with her fear. Peter had taken her seriously before—that mattered more than anything. But now?

"A dinosaur… the very idea," she muttered under her breath, trying to coax herself forward, allowing her voice to be tinged with disbelief. But as she peered into the dim interior of the barn, a sliver of doubt crept into her thoughts. Peter didn't seem like the type to lie. And there had been someone in the barn earlier.

She pressed her lips together, ignoring the flutter of nerves in her stomach, and stepped over the threshold. She couldn't back out now—not with Peter and Olivia watching. And whoever had been in there earlier was surely gone. Otherwise, Peter would have spotted them. Wouldn't he?

SSarah gave her eyes a moment to adjust to the gloom. The darkness refused to settle into anything recognizable, leaving her vision caught between certainty and imagination. Shapes loomed where the light failed, their outlines indistinct, shifting as her eyes tried to impose meaning on them. The space felt larger than it should have, the shadows deep and watchful, as if the barn itself were holding its breath.

Her pulse quickened as her imagination rushed to fill in the gaps. Anything could be hidden there—anything at all. She swallowed hard, forcing herself to remember that fear had a way of animating empty spaces, turning nothing into something if she let it.

Sarah swallowed her nerves and forced a teasing tone. "You seriously want me to believe that a dinosaur wrote a message on the doors and then decided to take a nap?" she said, a faint waver in her voice betraying her unease.

Peter hesitated, caught off guard. The barn felt different now—less menacing than before. The deep shadows that had unnerved him earlier seemed less threatening, stirring doubt in his memory. But whether something was in there or not, caution was still the smarter choice. He couldn't understand how she could go in so boldly after scolding him for doing the exact same thing.

"I don't—" he began, but Sarah cut him off with a look, letting her stubbornness outweigh her fear. Stepping forwards cautiously, she skirted around the overturned barrel Peter had tripped over earlier.

With each step she took, the wooden floorboards creaked underfoot. Dust motes floated in the slanted rays of sunlight, adding to the eerie atmosphere. She could feel Peter and Olivia's eyes on her back.

A sense of urgency welled up inside Peter. H*e DID see something!* He was sure of it. They should be cautious and have a plan. "Sarah! Come out of there!" he hissed.

Ignoring him, Sarah continued exploring deeper into the barn. Her eyes darted to each shadow, every pile of debris, seeing no movement. She came to the tractor and took a deep breath, trying to steady her nerves, and peered around it towards the back of the barn.

Then, she saw it.

In the farthest corner of the barn, half-hidden by shadows, was a form. It was large and indistinct, but undeniably there. Sarah froze, her breath catching in her throat. She could feel the hairs on the back of her neck stand on end, a cold wave of fear washing over her.

A gasp escaped her lips, and one hand instinctively flew to her mouth. Her eyes widened in shock as the creature before her shattered her reality. Curled up on the wooden floor of the barn lay a magnificent dragon, its body as large as an automobile, with a long neck that arched gracefully and a head nearly twice the size of a horse's. Its emerald scales shimmered faintly in a shaft of sunlight filtering through the hole in the roof. Its long tail wrapped around its body protectively, adding to its immense presence. It was unlike any living creature she'd ever seen.

Peter's insistent calls for her to get out faded into the background. Sarah could only stare, rooted to the spot.

As Sarah studied it, it began to seem less like a fire-breathing monster of legend and more like a wounded animal in need of care. Its chest rose and fell unevenly, each shallow breath accompanied by a faint, raspy wheeze that sounded painfully labored. One of its wings lay crumpled and motionless at its side, a clear sign of injury.

Sarah's legs were shaking, so she slowly knelt on the floor. Taking a cautious breath, she whispered, "It's a... dragon," the words tasting strange and surreal on her tongue. "And he's hurt!" she quietly exclaimed.

Despite the dragon's size and the strangeness of the situation, she could see it was a creature in need. Right now, this wasn't a terrifying beast—it was something vulnerable, something that needed help.

Growing up in the countryside, Sarah had learned to recognize the signs of an injured animal. She had nursed birds with broken wings and cared for small creatures like squirrels and hedgehogs, her heart always aching to see anything in pain. Big animals didn't scare her as much as they might have frightened the children in the village. This creature was far larger than any horse she had ever seen—immense and imposing—but even so, the instinct to care for it stirred within her.

As she gazed at the wounded beast, Sarah found herself drawn to it. The fear that had gripped her began to melt away, giving way to a sense of pity and a feeling of responsibility.

The dragon hearing her stirred, its colossal head lifting with a weak groan. It focused its gaze on Sarah. Sarah instinctively moved back. *What had caused this magnificent creature so much pain? Was she safe being so close?* Yet, as she met its gaze, she saw something unexpected—fear. Fear in the eyes of a dragon. The sight made her heart clench. Whatever had caused this majestic creature so much suffering, it had left it vulnerable and scared.

The enormous reality of what was happening struck her, and for a fleeting moment, her courage wavered. She leaned back slightly, her head spinning. This couldn't be real—it was impossible. Her hands gripped the floor for stability, grounding her as the weight of the moment threatened to pull her under.

But then the dragon let out another wheezing groan, its entire body sagging against the barn floor as if even holding its head up was too much. The sound snapped Sarah out of her hesitation. This WAS real. Whatever danger might be present, this creature was hurting. It needed her.

She turned toward the barn door, her voice rising as she called out. "It's a dragon!" she shouted, her words echoing in the dusty, shadowed interior. "He's hurt! Fetch a bucket of water from the pump!"

Outside, Peter and Olivia froze, exchanging wide-eyed, bewildered glances. Peter's jaw dropped, his mind unable to believe what he'd just heard.

"What?!" he finally managed to blurt out, his voice barely a squeak.

"A dragon?" Olivia echoed, her wide eyes lighting up with wonder.

Back inside the barn, the dragon's golden eyes opened toward the sound of Sarah's raised voice, its weary gaze filled with confusion. It tried to rise again, its massive chest heaving with the effort, but it quickly sank back to the floor with a muffled thud. The urgency of the situation sank in for Sarah. This creature needed immediate care.

Sarah turned her head back toward the dragon, urgency and determination flashing in her eyes. "Peter, fetch a bucket!" she shouted, her voice cracking with desperation. "He's injured!"

Chapter 8

As Peter and Olivia hurried off in search of water, the silence in the barn enveloped Sarah, broken only by the dragon's labored, raspy breathing and the soft creak of the floorboards beneath her.

Far from the quiet of the barn, in a stark military office on the continent, Field Marshal Wolfram Guilder addressed a group of officers, his voice steady but charged with intensity. A man both revered and feared, Guilder's fervent patriotism was matched only by his relentless pursuit of knowledge long forgotten. To many of his peers, his obsession with the occult bordered on lunacy, but to Guilder, it was untapped potential—a realm of power that modern men had foolishly abandoned in their blind adherence to the ideology of modern science.

Though the Führer himself dismissed the occult as nonsense, others in the party held a deep fascination with it. Their belief in the occult, entwined with Aryan myth and mysticism, fueled Guilder's exploration and research into ancient relics and esoteric rituals. To Guilder, the search for such secrets wasn't foolish; it was the key to absolute power, a force he believed would ensure the Reich's supremacy. It was this belief that drove his fervent support of Krammer's work.

Captivated by the prospect of harnessing ancient and arcane knowledge, Guilder threw himself into the expeditions Krammer orchestrated, convinced that what the world called "magic" was simply science and nature misunderstood. To him, uncovering these secrets wasn't madness; it was enlightenment. And with Krammer's guidance and breakthroughs, the path to that enlightenment seemed closer than ever.

Krammer had accomplished what others deemed impossible, producing results that defied conventional science. The machines he built and the phenomena they unleashed hinted at forces beyond the comprehension of even the brightest minds in the Reich.

Where others saw an unhinged scientist, Guilder saw a visionary—a man who had bridged the gap between mysticism and practicality. To Guilder, Krammer's work wasn't just important; it was indispensable. If Krammer could unlock the secrets of arcane forces, the Reich would wield power unmatched in human history.

Now, as Guilder's words echoed through the room, the gathered officers listened in uneasy silence. For some, his conviction was inspiring; for others, deeply unsettling. Yet none dared challenge him, for Guilder's unwavering belief and authoritative presence were as commanding as the rank he bore.

"Meine Herren," he boomed, his voice filled with urgency, "We cannot continue down this path with the limitations of conventional tactics! The Allies have established a foothold in France, tightening their grip on the skies, their forces weaving into Europe like an unyielding serpent. In the East, the Red Army has shattered our lines and is now advancing toward

East Prussia and Poland. The Wehrmacht is unable to mount effective counterattacks, and our reserves are overstretched. We are at an ever-growing disadvantage!"

A tense silence settled over the room after Guilder voiced what few dared to acknowledge. He paced before the assembled officers, his shadow stretching across the wall like a menacing claw, amplifying the weight of his words.

"But," Guilder continued, his voice dropping to a low, menacing growl, "we now possess a new asset—a weapon beyond anything the Allies could have anticipated. Something they cannot—"

"With all due respect, Field Marshal," an officer interrupted, his weathered face set in a skeptical frown and his steely blue eyes locked on Guilder. "The situation is dire, yes, but surely you don't mean to suggest we deploy something so… unnatural?"

Guilder cut him off with a sharp gesture and continued. "Imagine, gentlemen," he boomed, his voice rising with fervor as he began pacing the room. "We begin with the new American airfields! Their weapons, their planes, their personnel—none of it would stand a chance against what we now have! And with only that, Germany would again dominate the skies over the continent!"

A collective muttering rippled through the room. The notion of deploying monsters in warfare was an uncomfortable one, perhaps too much for the experienced officers.

Guilder, sensing their hesitation, pressed on. "The true brilliance of making use of this weapon lies not just in its destructive power," he declared, his voice hardening with newfound resolve. "Imagine the fear and chaos unleashed behind enemy lines! These creatures tearing through supply depots, shredding communication hubs—while their soldiers scatter in terror. The very lifeblood of their advance would collapse into ruin!"

Another officer, younger than the first, found his voice, though it wavered slightly. "You cannot be serious, Field Marshal! They're beasts—more a liability than a weapon! It's like unleashing a stampede of elephants and hoping they trample an enemy or two, while praying they don't crush your own men in the process."

A ripple of chuckles spread through the room at the clumsy analogy, but Field Marshal Guilder's expression remained unyielding, his stern gaze silencing the laughter almost as soon as it began.

Guilder straightened, a steely glint flashing in his eyes. "These are no beasts, Captain," he retorted sharply. "These are our brothers—the best of us. They are the Edelweiss!" He paused, letting the weight of the name settle over the room, his gaze sweeping across the assembled officers.

"Herr Krammer and I chose the most fanatically loyal subjects. They were trained and loyal soldiers before and they still are; Loyal to the Reich, obedient to their orders, and unwavering in their professionalism—they will execute their missions flawlessly!"

The room remained silent, his words hovering over the gathered officers like a storm cloud.

Finally, an officer cleared his throat, his voice laced with trepidation. "Field Marshal," he began, "how exactly do you propose to… deploy these… Edelweiss?"

Guilder clapped his hands together, the sound echoing through the room. "I propose a swift and decisive strike, carried out in the evening to maximize the element of surprise.

These can attack in complete silence," he declared, his voice resonating with conviction. "before the enemy knows they're there, before they can react. Destroying everything. When all is in flames, they will leave as silently as they arrived. Fear will be their weapon, chaos their victory cry!"

A somber acquiescence settled upon the officers. Unease rippled through the room like an unspoken undercurrent; the deployment of mythical creatures—things pulled from ancient tales and used as living weapons—had the potential for disaster. The unpredictability of such beasts in battle loomed foremost in their thoughts.

Yet, as the officers exchanged uneasy glances, a shared realization began to crystallize. Germany's resources were stretched to the breaking point, its tactical position deteriorating rapidly, and its industrial capabilities crumbling under relentless Allied bombardment. Time and viable options were slipping through their fingers like sand in an hourglass. Desperation had a way of dulling even the sharpest skepticism, and Guilder's audacious plan, outlandish as it seemed, carried an undeniable allure. The promise of a bold, game-changing action sparkled like a beacon amidst the gathering gloom, outweighing the creeping fear of calamity.

More pragmatic minds among them calculated the risks with cold detachment. If Krammer's creatures succeeded, the glory would be theirs to share, cementing their place in the annals of history as saviors of the Reich. If they failed, the blame would fall squarely on Guilder and Krammer—two figures already shrouded in controversy. For the rest of them, the gamble held little personal risk.

One by one, the officers gave their nods of approval, not out of conviction, but out of necessity. Whatever unease lingered was buried beneath the grim realities of the war.

Chapter 9

T he bucket felt heavy in Sarah's hands as she knelt, her knees pressing into the dusty barn floor. She pushed it closer to the dragon, her heart hammering in her chest. Moments before, Peter had handed her the bucket, rambling nervously about how dangerous a dragon could be, his words a chaotic jumble of warnings and reasons dragons can't exist. Now he stood in stunned silence, his wide eyes fixed on the creature before them, the reality of it far beyond anything they had ever imagined. Behind them, Olivia lingered near the door, her small frame frozen with wonder.

Sarah's mind was a whirlwind of conflicting emotions—disbelief and a strange protective instinct. The dragon, larger than any horse she'd ever seen, lay sprawled across the barn floor. Its massive chest heaved with labored breaths, each one dragging a faint, raspy wheeze from its throat. Despite the razor-sharp claws and scales that glinted like armor in the fractured sunlight, the creature radiated vulnerability. Its wing, tattered and limp, splayed out awkwardly, and its movements were slow and unsteady.

"Here," Sarah said gently, her voice trembling but steady enough to convey her intent. She carefully nudged the bucket closer to the dragon's enormous head, the water inside sloshing softly. "Drink."

The dragon's golden eyes were open, their brilliance dulled by exhaustion and pain. They locked onto Sarah, and for a fleeting moment, she froze, the enormity of its gaze overwhelming. It felt as if the creature could see into her very soul, weighing her intentions. Then, slowly, it shifted its head toward the bucket, its movement accompanied by a low, wheezing groan.

Sarah held her breath as its massive snout dipped toward the water and it began to lap at the cool liquid with surprising delicacy. As the dragon drank, a low rumble echoed from its throat, a sound strangely mournful.

Peter crouched beside her, his curiosity overcoming his fear. "It's a dragon, Sarah. A real dragon."

Sarah reached out tentatively, her hand trembling as she placed it on the bucket to steady it. The dragon finished drinking and let out a low, rumbling groan—a sound that resonated through the barn. Its eyes closed again, its massive head resting on the floor as if the simple act of drinking had drained what little energy it had left.

Peter leaned in for a closer look. "That wing looks awfully bad," he explained. "The bone is broken. I'd say he needs a splint to keep it immobilized."

He paused, his brow furrowing as the practical Boy Scout in him weighed the task at hand. Splinting a person was one thing, but this? This was a creature out of myth, a being that could crush him with a single swipe. *Would it even let him get close enough?*

Still, the dragon hadn't done anything threatening, which gave Peter a glimmer of assurance that the creature meant no harm to them. If it had wanted to eat them, surely it would have done so by now.

"Well," Peter said after a moment, straightening slightly, "maybe he'll let us help him. And the motto is 'Be prepared,' right?" His lips quirked into a small, nervous smile. "I'll need something sturdy for a splint—wood, cloth, anything that'll hold. Do you have anything in the cottage we can use?" His hazel eyes looked to Sarah, seeking her permission.

Sarah's gaze lingered on the dragon's injured wing. She could see the strain in its shallow breaths, the shudder in its massive frame. Finally, she nodded. "There are linens and rags in the cupboard by the kitchen," she said.

Peter stood and headed out the door, Olivia quickly following on his heels. Left alone with the dragon, Sarah swallowed hard, her hands trembling slightly. The barn felt unnaturally quiet.

The dragon let out a soft sigh, its golden eyes half-closed in exhaustion. Sarah watched, her chest tightening as she noticed a single tear trace a glistening path down its cheek. Sarah's breath caught in her throat. He was sad. The sense of empathy in her chest grew. It wasn't just a beast; it was a sentient creature. The realization dawned on her as she recognized the depth of emotion in the dragon's eyes.

Peter and Olivia returned, arms laden with supplies — a collection of wooden slats scavenged from a broken fence and a bed sheet liberated from the cottage. Setting the materials down carefully, Peter glanced toward the dragon.

"Do you think… it wrote that?" he asked in a hushed tone, gesturing toward the carved message on the barn door.

The dragon's head lifted slightly, its golden eyes locking onto Peter. Slowly, with deliberate effort, it gave a small, deliberate nod. The air crackled with a sense of the impossible. This truly wasn't a beast; this was a creature with a mind, with the ability to communicate.

"Blimey! It understands us!" Peter exclaimed, excitement coloring his voice.

Olivia took a tentative step forward and stood next to her brother. "Do you... have a name?" she asked softly.

The dragon grunted with the effort, but with a great rasp that echoed through the barn, it shifted itself. With painstaking effort, it scraped a claw across the wooden floorboards, the deep gouges forming a single word: **ANSELM**

The children stared, speechless.

After what seemed like ages, Peter finally found his voice. "Where did you come from, Anselm?"

The dragon attempted to answer, his golden eyes replete with effort, but a sharp wince and a low grunt of pain escaped his throat as he shifted his weight. Sarah, witnessing the immense strain the dragon was experiencing, instinctively placed a calming hand on his snout. She was unaware that she had moved close enough for the dragon to bite her had it intended to.

"Look at him," she said softly, her voice steady despite the situation. "He's in a lot of pain. He needs rest before we begin peppering him with questions."

Peter nodded, his Boy Scout instincts kicking in. He approached Anselm, keeping his movements slow and deliberate. Now that he knew the dragon was intelligent, it didn't seem as threatening. More like a wounded companion. Still, the size and power of the creature weren't lost on him. In the back of his mind, he knew the risk hadn't completely disappeared.

Even so, a surge of excitement ran through him. A dragon.

This was more than an adventure—it was something beyond anything he could have imagined. And for better or worse, they were in the thick of it.

"Let's see what we can do about that wing, then," Peter said, gesturing to the limp and crumpled wing.

The dragon's eyes followed him, but it didn't move. "Don't worry," Peter said, his voice shaking. "I learned enough about this from first aid practice with the Scouts and when we were assisting ambulance drivers. I know what I'm doing. It might hurt a bit, though. So, um… please don't eat me, right?"

A low rumble emanated from Anselm's chest. Peter froze a moment before realizing it wasn't a growl—it was more of a sound that could be interpreted as amusement and reluctant agreement.

Sarah continued stroking the dragon's rough hide in a comforting gesture. "It's alright, Anselm," she murmured. "Hold on, won't you? How about a bit of food after this? Bet you're famished."

Anselm responded with a weary, low grunt, his massive body relaxing slightly into the barn floor. His golden eyes blinked slowly before closing.

Taking a deep breath, Sarah got to her feet and moved toward the doorway. "I'll go and fetch something for you to eat," she said, glancing back at the dragon. "Olivia, you stay with him, alright?"

Sarah disappeared through the door, leaving Peter and Olivia alone with the injured creature.

Olivia hesitated, then knelt down near the tractor, still wary of the dragon. She offered a reassuring smile. "We'll get you fixed up," she whispered to the dragon.

Anselm opened his eyes and regarded her for a long moment, his golden eyes showing gratitude. Then, with a heavy, rattling sigh, his eyes closing again as exhaustion overtook him.

Peter laid out the supplies for the splint, his movements steady as he recalled the lessons ingrained in him. He had learned the basics from the Boy Scout Handbook for Boys, but his real education came from watching first-hand while his Troop assisted the local ambulance service. He had watched many times as bones were splinted and injuries tended, filing away the knowledge for a moment like this—though never in his wildest dreams had he imagined tending to a creature like this.

Taking a deep breath, Peter assessed the condition of the wing. He grabbed the wood slats and sheets, trimming the wood with his penknife into manageable lengths. His hands moved with calm precision as he worked, each cut deliberate.

"I'm just going to lift this, alright?" he said in a hushed tone to the dragon. The dragon let out a low, quiet moan but remained still.

He then gently lifted the dragon's bent wing, using a strip of bedding as a makeshift sling to hold it steady. The dragon winced, its massive body tensing, but managed not to move. With careful precision, Peter positioned a wooden slat along the bone to create a splint. He worked quickly but gently, with deliberate movements, knowing that speed was essential to minimize the dragon's discomfort. Using strips of the sheet, Peter secured the slat, knotting the fabric firmly and carefully, checking his work to ensure it would hold. His hands shook slightly as he tied the final knot.

He stepped back, satisfaction on his face as he surveyed

his handiwork. "Well, that should hold it steady," he said, brushing his hands on his trousers. The dragon's chest rose and fell with a labored rhythm, its exhaustion evident.

It was then that something caught his attention—a flash of red, white, and black peeking out from beneath the dragon's massive tail. Curiosity piqued, he crouched down for a better look. "What's this, then?" he muttered, reaching toward the crumpled fabric.

With a gentle tug, he pulled the cloth free and began unfolding it. As the fabric unfurled in his hands, Peter's heart skipped a beat—it was a flag. His breath caught as he recognized the unmistakable symbol emblazoned on it: a black swastika in a white circle, centered on a red background. A cold, sharp jolt of fear snaked down his spine.

Partly wrapped in the flag was a small leather suitcase. The dragon must have been using the flag as a makeshift bindle. Peter hesitated before pulling the case aside, the Nazi emblem on the flag making his stomach churn. He lifted the lid of the suitcase and peeked inside.

The first thing he noticed was a clunky black movie camera, its worn leather strap coiled to the side. Beside it lay a smooth amber stone, about the size of an ostrich egg, its surface etched with intricate rune-like symbols that shimmered faintly in the dim light. Peter's breath hitched. He had never seen anything so strange, so mesmerizing.

Slowly, he reached out and picked up the stone. The moment his fingers touched its surface, he was surprised by a warmth that seemed to radiate from its core.

He set the camera and stone aside carefully and delved deeper into the suitcase. BBeneath the camera and stone were a stack of blueprints, handwritten notes, and photographs.

The photos showed men in lab coats standing around unfamiliar machinery. The papers were covered in dense German text, each page bearing a Nazi insignia stamped prominently at the top. Peter didn't need to read the language to understand this was something serious.

Just then, the sound of footsteps and Sarah's cheerful voice broke through his thoughts.

"How about some eggs, Anselm?" she called out, her tone light and hopeful as she stepped into the barn carrying a basket. "Do dragons eat eggs? Mum's not going to be happy about not having any—"

Sarah's voice trailed off as fear gripped her as reality set in. How would she explain a dragon to her mother, who was due back in a few hours? Panic clawed at her throat.

"Mum! What will I tell Mum?!?" she cried, clutching the basket to her chest. The question burst from her lips, shattering the surreal excitement of discovering a dragon.

Peter, his gaze fixed on the flag, didn't miss the rising panic in Sarah's voice. He understood her fear; her mother wouldn't understand; no adult would. But the Nazi materials changed everything. This wasn't just about explaining a magical creature to her mother. They were potentially entangled in something far more dangerous, with larger implications.

Peter met Sarah's frantic gaze and held up the flag, the swastika showing in the faint light, its dark symbolism casting a shadow over the room. "Sarah," Peter declared, "we've got bigger issues than your mum."

Chapter 10

Sweat beaded on Sarah's forehead as she stood there clutching the basket of eggs. Her heart thumped with a mix of anxiety and dread. Figuring out how to handle her mother was a large enough problem, but the discovery of the Nazi flag had cast a longer shadow.

Peter and Olivia stood beside her, their faces etched with concern mirroring Sarah's own.

"Mum will be home soon. What do I do?" Sarah whispered, her voice tight with a knot of conflicting emotions. A part of her yearned to tell her mother, to blurt out everything about the strange, magnificent creature. It would be so easy. But another, protective and cautious part held her back. *What would her mother do if she found out?*

The idea of explaining a dragon to her mother felt absurd, even comical, for a moment. But then dread crept in. Sarah knew her mother loved her fiercely, but helping a dragon? That was something else entirely. Her mother was practical, rooted in a world where dragons didn't exist.

Would she call the authorities? The thought made Sarah's chest tighten. *What would they do to Anselm? Would they drag him away, lock him up, subject him to terrible experiments—or worse, kill him outright?*

She looked out the barn doors and saw the shadows in the yard had grown longer with the late afternoon sun. Time was running out. "She won't understand, not really," Sarah said, her voice shaking. "If she sees..." she trailed off, her eyes returning to Anselm.

A soft sound from him startled her, and Sarah's gaze locked with Anselm's. He let out a low rumble that vibrated through the barn. Sarah wasn't sure if he was expressing understanding, or if he was trying to tell her something. But one thing was certain – they had to figure this out.

Taking a deep breath, Sarah straightened her shoulders and focused.

"Mum'll be home soon," Sarah repeated, this time less frantic, more thoughtful. She furrowed her brow, working through the problem aloud. "She won't understand if she sees Anselm, will she? So we can't let her find out. But he needs looking after, and I can't stay out here with him all night. She'll know something's up if I do."

"And Olivia and I can't stay here all night either," Peter added. "Our mum'll be wondering where we've got to."

Peter's mind was whirling as he tried to formulate a plan that addressed all the challenges they faced. He prided himself on his ability to strategize, but every idea seemed to run into the same insurmountable roadblocks. They had to be sure to keep Anselm hidden from Sarah's mother, yet the dragon was injured and desperately needed care. None of them could stay with him overnight, leaving him vulnerable. And then there were the Nazi materials Anselm had brought with him—vital information the authorities would definitely want to know about. But how could they hand it over without exposing Anselm? If they revealed Anselm's existence, the authorities might view him as a threat and harm him. No matter how Peter turned it over in his mind, each solution unraveled in the face of these conflicting needs.

Olivia stated the only short-term solution, leaving Anselm on his own. "If Anselm stays quiet, maybe your mum won't know he's here."

Sarah nodded slowly. "What about water?" she asked. "He'll need loads of it, won't he?"

Peter glanced around as he thought. "We'll grab every bucket we can find—anything that holds water—and leave them all filled up for him," he suggested. "That way, he won't need them topped up."

Sarah nodded, "Alright," she said, her voice gaining a note of confidence. "We ask Anselm to be quiet, leave plenty of water inside…" Sarah hesitated, the worry in her eyes returning. "But he's so injured," she said softly. "And needs more than just water. What if he gets worse overnight?"

Peter shook his head. "We'll have to sort it out tomorrow, won't we? Right now, it's about keeping him hidden." He continued, his voice gentle yet unwavering. "If your mum catches you sneaking out to check on him, she'll twig what's going on."

Peter met Sarah's gaze earnestly. "We'll have to hope for the best until morning. Promise me you won't go out tonight."

Sarah hesitated, her lips pressing into a thin line as she looked at the floor. She didn't want to leave the dragon alone, but Peter was right. If Mum found out, the whole situation could spiral out of control.

"Alright," she said reluctantly, lifting her gaze back to his. "I promise. But first thing tomorrow, once Mum's off to work, I'm checking on him."

Satisfied, Peter gave her an approving nod. Olivia, standing close by, offered Sarah a small, encouraging smile.

Suddenly, Sarah remembered the basket of eggs she was holding. She approached the dragon. "These are for you," she said softly, setting the basket near him. "I don't know what dragons eat, and I know it's not much, but hopefully, this'll do you until tomorrow."

Anselm winced as he moved, but with surprising grace, he tilted his head in what Sarah took to be a gesture of gratitude.

Hunger was etched across his features as his massive head moved to investigate the eggs. He nudged them with his snout, hesitated, then drew back slightly, as if wishing the eggs were prepared. Finally, he swallowed one whole. He paused, his golden eyes narrowing as if contemplating the strange sensation. The next one he bit into, but immediately recoiled, his head jerking back. The sharp crunch of the shell and the slimy yolk spilling onto the floor seemed to catch him off guard. He shook his head, a look of mild disgust crossing his face.

Watching him, Sarah couldn't help but smile, even with the worry knotted in her chest. "Not a fan of the shells, then."

With a sigh and a rumbling sound of displeasure, Anselm conceded defeat and gobbled down the rest of the eggs whole.

"We'll sort it," Sarah whispered, her hand gently running over his rough scales. "Tomorrow, we'll find you something proper."

"It's getting late," Peter said, his tone tinged with guilt for leaving. "We should probably head back. C'mon, Liv. See you tomorrow, yeah?"

Olivia hesitated, then stepped forward, wrapping her small arms around Anselm's massive neck in a timid hug. The dragon, despite his fearsome appearance, seemed to shrink slightly under her touch. A low rumble, almost like a contented purr, vibrated through his chest. Closing his golden eyes, Anselm nuzzled his head gently against Olivia's small form, his movements careful and tender.

Pulling away, Olivia turned to Sarah, "Bye, Sarah," she said shyly. Then, without another word, she ducked behind Peter, slipping her hand into his for reassurance, and stole one last glance at Anselm before the two stepped out of the barn and headed down the lane toward home, their footsteps fading into the night.

Sarah watched them leave—two kids she barely knew before today—and felt a warm sense of camaraderie. They were in this together.

Sarah stayed with Anselm, talking to him as he dozed off. Despite the language barrier, a sense of understanding passed between them. Anselm's golden eyes seemed to hold a wealth of knowledge, and Sarah felt hope. Maybe, tomorrow, they could figure out a better way to communicate.

The familiar rattle of her mother's bicycle on the gravel driveway signaled it was time to leave. With a final glance at Anselm, Sarah slipped out of the barn. As she walked back toward the farmhouse, a new worry bloomed in her chest. A few eggs wouldn't be enough. *Where would they find enough food to sustain a dragon? Would he eat a chicken? A sheep?* And then there was the suitcase—the Nazi flag and the strange artifacts inside it. A nagging feeling clung to her, refusing to let go. Those items held a mystery that demanded answers. Whatever tomorrow held, she knew it would be unlike anything she had ever faced before.

Chapter 11

A crisp evening air settled over a newly established Allied airfield in France. Floodlights cast an artificial daylight on the runway, illuminating a row of P-47 Thunderbolts that gleamed like new under the harsh lights.

A lone cricket chirped defiantly against the backdrop of activity on the base. Corporal Evans made the final adjustment to the P-47's Pratt & Whitney R-2800 Double Wasp radial engine. A satisfying click echoed softly, a comforting sound along the quiet runway.

Here, behind the lines, the war felt distant, like a storm on the horizon, held at bay by the pilots he supported. He wiped his grease-stained brow, the metallic tang in his nose a familiar friend. Sleep, after a long day, beckoned.

The rhythmic thrum of a jeep engine shattered the fragile peace. Miller, his youthful face creased with worry lines that seemed to deepen by the day, pulled up beside Evans. The endless job of ensuring everything was ready weighed heavily on him. Tracking the status of equipment, managing unreasonable demands from superiors, and the constant longing for home added to his burdens. Each day felt like a balancing act, where even a minor slip could have dire consequences.

"Hey, buddy? Think she'll make tomorrow's patrol?" Miller asked.

Evans stepped back from the aircraft, wiping his hands on a rag. "Yeah. She's good to go. Just finishing up."

A series of pops crackled from the heart of the base, like firecrackers going off. Both men spun around, recognizing it as the sound of gunfire. Their eyes darted to the tree line separating the rest of the base from the runway.

An unsettling silence followed. Then, a blinding flash and thunderous sound erupted. A plume of orange fire shot skyward, casting an eerie glow across the previously peaceful airbase.

Miller shook off his shock and came to his senses, throwing the vehicle into gear and shouting, "That was the fuel depot! Get in! We're under attack!"

Evans stared, a tightness gripping his gut. It couldn't be an attack—it was too quiet. *Where was the roar of aircraft or the whistle of incoming artillery?* This wasn't a normal attack. This was something else entirely.

The jeep swung around, tires spitting gravel as Miller gunned the engine towards the main base. But the horror wasn't confined to the fuel depot. Vehicles, tents, and a newly erected quonset hut were going up in flames as well.

A guttural shriek ripped through the night ahead of them. Evans swung his head around as one of the P-47s was bathed in the flickering orange glow of flames. Then another. Evans' breath caught in his throat as he realized they weren't random explosions. Something large and dark was streaking down the row of planes towards them, spewing fire like a monstrous blowtorch.

Miller, his youthful face etched with terror, slammed the

jeep into reverse. The ground rushed by in a blur as they fled in the opposite direction. But escape was a fading hope. The plane Evans had been working on suddenly became a twisted wreck, roaring into flames as they passed. Heart pounding, Miller jerked the wheel, executing a sharp Y-turn. The jeep skidded, tires screeching, before he shifted gears and got it going forwards once more.

A colossal shape passed overhead. Evans craned his neck, a strangled cry escaping his lips. A monstrous creature rushed past them, its wings shrouds of darkness and menace. Its roar, a deafening concussion of sound, shook the very ground.

With a sickening crunch, the creature landed directly in front of the speeding jeep, its massive form crushing a nearby water truck. In the harsh glare of the fires, Corporal Evans locked eyes with the beast – a dragon! Its crimson scales shimmering in the light of the burning aircraft.

The men's minds reeled as they struggled to comprehend the impossibility of the creature before them. The dragon's eyes, blazing like twin suns, fixed upon the jeep and its two occupants. Miller cursed loudly, and threw the jeep into a hard left turn, barely avoiding a direct collision with the beast's massive clawed talon as it took a swipe at the jeep.

The dragon let out an earth-shaking roar, its wings beating the air with a thunderous sound. Evans could feel the heat from its fiery breath even from meters away. It reared its head back towards the destroyed truck, and a stream of fire shot forth, engulfing it in a billowing explosion of flames.

"Get the rifle!" Miller yelled, his voice strained with fear as he swerved the jeep around obstacles, narrowly dodging another blast of fire from the dragon.

Evans fumbled for the rifle in the back of the jeep—an M1

Garand. Bringing it to his shoulder, his hands trembled as he prepared to fire. He looked back at the airfield, now a chaotic scene of burning planes and scattering survivors. The dragon, reveling in the panic and destruction it had unleashed, let out a triumphant bellow, its eyes locked onto the two men in the jeep.

Evans emptied the M1's clip at the dragon, the metallic ping echoing as the last round was fired and the empty clip popped out. But the shots bounced harmlessly off the dragon's scales, his desperate scream of frustration swallowed whole by the dragon's earth-shaking roar.

The dragon reared back once again, its crimson scales glowing with malevolent heat. Miller and Evans both tried to shrink back into their seats in a futile attempt to evade what was coming.

The dragon's fiery breath washed over the jeep, a searing inferno which consumed everything.

The world dissolved into blinding white, the last sound reaching their ears was the deafening crackle of flames.

A metallic crunch echoed through the night as the flaming jeep collided with the burning remains of an aircraft, leaving an eerie silence in its wake.

A hurricane of wind erupted from the dragon's wings as it slowly launched itself skyward. Two other colossal shapes materialized from above the smoke and ash, their roars echoing across the devastated airfield.

The three monstrous forms circled overhead, then disappeared into the night. The smoke slowly began to clear, revealing the horrifying extent of the carnage. No human soul stirred. The once-bustling airfield was reduced to an ashen wasteland. In the heavy, acrid air, only silence remained.

Chapter 12

Sarah sat hunched beside Anselm, her heart heavy with worry. She gently stroked his scaled hide, each labored breath he took resonating through her fingers. Each exhale was a reminder that he wasn't improving. The makeshift splint seemed to be holding, but uncertainty gnawed at her. The wheeze in Anselm's breathing indicated that he was hurt far beyond what they could handle on their own.

The creak of the barn door sent a jolt through Sarah before she realized it was Peter and Olivia.

"Your mum?" Peter asked quietly.

"She left ages ago," Sarah replied, her voice hoarse. "Won't be back till dusk."

Peter looked at Sarah, a question burning in his gaze. "Did she suspect?"

"She was too knackered last night to notice much… well, almost," Sarah said with a wry glance at Peter and Olivia. "She wasn't too thrilled about there not being any eggs."

Sarah cast a worried glance at the dragon, its massive frame barely rising and falling with each strained breath. Her eyes then returned back to Peter and Olivia. Now that the immediate threat of discovery was gone, the gravity of their situation could settle in, forcing them to contemplate the difficult decisions they needed to make.

Peter broke the silence first, his voice low and steady. "We need to figure out what to do next," he said, though the words felt inadequate given the enormity of the task.

He began pacing back and forth, his mind a whirlwind of thoughts and ideas. The gravity of their situation bore down on him, every scenario he considered leading to more questions than answers. Anselm, lying motionless save for the rise and fall of his labored breathing, followed Peter's movements with his golden eyes.

With a low groan, Anselm shifted his body, his massive frame trembling with the effort. Wincing painfully, he nudged the suitcase forward, its leather surface scuffed and weathered, until it slid into view, out where it could be seen by the children.

A tense silence descended upon them, broken only by Anselm's ragged breaths. Peter's eyes went to the crumpled Nazi flag, and a cold dread washed over him. The flag wasn't just a symbol of the enemy; it was a chilling reminder that something big was going on. They needed to know what.

Taking a deep breath, Peter asked, "Sarah, would there be any butcher's paper in the cottage? We need to know what Anselm was doing with that flag and those objects."

"I think so," Sarah replied suddenly understanding. "I'll go get it and something he can write with."

Turning back to Anselm, Peter continued, "Anselm, I know you're hurt, but you've got to tell us—why are you here?"

Anselm, pain evident in his eyes, nodded in agreement.

Sarah returned with the paper and a box of crayons.

Anselm maneuvered himself upright with great effort,

lowered his head, and forced himself to focus. His three clawed fingers grasped the crayon awkwardly, revealing the difficulty of using a tool designed for human hands. With a slow, laborious movement, he managed to scrawl a message on the paper. The message in broken English: "**STOLE TO STOP THEM. TAKE TO AUTHORITIES. MAKE THEM LISTEN OR MANY MORE DRAGONS**"

Peter stared at the message, his face pale. "Blimey," he muttered. "Many more dragons? What does he mean by that? Are the Nazis making more of them? Are they already out there?"

Anselm began coughing, a terrible sound, like rocks grinding together accompanied by the faint crackle of embers.

Sarah's frustration spilled out in her voice. "He doesn't need the authorities! He needs a doctor, someone who can help him."

"Sarah, he's trying to help us. He's—he's trusting us to help him and stop… whatever this is." Peter gestured toward the suitcase and the flag. "If we want to help Anselm, we should do as he says," he said firmly, his eyes fixed on Anselm's message. "We need to take the contents of the satchel—the camera, the stone, and the papers—to the authorities. It's our best chance. Maybe whoever understands the papers and the stone will also know how to heal a dragon…." His voice trailed off as his gaze returned to Anselm.

Hope sparkled in Sarah's eyes. Perhaps the authorities did hold the key to both problems.

Peter thought about where to find the authorities they needed.

"The base on the coast," Peter suggested. "It's the closest, that's where we need to go."

73

A wave of unease washed over Sarah. The base was kilometers away, far too distant to reach on foot. But as she looked at Anselm, his breaths shallow and labored, she couldn't believe there weren't other options. "It's too far, Peter. Why can't someone nearby, in the village help Anselm?"

"This is bigger than Anselm. The Nazis are up to something the military needs to know about," Peter countered, his voice firm. "We need to tell someone at the top."

Peter paused, a glint sparking in his eyes. "You are right, though, it is too far, unless…" Peter glanced towards the doors of the barn, where outside there was a large tarp billowing slightly in the breeze. Beneath the tarp, Sarah knew, sat her father's pride and joy – a gleaming black 1938 Morris Eight.

Sarah's father had always babied the Morris Eight, treating it with an affection that bordered on reverence. He had purchased it before the war, a decision that had sparked heated arguments with her mother, who thought it an unnecessary luxury. Yet, her father had insisted, he had to have it.

It soon became a centerpiece of family adventures. They would pack a picnic basket and head out for leisurely tours of the countryside, the car gliding smoothly over the rolling hills and through picturesque villages. After which, her father would always meticulously clean it after every trip, polishing the chrome hubcaps and ensuring the spoked wheels gleamed. The elongated fenders and running boards were always free of dirt, and the interior was spotless, smelling faintly of leather and motor oil.

The thought of using her father's car for a high-stakes mission filled Sarah with dread. "Peter, no!" she protested, her voice trembling. This wasn't just about getting into trouble— it was about risking her father's most treasured possession.

Sarah folded her arms tightly across her chest, staring at Peter in disbelief. She had only met him and Olivia the day before, and now here he was, standing there, asking to take her father's car. A car! And he was only thirteen! The sheer audacity of it left her speechless for a moment.

Peter squared his shoulders, his hazel eyes meeting hers. "I know how it sounds," he admitted. "But what choice do we have? You said it yourself, we need to help Anselm—and we can't do that without getting the authorities at the base involved."

"You can't be serious," she finally said, her voice filled with both shock and frustration. "You're just a kid! You've barely known me a day, and now you're asking to drive my dad's car?"

He hesitated, looking as earnest as he could manage. "I've driven before. A tractor, anyway," he added quickly when Sarah's eyebrows shot up in disbelief. "It's not that different. It will be fine!"

Sarah's arms dropped to her sides as she gawked at him. "A tractor? Peter, that's not the same thing at all!"

"It's close enough!" he insisted, his voice firm but not unkind. "Look, I know how this sounds, but think about it – we need to get to the base fast. What other options do we have?"

Her gaze went toward Anselm, who lay injured nearby. Her mind raced. The thought of Peter, a boy barely older than herself, behind the wheel of her father's car was absolutely mad. But then again, what choice did they have?

She bit her lip, glancing between Peter and the dragon. "What about the constable?" she suggested. "We could tell him. He'd know what to do."

Peter shook his head, having already anticipated the idea. "The nearest bobby is in town—the same town as the base. We'd still need to drive there to reach him."

Sarah frowned, trying to think of another option. "Alright, but what about the veterinarian? Mr. Clark's in the village. He could help Anselm, and he's closer."

Peter's face tightened. "A vet might know how to help a horse or a cow, but this is a dragon. You think Mr. Clark has a manual on how to take care of a dragon?"

"Well, no…" she admitted, her voice faltering.

"And what if he blabs to the locals?" Peter said, his tone sharp. "You know what people can be like. They'd lose their heads, and before you know it, there'd be a mob with pitchforks storming up here. They'd kill him out of fear!" His voice dropped, and his gaze shifted toward Anselm. "He wouldn't stand a chance if word got out."

Sarah's shoulders slumped, her heart sinking. "But… we can't just leave him like this."

"We won't," Peter said firmly, his voice steady. "The base is our best chance. They're the only ones who might have the resources—the people—to help him properly."

"This is insane," Sarah muttered, more to herself than to Peter. "Absolutely insane." Her mind raced, grasping for something—anything—that didn't involve letting a thirteen-year-old boy drive her father's beloved car. But every idea she considered fell apart as quickly as it came.

As if sensing her hesitation, Anselm nudged her gently with his snout. He grunted painfully, then managed to push the suitcase toward her, reminding her of the importance of informing someone in charge. Sarah's heart melted, and tears welled in her eyes as she looked at him.

She turned to Peter, with no room for argument. "Fine," she said reluctantly. "But if you crash it, Mum will have your hide"

Chapter 13

The Morris Eight had a short, curved hood that gave it a neat, compact look. Under the hood, it housed a reliable four-cylinder engine. Not the fastest or best performance, but steady and dependable, with more than enough power for a 13-year-old driving for the first time. Thankfully, Sarah's father had insisted on keeping a small petrol reserve in the barn "for emergencies," a foresight that now felt eerily prophetic.

This car, Sarah's father's pride and joy—a pre-war beauty he'd saved years to afford—now rumbled precariously under Peter's uncertain touch. Peter was enjoying the rumble of the engine, feeling like he'd gotten the hang of driving. Barely tall enough to see over the dashboard, his young frame dwarfed in the leather seat, he had contorted himself into an awkward yet surprisingly effective driving position, his eyes glued to the winding road ahead. His confidence growing with each kilometer, the ease of maneuvering the Morris Eight lulling him into a sense of mastery over the vehicle.

Peter turned to grin at Olivia, who was sitting next to him.

The car began to drift off the road, jolting Peter back to reality. The tires squealed in protest as Peter overcompensated and the car wove to the opposite side of the road. Sweat slicked his palms despite the cool morning air. Olivia's grip on her seat was a vice, her wide eyes mirroring his own. They couldn't afford mistakes. Not with Anselm's life hanging in the balance.

As he accelerated, the Morris Eight responded with a throaty growl that reverberated through the cabin. His earlier confidence had given way to a newfound respect for the machine and the skill required to control it. Yet, as they picked up speed, the steering began to feel smoother, and Peter started to feel at ease once more.

Olivia held on, her silence punctuated only by the occasional gasp as Peter navigated a sharp curve or avoided an oncoming vehicle.

Reaching a sharp bend, Peter misjudged the turn, and the car veered off the road, crashing through the underbrush. Olivia screamed, gripping the edge of her seat as Peter's heart pounded in his chest. He slammed on the brakes, and the car jolted to a halt, half-hidden in the tall grass. For a moment, they sat in stunned silence, the only sound the ticking of the cooling engine.

"Sorry, Liv," Peter whispered, his voice trembling. "I guess I've… I've never really driven before. Not for real."

Olivia's grip on her seat loosened slightly, her breathing ragged but steady. "It's okay," she said softly. "Just be careful."

Peter nodded, swallowing hard. He restarted the engine and carefully reversed the car back onto the road, his hands shaking as he maneuvered the wheel.

Sarah had trusted him—trusted him with her father's car, with the chance to help Anselm—and here he was, nearly proving her fears. He couldn't afford to be reckless. Not with Olivia sitting beside him. And not with Sarah, back at the farm, counting on him to get them to the base and back safely.

After that, his knuckles went white on the wheel. This time, Peter kept his focus, navigating each curve and stretch of road with care. Every imperfection in the road now seemed magnified, shaking his confidence with each bump and dip. Peter's earlier bravado had been replaced by a caution. He wouldn't let them down.

They managed to make it safely to the outskirts of the town bordering the military base. The Morris Eight, now bearing scratches from their off-road excursion, continued to rumble faithfully under his extra careful guidance.

The town came into view, its narrow streets alive with the morning bustle of activity. Delivery vans rattled over cobblestones, shopkeepers propped open doors to let in the cool breeze, and bicycles wove through the crowd, their bells ringing cheerfully. Yet, beneath the veneer of everyday life, the tension of war lingered. So close to the Kent coast, the town had borne its share of the war's weight.

Before the D-Day landings, a little more than a month earlier, German long-range artillery stationed across the Channel on the French coast had shelled the coastal communities. A few of the town's buildings bore the scars—jagged cracks spidering up stone facades, boarded-up windows, and fresh patches of mortar where shrapnel had struck. For years, the residents had lived with the terrifying unpredictability of the barrages, seeking shelter in hastily dug trenches or basements when the warning sirens wailed.

Now, with the landings pushing the front lines farther away, the shelling had ceased, but the memory remained vivid in the minds of those who lived here.

Peter navigated cautiously, keeping to quieter streets as they ventured further in. Olivia's wide-eyed silence spoke volumes, her gaze darting around in wonder, so different from the quiet countryside she was accustomed to.

Peter eased the car down the narrow streets, the cobblestones rattling the vehicle as he gripped the steering wheel tighter. The stiff clutch and heavy steering demanded every bit of his small frame to maneuver. As they inched along, Peter's heart raced with the fear of being caught; he was only thirteen, far too young to be driving—and in a vehicle he didn't exactly have the proper permission to be driving, anyway.

The streets were bustling with a mix of military vehicles, bicycles, and pedestrians going about their wartime routines. Spotting a parking space proved to be quite the challenge. Every street seemed occupied, either by a stationary military truck or makeshift stands selling rationed goods.

"There!" Olivia exclaimed, pointing excitedly at a small gap between two trucks. It was a tight fit, but Peter carefully maneuvered the car into the space, wincing as the car jostled over the curb. He killed the engine and sat for a moment, heart pounding with a mixture of relief and exhilaration.

Peter gave Olivia a weak smile and small nod, which she returned. Together, they opened their doors and stepped out of the car.

Olivia watched Peter retrieve the case from the back seat and lift it into the boot, which he closed with a click. Peter felt a pang of worry about leaving such important things unattended in a busy town, but it was safer than carrying them.

Taking Olivia's hand, Peter glanced around the square, orienting them towards the military base. It was a brisk walk away, through the heart of town. People bustled about, and soldiers marched by, creating a bustling backdrop to their mission.

As they approached the military base, guarded by uniformed soldiers and surrounded by barbed wire-topped fences, Peter felt a mix of nerves.

At the imposing gate stood a lone young soldier on guard duty. He ignored them until they were standing close, then scrutinized them intensely.

"We need to speak to someone in charge," Peter blurted, his voice cracking.

The soldier, unsurprisingly, replied with a mixture of amusement and annoyance. "I don't think so mate."

"You don't understand, we have information vital to the war effort," Peter pleaded.

The soldier raised an eyebrow, curiosity piqued despite his irritation. "You do, eh? Let's hear it then."

"We're under strict instructions to only share the information with someone of authority," Peter responded, trying to sound authoritative himself.

"Who instructed you, eh?" the soldier challenged unmoved.

Peter hesitated, realizing that he had failed to come up with a good reason for two kids to enter a military base, "It's classified," he said, hoping to sound convincing.

The soldier's expression hardened, clearly unimpressed. "Classified, huh? Look, kid, I don' have time for your games. Beat it"

Olivia, sensing Peter's desperation, blurted out, "We need to tell someone about the dragons!"

A beat of stunned silence followed. Peter whipped his

head around to glare at Olivia. A surge of panic flooded through him. The soldier's amusement vanished along with his tolerance. His posture stiffened, his gaze turning stern. He wasn't going to waste his time talking to children anymore.

"Leave now, little man. I've had me fill of your nonsense." The soldier barked, his voice filled with annoyance. Peter opened his mouth to argue. "Now! Before you get into real trouble."

The dismissal stung, but Olivia tugged on his sleeve, her eyes wide with fear. The soldier had given her a fright, and pushing their luck wouldn't help. With a defeated sigh, he turned and started walking away, the weight of the impossible situation pressing down on him. The soldier's words echoed in his ears. They were just kids, with a story no one would believe. Yet, if they failed, Anselm's life—and perhaps the country's fate—would be jeopardized. Everything depended on them finding a way onto the base.

Peter and Olivia retreated from the base and found a quiet spot a short distance away, hidden by a tall formal hedgerow. Peter clenched his fists, frustration tightening his throat, while Olivia looked down, her face pale.

Olivia glanced up at him, her small hand reaching out to grip his sleeve. "Peter... that soldier was really mad."

Peter kicked a stone in the dirt. "He wouldn't even listen. He thinks we're making stuff up."

Olivia's brows knit together. "But we're not. He doesn't know about Anselm."

Peter nodded, his jaw tightening. "No. He doesn't." He scuffed the ground with his shoe, his voice dropping. "We're just kids. Why would anyone take us seriously?"

He swallowed hard and glanced back toward the base. For a fleeting moment, he considered climbing the fence—but the image of angry soldiers, shouting and dragging them away, made his stomach twist. Then another image followed: Anselm, hurt and helpless. Sarah, trusting him to succeed.

"I'm scared, Liv," he admitted quietly. "What if we can't find anyone who'll help?"

Olivia tightened her grip on his sleeve. She didn't say anything—she just looked at him, certain he'd think of a way.

Peter shook his head, doubt pressing down on him. "Don't look at me like that. No one's going to believe us."

He stared back at the base, the gates tall and unyielding, then let out a heavy sigh. "Come on," he muttered. "Let's head back to the car."

Olivia's eyes widened. "But—"

"It's no use," Peter said, cutting her off. "They won't let us in. I don't know how to make them listen."

He turned and started walking. Olivia followed, her footsteps dragging on the gravel. Each step felt heavier than the last. He couldn't shake the feeling that he'd failed—not just Olivia, but Sarah... and Anselm.

Sarah's face rose unbidden in his mind—not the one arguing against the plan, but the one that had trusted him enough to hand over her father's car. She'd taken a risk, knowing what she could lose, and believed in him anyway.

His pace slowed. If Sarah could take that risk, how could he walk away now? How could he give up when Anselm was counting on them?

Peter stopped and turned to Olivia. She looked up at him, worry etched across her face. The town hummed around them, oblivious.

He took a deep breath.

"Alright," he said. "We're not giving up. We'll try again. We have to find someone who'll listen—even if we're just kids."

He glanced back toward the base, fear still knotting his stomach, then met Olivia's eyes.

"Okay, Liv. We'll try again."

Olivia's eyes widened with surprise, but then a spark of hope flickered in her expression. "What are we going to do?" she asked cautiously.

Peter hesitated, glancing back toward the base. "I don't know yet," he admitted, "but we'll find a way. There's got to be someone there who will listen. We just have to find them. We'll have another go at getting onto the base."

Olivia bit her lip. "Okay. But... you go first, right?

Peter gave her a smile. "Yeah. I'll go first." He took a deep breath, nodding to himself as much as to Olivia. Even though his hands shook, and every instinct told him to turn back, he knew they couldn't. They were all Anselm had.

Peter led Olivia around the perimeter of the base, their footsteps soft against the gravel. They spotted another gate where a soldier stood, distracted as he checked a vehicle. Peter saw their chance. A small guardhouse stood near the gate, flanked by concrete barriers that led up to it. He knew those barriers would provide perfect cover. The rhythmic thump of truck engines would mask any noise they made.

"Come on, Olivia," he whispered, pulling her along.

They slipped through the gate unnoticed, their hearts pounding as they ducked behind the barriers. Peter pressed his back against the cold concrete, his breath coming fast and shallow. Olivia crouched beside him, her eyes wide with nervous energy. For a moment, neither of them dared to speak.

Quickly, they darted behind the small guardhouse.

Peter peered around the corner of the building to take in their surroundings. Trucks rumbled past, soldiers moved about the base. The guard at the gate remained oblivious to their presence.

"Right," Peter whispered, turning back to Olivia. "We need to figure out where to go next. Somewhere with officers—someone in charge."

"How will we know who's in charge?" Olivia asked, her voice barely above a whisper.

Peter hesitated, his mind racing. "Look for someone with the most stars on their uniform, I suppose," he said, his tone laced with a forced confidence. "We can't just wander around aimlessly. We need to look like we know what we're doing."

He scanned the base again, his gaze flitting over the rows of barracks and the tall radio tower looming in the distance. "They'll have a command building, I reckon," he said. "That's where the officers will be. It's bound to be near the centre of the base."

Peter turned back to Olivia, his face set with determination. "Let's go. If anyone asks, we're with someone—an uncle or something."

Peter had just begun to lead Olivia from behind the guardhouse, toward the nearest row of buildings when a shadow fell over them. Before he could react, a strong hand clamped down on his shoulder, followed by another on Olivia's arm.

"And where do you lot think you're off to, then?" a soldier growled, leaning in close, his face inches from theirs.

Peter's heart hammered against his ribs. "We… we're trying

to find our…. uncle, sir" he stammered, grasping for a reason. "Private John Thompson. Our mum said he's stationed here and we were supposed to meet him."

The guard narrowed his eyes, clearly unconvinced. "I don' know any Private Thompson," he said sternly. "You lot can't just stroll onto a military base, you know."

Trying to look as sincere as possible, willing the guard to believe the truth, "Please, sir, We have vital information for the war effort, sir." Peter insisted, trying to keep his voice steady.

The guard raised an eyebrow and leaned in to Peter's face. "Really? Come on then, what's so important that you kids think it's worth the trouble you're going to get into for sneaking onto the base?"

"We can only tell the person in charge, sir" Peter replied, his voice wavering but determined. He glanced at Olivia, who kept silent this time.

The guard eyed them sternly. "I'm going to have to call this in, you know." he said, reaching for his radio. Peter saw a ray of hope, "Yes. Please, sir. Call whoever is in charge. We need to speak to them urgently!" The guard directed them to wait in the small guardhouse while he stood outside to make the call.

While they waited, Peter paced nervously while his mind raced, rehearsing what he would say when the guard returned. Olivia sat on the edge of a wooden bench, her legs swinging as she fidgeted with the hem of her dress. The minutes dragged on, each second feeling like an eternity.

The guard returned with another soldier. "Right, you two," he said. "This private here's going to take you back to the main gate. You can't be wandering about playin' games."

"We're not playing games!" Peter protested. "If you'd just listen—"

The guard ignored him. They were marched back to the gate, where the first sentry's irritation was already written across his face.

"Didn't I tell you two to clear off?" The soldier turned and called to an older man nearby, who was smoking a cigarette and chatting with a lorry driver outside the fence. The man was wearing a flat cap and had a face weathered by time and the sun. His broad shoulders and rough hands were the product of a lifetime of labor. "Mister King, sir, could you please give us a hand here?"

Defeat settled over Peter like a shroud. The look of despair was in his eyes as he stole a glance at Olivia. Her lower lip was trembling, and a fat tear welled up in one eye, threatening to spill over. But she quickly blinked it back. They couldn't give up. Not yet.

"What's all this, then?" the old man asked, his bushy eyebrows furrowed with curiosity as he looked at Peter and Olivia. His voice, surprisingly gentle for his weathered appearance, rumbled like distant thunder.

"These two 'av been caught snooping around, sir," the guard explained. "An' I'm struggling to decide whether to send 'em home or lock 'em up. What do you think I should do with them, sir?"

The old man eyed them for a moment. "Ah… I understand. Hand them over to me, soldier, I'll see to it they're sorted properly."

"Much obliged, sir," the soldier replied, giving the kids a threatening glare before returning to his post.

The old man turned to Peter and Olivia. "Alright, kids. This isn't a place for messing about."

"But sir, we're not messing about—we really do have important information, honest!" Peter protested as the old man led them away. Panic clenched at Peter's gut. They were getting further away from where they needed to be.

The man shook his head. "I'm sure you think you do. Now come along, let's get you back to where you're meant to be."

Defeated once more, Peter and Olivia were led away, their hopes dimming but not extinguished. They had to find another way to make the authorities listen. Anselm's life depended on it.

Peter silently vowed not to give up. He turned and stood directly in front of their escort. "I know we're just kids, sir, but we really do have important information for whoever's in charge. And we're not going to give up," Peter insisted, his voice unwavering despite the odds against them.

The man regarded Peter, taking a long drag on his cigarette, the glowing ember momentarily illuminating his face. "Alright, listen here. I'll strike you a deal. I'm not one of the top brass, but I'm with the Home Guard, and I know the ones who are. You tell me what you've got, and I promise, if it's something they need to hear, I'll see to it they do."

Peter felt a glimmer of hope. Maybe, just maybe, they had found someone who would listen. "Thank you, sir."

The man introduced himself. "Thomas. Thomas King."

Peter hesitated for a moment before taking the offered hand. "Thank you, Mr. King. I'm Peter, and this is my sister, Olivia.

Olivia offered a shy nod. Mr. King smiled kindly at her before leading them to a small park. A monument to the Great War, its surface etched with names stood in the center, honoring the men from the town lost during the First World

War.

Mr. King turned to them, his expression patiently reserved. "Right then, lad, let's hear this information you think is so important."

Peter glanced at Olivia, who gave him a small nod. His best chance was to tell Mr. King about the suitcase. If he mentioned Anselm, the man would think he was pulling his leg.

"Er, right, sir. It's about… well… we came from a farm in Bedfordshire and… um… we've got some things that came crashing through the roof of our mate's barn." He winced as the heat of embarrassment crept up his neck, realizing how absurd it sounded.

"Fell through the roof of your friend's barn… from an airplane, was it?" Mr. King guessed.

"No… not exactly, sir," Peter replied, hesitating. "It's… complicated," he admitted, shifting uncomfortably. "But it's really important. Someone at the top needs to see them."

Mr. King raised an eyebrow, looking at Peter intently. A flicker of something danced in his cloudy blue eyes for a brief moment, then his expression became curious. "Hmph… Not from an airplane."

Peter's mind raced, each passing moment feeling like their chance to save Anselm was slipping further away. He had to convince Mr. King of the importance of the suitcase, but how? *Could he mention the stone with the strange markings? Would that make Mr. King think they were mad?* Peter bit his lip, glancing at Olivia, who was watching him anxiously.

There was no other way. He'd have to show him. His voice cracked as he stammered, "They're in the car, Mr. King. In a suitcase."

Mr. King studied him for a moment, then gave a short nod. "Alright, let's take a look, then."

He followed the kids back to the car. Peter paused before opening the trunk, praying that Mr. King would recognize the importance. He opened the trunk. "Under the flag, in the suitcase, sir."

Thomas raised an eyebrow at Peter as he recognized the enemy flag, then moved it aside to get to the suitcase. Peter felt a bead of sweat roll down his temple. This was it. Their only chance.

Mr. King opened the suitcase. Inside were the papers, photos, the camera, and the strange stone. He pulled out the papers and began to look them over. All in German, and they looked official. They were plans for something. Each page with a stamp of the German eagle over a swastika. The camera too had German labels.

Thomas lifted the stone from the satchel, a look of puzzlement crossing his face. "This thing doesn't quite fit with the rest, does it?" he murmured, turning it over in his hands. "It's... oddly warm," he added, studying it. "Feels like it's been sitting near a fire."

He held it up to examine the strange symbols etched across its surface.

"Well," Mr. King muttered, placing the items back in the case, his tone calm but curious, "this does seem to be something, possibly important. But I need to know—where exactly did you come by them?"

Peter hesitated, choosing his words carefully to steer clear of mentioning Anselm. "Um, well, sir, someone gave them to me—they brought them over from Germany. Said it was really important they got to the authorities"

Mr. King frowned, his eyes narrowing slightly. "Didn't you say before they fell through the roof of a barn?"

Peter nodded, trying his best to keep his story straight. "Yes, sir. They did. The person who… stole them—he… well, like I said, it's complicated, sir."

Mr. King studied Peter's face for a long moment, his expression unreadable. Finally, he sighed. "Peter, what you've got here may be important, but I can't take this to the authorities without knowing the full story. You'll need to explain what's so complicated, lad."

Peter felt a lump in his throat. He didn't want to mention the dragon, but he knew the items were vitally important. Olivia looked at him with wide, anxious eyes, silently urging him to tell the truth.

Sweat prickled on his forehead despite the cool morning air. Deciding the best thing to say felt like a tightrope walk, his stomach twisting with anxiety.

Finally, Peter gave in. "I swear on my honor, sir, the items didn't fall through the roof on their own… they were carried by a," Peter felt his mouth become dry, "a…dragon. He fell through the roof."

There was a moment of silence. The old man took a long drag of his cigarette, exhaling slowly. He studied Peter and Olivia for a long moment, his weathered face unreadable.

Stupid! Why had he mentioned Anselm? This might have been the only chance to report everything to someone in authority and he'd blown it.

"A dragon." Thomas repeated, his voice quiet.

Peter nodded earnestly. "Yes, sir. A dragon. I swear! On my honor! It's the truth!"

The old man chuckled softly, shaking his head, something

dancing in his cloudy blue eyes. "Well, I'll be... A dragon."

"It's true, sir, my brother never lies," Olivia insisted desperately, her voice trembling. "He's real."

The old man regarded them thoughtfully. "It's alright. I believe you."

Peter was shocked. "You do?" He believed? This man must be crazy. Believing kids talking about dragons. "You believe we got the suitcase from a dragon?"

Mr. King closed the suitcase in the boot and looked at the children calmly. "I don't know. But I know someone who claims he saw a dragon not two days ago, and I trust him. He's been a laughingstock ever since he reported it. If what you're saying is true, he'll be very relieved to know he's not mad." A spark of curiosity showed his eyes, tempered by skepticism, but there was something else—he was intrigued.

Peter nearly collapsed with relief as Olivia threw her arms around him, the sense of reprieve washing over them both. "Thank you, Mr. King! Thank you so much!"

Thomas then directed the kids down the street, "Come on, then" His voice surprisingly gentle for such a large man. "let's find Orville."

They made their way through the bustling streets to a nearby pub. The sign above the door read "Rosewood" and the sounds of laughter and conversation spilled out into the street as they entered.

Inside, the air was thick with the smell of tobacco and the chatter of locals. A few patrons cast them curious glances as they entered, but their attention quickly returned to their drinks. One patron against the far wall, though, a woman with fiery red hair and an enormous grin, turned her attention on them. Her gaze was unnerving, and Peter couldn't help but feel a prickle of unease run up his neck.

Mr. King led the children to a corner table where an older man with a bushy mustache and a faraway look in his eyes was nursing a pint.

"Orville," Mr. King called out, guiding Peter and Olivia to sit down. "I'd like you to meet…"

Peter, interrupted politely, "Peter, sir. And my sister, Olivia."

Orville looked at the children, startled. He clearly expected them to be making fun of him. But their serious expressions held him captive.

Mr. King leaned in closer to Orville, his voice dropping to a low murmur. "These two—Peter and Olivia—they've come across something. Let's just say it's something that could have a bearing on the war effort." His eyes met Orville's meaningfully. "And what they've found… well, it's connected to what you saw the other day, Orville."

Orville's eyes widened, and for a moment, hope flickered across his face. His eyes softening. "Did they see it?"

As Peter was about to answer he noticed the woman at the back of the pub again, her eyes still fixed on them with the same disconcerting grin. Her eyes seemed to bore into them.

Peter tore his eyes away from the woman and met Mr. King's gaze, his expression tense. He gave the slightest tilt of his head in her direction, his brows raised meaningfully, hoping Mr. King would catch on. Then, barely moving his lips, he whispered, "That woman, sir."

Mr. King's gaze shifted toward the woman, picking up on Peter's subtle signal. He studied her for a moment, his eyes noting her posture and the hint of a grin, carefully assessing whether she posed a threat. He remembered seeing her loitering around before, especially when Orville was around.

At last, he gave a small nod, his voice calm but resolute. "Right you are, lad," he said, keeping his tone light. "Let's be on our way. This isn't the place for this sort of discussion." He turned smoothly, motioning for the others to follow as they headed toward the exit, casting a casual glance back at the woman.

As they were leaving the pub, Peter looked back towards the woman. Her unsettling grin hadn't wavered, and her eyes, sharp and cold as chips of ice, were still fixed on them.

Outside, the group moved through the town and back to the car. Peter felt relieved and excited that they had succeeded in their mission. Mr. King would take the suitcase to the authorities and in doing so maybe they could find someone to help Anselm.

Back at the car Thomas retrieved the suitcase from the boot, and popped it open with a snap. Nestled inside was the camera and the strange, carved stone, and underneath the stack of papers stamped with a symbol Orville recognized all too well – the German eagle clutching a swastika. Orville's eyes widened as he took in the symbol.

"Well…", he murmured, a nervous flutter settled in his stomach.

Orville leaned closer, his gaze fixed on the papers. His breath caught in his throat as he pulled them out of the suitcase.

"Undeniably German. Schematics… plans, don't you think?. Something big." He shook his head, exhaling slowly.

Thomas placed a hand on Orville's shoulder. "The kids here, Peter and Olivia, found these on a farm. They say they were brought from Germany."

Peter piped up nervously, "Mr. King, we really need to

get moving. She's followed us." His eyes looked back in the direction of the pub, seeing the woman with the unsettling grin casually working her way up the street.

Thomas motioned for Orville to close the suitcase as he looked back towards the woman. "Right then, everyone in the car. Let's be off, shall we?"

They all piled into the vehicle, with Thomas taking the wheel. Peter in the passenger seat beside him, Olivia on his lap, while Orville settled in the back, still engrossed in the paperwork. His brow furrowed in concentration, and occasionally a muttered phrase escaped his lips, "...unlike anything I've ever seen... and these symbols...?" Thomas started the engine, and Peter felt a surge of relief.

But when he glanced back, his stomach lurched. The woman stood in the street, her unnerving grin fixed on them as she watched the car pull away. An eerie, uncontrolled giggle escaped her, and her cold, calculating gaze didn't waver as they disappeared down the street.

Peter's chest loosened, a sense of calm beginning to settle over him. He felt their worries might finally be behind them. Once they reached the base, not only would they be safe, but they'd get the help they desperately needed—people who would know what to do with the strange papers, who could help Anselm, and who might finally make sense of it all.

But as Mr. King turned the car out of town and away from the base, Peter's relief faded, replaced by a sinking feeling. He looked at Mr. King, brow furrowing. *Where was he taking them?*

"Hold on, Mr. King, where are we heading?" Peter asked, alarmed.

"Back to your barn in Bedfordshire," Mr. King replied calmly.

"But shouldn't we be taking the items to the authorities?" Peter protested.

Mr. King kept his eyes on the road. "If I walk in there talking about dragons, they'll lock me up with you," he said evenly. "I need to know exactly what I'm saying before I put my name to it."

Then he glanced at Peter, his expression reassuring. "Aye. We will, Peter. But first, I need to see... it with my own eyes. That's something the authorities need to know about as well."

Olivia squeezed his hand, her eyes wide with concern.

Peter felt torn, anxiety gnawing at him. It was crucial to get the items to the authorities, yet proving the dragon's existence to Mr. King was important as well. The older man didn't seem like he meant any harm to Anselm.

"Alright," Peter said finally. "But please, we must hurry!"

Taking Peter's direction, Thomas accelerated the car down the road. Orville, in the back seat, continued to examine the papers muttering to himself. "These documents... they're blueprints for something big."

"Alright, lad," Thomas rumbled, his voice gentle, "tell us everything. About the barn, the suitcase, and the dragon."

At the mention of the dragon, Orville looked up sharply, his eyes wide. He'd been mocked and dismissed as a fool for reporting that he'd seen a dragon.

Peter looked at Olivia who nodded encouragingly, then forward at the road. Every moment felt like a ticking clock, each second wasted time.

Peter hesitated for a moment, then launched into the story. He spoke of Sarah's discovery of the hole in the roof of the barn, finding the suitcase with its contents. He needed to tell Mr. King everything, but mentioning Anselm to strangers made his stomach churn. Yet, the dragon's condition was worsening, they couldn't afford to waste time. His voice dropping to a hushed whisper as he told them about the injured dragon.

Silence hung in the car as Peter finished. He stole a glance at Orville in the rear-view mirror. The man's face was pale, his eyes wide with a mix of shock and... relief?

A choked sob escaped Orville's lips. "A dragon," he whispered, his voice thick with emotion. "I knew it! I knew I wasn't crazy!" Tears welled up in his eyes, spilling over and tracing tracks down his weathered cheeks. "They laughed at me... called me 'Daft Orville and his flying serpent.'" His voice cracked as he spoke the cruel nickname, the pain of the ridicule still fresh.

"I reported it, you know. Straight away, but when I described it—" He gave a bitter laugh that caught in his throat. "Wings like umbrellas, a serpent body—they laughed before I even finished."

His gaze fell to his lap, his hands clutching his cap tightly. "The lads at the base made me the butt of every joke. The villagers weren't much kinder. Even Thomas here—" Orville hesitated, glancing at his friend, his voice softening. "Even you thought I'd lost my marbles."

Thomas shifted uncomfortably, his expression pained. "Orville, I believed that you thought—"

"It's alright," Orville interrupted. "I saw it in your eyes, mate. You thought I'd gone barmy." He let out a shaky breath and leaned back, staring out the window as the countryside blurred past. "But I wasn't mad, was I? I saw it. And now...

98

now you know I saw what I saw."

The car fell silent again, the weight of Orville's words settling over them. After a moment, Thomas looked back. "I'm sorry, Orville," he said quietly, his voice steady.

Orville didn't reply immediately, but the faintest hint of a smile touched his lips. "It's alright, Tom," he said at last, his voice soft. "You still stood up for me. What matters is… it's real. I didn't imagine it. And that… that's enough."

Peter took a deep breath and turned back towards Orville. "The dragon… Anselm, he's hurt—really badly. He really needs help! We thought—well, we hoped—that going to the authorities might mean finding someone who could do something for him."

Orville, his eyes widening. "The dragon is injured, you say?" Memories stirred – years spent at a Casualty Clearing Station during the First World War, the sights and sounds of mangled bodies etched forever in his mind. Instincts honed in those harrowing days, surged to the surface.

"Yes, sir," Peter continued, his voice steady but urgent. "When we found him, he was very weak—quite badly hurt. And he's getting worse. He needs medical attention, or he might die."

Orville spoke with renewed purpose, his expression serious. "Then we'd best get a move on."

With his eyes on the road, Thomas gave Peter a reassuring nod. "If anyone can help, it'll be Orville," he said with quiet confidence. "He's patched up plenty of injuries in his time."

The car sped along the road, the countryside blurring past. Peter looked at Olivia, hoping he had made the right choice. Anselm's fate—and perhaps much more—depended on what they did next.

Chapter 14

The car glided to a stop in the driveway, a plume of dust billowing behind it. As they stepped out, Sarah came running out of the barn, tears streaking her pale face. She cast a wary glance at Thomas and Orville.

"Peter! Peter!" Her voice was frantic. "Anselm won't wake up!"

Peter felt a cold wave of fear wash over him as he raced to the barn with Sarah, followed closely by Olivia, Thomas, and Orville. "What do you mean he won't wake up?" he asked as they reached the barn.

Sarah grabbed his arm, her eyes wide with fright, and dragged him inside the barn. "I tried everything! He's just lying there, barely breathing! I don't know what to do!"

Inside, the massive creature lay on its side, its scales dulled, its breathing labored and shallow. The air was thick with the smell of dust and something else—a metallic tang, like blood.

Orville saw the dragon, and a lump formed in his throat. Amazement, fear, and a powerful wave of vindication washed over him all at once. He remembered that evening on the Dover cliffs with Thomas, just days ago. He'd seen it then— clear as day against the twilight sky—a dragon, wings wide and powerful. He hadn't doubted himself for a moment, yet when they'd made their report, no one believed him. People in town had broken into laughter whenever he walked by, calling him a fool, asking him to "give their best to the fairies" next time he was on watch. The memory of their laughter still echoed, raw and sharp.

But now, here it was—undeniable, magnificent, and real. A dragon lay before him, scales faintly gleaming even through the dirt and blood. He hadn't imagined it. He hadn't been mad. He had seen it. He had been right.

Thomas stood frozen at the doorway, his breath catching in his throat as his eyes locked on the massive creature. His usual calm exterior cracked under the sheer impossibility of the sight before him. He felt lightheaded, as though the air had been sucked out of the barn.

"I don't believe it," he murmured, his voice barely audible, almost lost in the heavy stillness. He rubbed the back of his neck, his hand trembling slightly, then ran it down his face as if trying to ground himself. His knees felt weak, and he steadied himself against the door frame, his gaze never leaving the dragon. "A dragon... a proper dragon."

Orville shot him a sideways glance, but Thomas raised a placating hand. "Alright, mate," he said, his voice tinged with awe. "You were right. There it is."

Peter knelt down beside Anselm, his face taut with worry, his hands hovering helplessly. Sarah knelt by Anselm's head, her lips trembling as she touched the dragon's forehead. "Help him," she pleaded, her voice barely a whisper, full of desperation.

Orville took a deep breath, steadying himself, willing his hands to stop trembling. "Alright," he managed, though his voice wavered, the thrill of what he was witnessing still rattling through him. He removed his coat, rolling up his sleeves with a purpose, and stepped forward carefully, a cautious reverence in his movements.

Steeling himself, he cleared his throat and said, "Right then... let's see what we can do."

Orville began at the top of Anselm's head, his fingers brushing over the textured scales as he marveled at their rough yet smooth surface. The sight of the enormous creature, injured but alive, sent a renewed thrill of awe coursing through him. Warmth radiated from the dragon's massive body, but the sharp wheeze accompanying each rise and fall of its breath was a sobering sign of its fragile state.

He worked his way down the dragon's long neck, his hands moving with care, searching for the source of the dragon's distress. His fingers brushed against each ridge and curve with deliberate precision, his focus sharp as he reached its broad torso.

As he continued his inspection, Orville's gaze caught on the deep, ragged gashes along Anselm's belly, mostly hidden but unmistakably severe. For a moment, the sight transported him back to the battlefield—the suffocating stench of blood, the unending wails of the wounded, the desperate scramble to save lives. The memories surged forward, threatening to paralyze him, but he pushed them aside with practiced focus. Wound care was wound care, whether for a human soldier or for a creature that defied every law of nature.

"Let's get him rolled over," Orville commanded urgently, "Thomas, Peter—lend a hand."

Peter and Thomas moved swiftly to assist. Together, they carefully shifted the dragon.

Their shock was palpable as they beheld the large bleeding

gashes across Anselm's abdomen, as though a massive claw had torn through the scales and into the soft flesh underneath.

"We'll have to move fast," Orville said, his voice tight. He turned to Sarah. "I need clean clothes to clean the wound—antiseptic if you've got it, or alcohol. Even vinegar will do in a pinch. And bandages, plenty of bandages!"

Nearly panicked by the urgency, Sarah raced to the farmhouse without hesitation, Peter close on her heels. Moments later, they returned with clean cloths, sheets, a bottle of Dettol antiseptic, and a bottle of vinegar. Orville took the supplies, setting them down carefully.

He poured a small amount of antiseptic directly onto his hands, rubbing them together thoroughly before turning to Anselm. With measured precision, he poured more antiseptic onto a cloth and began cleaning the wounds, mindful not to startle the dragon. Anselm stirred slightly, his breathing shallow. A pained snort rumbled from his throat, sending shivers down Sarah's spine.

"We must slow the bleeding," Orville muttered, his brow furrowed in concentration. Orville reached for the pile of clean sheets Sarah and Peter had brought, swiftly tearing them into strips. "Peter, keep pressure on with these cloths. We need to stem the flow."

Peter did as he was told and pressed the cloths against the gash, feeling the warmth of the dragon's blood seeping through. Orville worked quickly and methodically, applying more antiseptic. With practiced hands, he began to wrap the sheets tightly around the dragon's abdomen.

Anselm's massive form required repositioning him with care to fully secure the bandages around his torso. Peter, Thomas, and Orville worked in tense coordination, straining against the dragon's weight as they gently shifted him from side to side.

"Steady on," Orville murmured, his voice calm as he adjusted the bandage. "We'll have this sorted in a moment."

Peter and Thomas braced themselves, their arms trembling slightly under the effort. Supporting Anselm's immense weight while Orville worked demanded every ounce of their strength, but Anselm's labored breaths focused them on the intense urgency.

Finally, Orville finished securing the bandage with a firm knot, ensuring it was snug but not constricting. He stepped back, wiping the sweat from his brow. "There. That should do it for now."

Peter stepped forward, handing Orville a cloth to clean his hands. "What else can we do, sir?"

Orville sighed, his gaze lingering on the dragon. "We need to keep him comfortable, monitor the injuries, and make sure he doesn't get worse. But beyond that…" He trailed off, leaving the rest unsaid.

Sarah gazed at the bandaged dragon, her hands trembling. "Sir, will this be enough?"

Orville drew a deep breath. "We've done what we can for now. It's hard to say. He's got a chance. Has he been eating or drinking anything?"

Sarah shook her head, worry etching lines on her forehead. "Only a few dozen eggs and water in the last few days."

Orville frowned. "He must be absolutely famished. A creature of his size needs far more nourishment than that, especially with wounds as serious as these."

"Come on, Anselm," Sarah whispered, her voice thick with emotion as she gently stroked the dragon's face. "You have to be okay. Please be okay."

Chapter 15

The afternoon sun hung high in the sky, casting sharp shadows across the landscape below. A formation of twelve B-17 Flying Fortresses droned steadily toward their target deep in the heart of Germany. The hum of their engines reverberated through the air, each laden with bombs destined for factories that supplied the Nazi war machine.

Captain Jack Morrison's confident expression spoke of countless hours spent in the air. A veteran of thirty bomber missions, he gripped the yoke with a seasoned precision. His co-pilot, the young and eager Lieutenant Samuel Jenkins, monitored their course while the other pilots in the flight followed their lead, keeping the formation tight. The intercom crackled with chatter from the other bombers, the crews exchanging nervous banter to ease the tension.

"Looks like our little friends have reached their limit. They're turning back for England.'" Jenkins noted, watching their fighter escorts, P-47 Thunderbolts, peel away and head for home. "Damn shame they can't launch from France anymore."

A series of crippling attacks on new Allied airfields in France had severely hampered their ability to fly fighter missions into Germany. Now, all escorts were launching from England.

The P-47 Thunderbolts, with their limited fuel range, simply couldn't make the round trip from England and still provide protection for the entire mission. They were forced to turn back sooner, leaving bombers vulnerable as they entered German airspace.

"Eyes peeled!" Jenkins called through the intercom. The young gunner at the waist, Henderson, barely out of his teens, swallowed hard, checked his machine gun, betrayed by the tremor in his hands.

The drone of the engines thrummed a monotonous beat. Everyone on board was scanning the endless blue canvas above for the telltale glint of Messerschmitts. The deeper they penetrated into German airspace, the thicker the silence seemed to grow, broken only by the rasp of nervous breaths.

A curt but urgent call echoed through the intercom, "Mark Eight! Bogeys at five high!" The tail gunner's voice held a practiced edge, not panic. Morrison acknowledged, his own focus already glued to the sky above. Muscle memory kicked in as his hands tightened on the controls.

Morrison twisted in his seat and scanned the sky, expecting the familiar silhouette of a German fighter. Instead, his breath caught in his throat as he squinted at three dark shapes plummeting from high above. They weren't the clean lines and sharp angles of German engineering. Their outlines were wrong and their forms moved with an unsettling grace, unlike anything he'd ever seen before. "Those aren't fighters..." Morrison muttered, his brow furrowing in confusion. "What the hell—?"

The shapes resolved into what looked like three massive birds descending upon the bombers from above and behind. With their wings tight against their bodies, they sliced through the air like living missiles.

A collective gasp echoed through the intercom, a mix of surprise and confusion. Over the roar of the engines, Morrison heard a startled cry from the flight engineer behind him who was manning the top turret.

Plane by plane, the .50 caliber machine guns came roaring to life. Tracer rounds streaked through the sky, but the targets twisted and dodged with unnerving agility, evading the bullets with ease.

The pilot of "Storm Front," further back in the formation, exclaimed into the radio, "They're dragons!!!" A beat of stunned silence followed, broken only by the staccato chatter of the machine guns.

The lead dragon, a monstrous beast with red scales and fiery eyes, slammed into "Eagle Eye." Its claws tearing into the fuselage with a deafening screech of rending metal.

Morrison watched in horrified fascination from the "Magnolia" as the dragon, its wings tucked tight, clung to the fuselage like a monstrous tick. A guttural roar erupted from the beast, shaking the very air, as its powerful legs propelled it towards a wing. The dragon ripped away the aileron with a sickening tear, then plunged its claws into the bomber's exposed wing, tearing open a gaping hole in the fuel tanks. Gallons of flaming fuel erupted from the wound with a fiery whoosh, trailing the bomber like a monstrous comet's tail. "Mayday! Mayday!" the frantic voice from "Eagle Eye" echoed in Morrison's headset, as the stricken bomber started to spiral downwards. He gritted his teeth, a cold fury replacing the initial shock. They weren't targets. To these beasts, they were prey.

The second dragon, a vast serpent with scales shimmering

an unnatural crimson, ignored the hail of .50-caliber rounds pinging off its hide like pebbles. It swooped down upon "Iron Lady," its immense form casting a monstrous shadow that engulfed the doomed B-17. With a deafening screech of metal tearing, the dragon's razor-sharp claws raked across the fuselage, tearing gaping wounds in the aluminum skin.

Twisting with unnatural agility, the beast caught the vertical stabilizer, and ripped the rudder off with a sickening snap. The impact sent a violent shudder through "Iron Lady," throwing the tail gunner, Miller, against his harness. Pain lanced through his arm, but adrenaline surged as he continued firing his .50 cal Browning machine gun in a desperate hail of bullets.

Suddenly, a colossal claw tore into the side of his compartment. Miller, momentarily stunned, watched in horror as the dragon, with a cruel twist of its wrist, forced the barrel of his machine gun to point directly at the bomber behind them, "Storm Front." The crew in "Storm Front" had no time to react. A torrent of bullets, ripped through the nose cone of "Storm Front," killing the nose gunner and flight crew.

As "Iron Lady" fell away, trailing smoke and fire, followed by "Storm Front", the dragon wasted no time. With a powerful leap, it propelled itself towards the next B-17 in the formation, its crimson scales glinting maliciously in the sun.

Sweat beaded on Henderson's forehead as he tracked the dragons through the waist gunner's sight on the "Magnolia." Each burst of fire he unleashed seemed to dissipate harmlessly in the air. The monstrous creatures twisted and turned with impossible agility, their scales glinting like obsidian in the sun.

"They're dodging our fire! What the hell are they?" Henderson shouted, his voice tight with fear and a hint of raw frustration echoing through the intercom of the "Magnolia."

The third dragon, its scales shimmering with an infernal glow as if stoked by an internal furnace, targeted "Flying Fortress." A deafening roar, like a mountain collapsing, erupted from its maw as it propelled itself towards the doomed B-17. With a bone-jarring impact, the dragon slammed into the side of the bomber.

A heartbeat of horrified silence followed. Then, a torrent of white-hot flames erupted from the dragon's maw, engulfing the open starboard gunner station in an inferno. The flames roared through the fuselage, an unstoppable wave of searing heat. Screams ripped through the intercom, cut short in horrifying succession as the fire consumed the crew.

The stricken B-17 shuddered violently. Black smoke billowed from the gaping hole in its side, trailing behind it like a tattered funeral shroud. Undeterred, the monstrous serpent began to crawl up the fuselage towards the cockpit. With a screeching roar, the dragon smashed the windscreen and let loose another blast of flame into the cockpit. The formation lost another bomber.

The pilot of "Mermaid," from the middle of the formation, panicked as a dragon pounced towards it. In a desperate, in-stinctive reaction trying to avoid the dragon his B-17 lurched dramatically, but the maneuver was a fatal miscalculation.

The belly of "Mermaid" slammed into the topside of "Win-drover," the B-17 flying directly below and behind them in formation. Both bombers, crippled and spewing black smoke, spiraled out of control, leaving a trail of debris in their wake.

Despite the best efforts of the bomber crews, the dragons'

assault was relentless. One by one, the B-17s were picked off, their once formidable formation falling into chaos. Flames and smoke filled the sky as the dragons tore through the bombers with savage efficiency.

At last, a dragon's monstrous shadow engulfed "Magnolia." Morrison and Jenkins wrestled the controls, the plane dipping precariously under the dragon's weight. "Bail out! Bail out!" Morrison roared into the intercom, the finality echoing in the cockpit.

Inside, the crew fought desperately against the impending doom. Morrison and Jenkins wrestled the controls as the ground below loomed closer.

The bomber struck the ground with a devastating impact. The once mighty Flying Fortress crumpled upon itself, the force of the crash tearing it apart.

Parachutes had blossomed across the sky as surviving crew members of the formation leapt from the crippled planes. For a brief time, there was hope of survival. But the dragons weren't finished. With a chilling efficiency, the beasts swooped down, snatching men from the air in turn like rag dolls. Screams echoed for horrifying moments - then died away into an unsettling silence.

Chapter 16

Orville checked on the dragon, his experienced hands hovering over Anselm's injuries. The creature's breath was still shallow and labored, his usually vibrant scales dull and cool to the touch. "He's in shock," Orville explained, his voice grim. "We need to get him warm. Blankets, anything."

Sarah dashed to the cottage, her heart pounding. She returned moments later, her arms full of thick quilts and blankets. Dropping them nearby, she knelt beside Anselm, tears welling in her eyes as she rested a trembling hand on his snout. "It's alright," she whispered softly, her voice shaky but soothing. "You're going to be alright."

Peter and Olivia helped throw the quilts over Anselm's enormous body, the fabric barely enough to cover his scale-plated sides. As Peter tucked the last edge in place, he glanced at Orville, curiosity flickering through his worry. "How do you know so much about this? The first aid?"

Orville straightened, his gaze lingering on the dragon for a moment. Sadness crossed his face, drawn from memories of a long-ago time. "Used to be a medic," he replied gruffly. "During the Great War. Seen my share of injuries, big and small."

He paused, his gaze shifting from the dragon to the worried faces around him. "Well. Let's be prepared for when he wakes up. He'll need sustenance to regain his strength. Sarah mentioned he's only had a few eggs since he arrived—nowhere near enough for a creature his size. See what kind of food there is around." Orville looked to Thomas, "Some meat?"

Thomas grunted in acknowledgment, his brow furrowing thoughtfully. "Right then, I'll see what I can manage." His gaze shifted to the dragon. "I reckon I saw some sheep across the way. That ought to do for starters." With that, Thomas turned and headed out the door.

"You know," Orville began, his voice calm and reassuring, "Thomas was a butcher, before his son took over the business."

Sarah, still kneeling next to Anselm with her brow furrowed in worry, offered a small smile. "Thank you for helping Anselm, Mr...?"

"Morris. Just call me Orville, and you're welcome." He turned to Peter. "Now, let's have another look at that suitcase, Peter."

Peter went outside to fetch the suitcase from the car while Orville pulled out the pages he'd set aside earlier. Skimming the pages, his brow furrowing as he studied the strange symbols.

Orville's eyes widened as he scrutinized one page. "These symbols... I know I've seen their like before." After a few moments his face changed as the realization came to him, "They're runes. Like the ones on the ancient stones in the countryside."

Peter returned, the leather suitcase clutched tightly in his hands. He set it down carefully near Orville who opened it revealing the amber stone, the rest of the papers, and the movie camera. He lifted the camera out and examined it, "wish we could see what was on the film. It needs to be developed." He returned the camera carefully back to the suitcase, and reached for the stone. It was warm in his hands. He turned it over, his gaze fixed on the intricate markings etched onto its surface. "Runes," he muttered, almost to himself. "These ARE runes! I'm sure of it."

He traced the etching on the amber stone with a finger, a distant look coming into his eyes. "I'd see old stones standing in the countryside when I was young. My grandma would tell me stories about them," his voice low and raspy. "Stories about the little people." He trailed off, the light coming in through the hole in the roof dancing in his rheumy eyes. "I haven't thought of those markings in decades. I never knew what they really meant. Still don't."

While they talked they failed to hear the crunch of gravel outside, followed by the creak of a bike stand snapping open.

Sarah's mom stood at the door of the barn, her brow furrowed in confusion and bewilderment. "Sarah! What's going on in here? Why is your father's car in the drive? Who are these people?"

Her gaze scanned the interior of the barn, taking in the strangers, overturned crates, scattered bandages, and then—
the massive form in the back, shrouded in her quilts.

A strangled gasp escaped her lips, her hand flying to her mouth.

Chapter 17

S arah leapt up upon seeing her mother, chastising herself for losing track of time. "Mum!" she exclaimed. Peter and Olivia instinctively stepped back, trying to blend into the shadows of the barn. Peter kept his eyes fixed on the floor. Beside him, Olivia clutched her hands tightly, her wide eyes darting between Sarah and her mother as she edged closer to Peter.

Sarah's mother stood frozen in the doorway, her face in complete shock.

"Mum! I can explain everything," Sarah promised frantically. But before she could speak further, a low rumble echoed through the barn. Everyone's attention snapped towards Anselm.

He didn't rise or open his eyes fully—just a clear bit of movement beneath the heavy lids and a sluggish lift of his massive head. It was a small sign, but for them, it was monumental joy. A wave of relief washed over Sarah, tears welling in her eyes.

Olivia, unable to contain her joy, let out a choked sob and went to the dragon's side. She sank to her knees beside him, her hand hesitantly reaching out to brush against his cool scales. "Anselm," she whispered.

Anselm's head dipped back to the floor, a faint exhale escaping his nostrils. It was barely a response, yet it spoke volumes. He was alive, he was aware. A collective sigh of relief filled the barn.

Sarah's mother, however, remained rooted to the spot, her eyes wide with disbelief. This wasn't a horse, a cow, or any animal she knew.

This was a monster.

She took a shaky step back, her gaze locked on the dragon. "That... that's not..." she muttered, her voice verging panic.

Her gaze shifted to the group gathered calmly around the barn. Strangers—an old man and a pair of children. Confusion painted across her face. Who were these people, and why were they here? What on earth had Sarah gotten herself into?

Sarah, sensing her mother's thoughts, approached her and squeezed her hand reassuringly. "Mum, it's okay. I will tell you about all of it." She took a deep breath, bracing herself for the most unbelievable story she'd ever tell.

Orville stepped forward, offering a polite nod as he set down a sturdy wooden produce crate. "Ma'am, would you like to sit down? I'm Orville Morris," he said gently, keeping his tone calm and reassuring. "I know this isn't something one expects to see in their barn."

He glanced at the dragon, then back at her, his expression tinged with unease as he sought to diffuse the tension. "Your daughter and her friends have come across something rather extraordinary... well, it's quite out of the ordinary, isn't it?" He paused to collect his thoughts before continuing, "Rest assured, ma'am, we're here to assess the situation properly, to understand what we're dealing with, and then to report it through the appropriate channels," he said, then quickly added, "And, of course, to help."

Sarah's mother stood unmoving, her eyes fixed on him with a blank stare, struggling to process what she was seeing and hearing.

He gestured toward the crate. "Please, ma'am, if you'd care to sit for a moment and collect your thoughts, take it all in at your own pace."

Sarah's mother sank onto the crate without a word. Her hands trembling, but as she looked at Sarah, she began to overcome her shock. She reached out and gripped her daughter's hand tightly, her voice trembling but firm. "Sarah... what on earth is happening? Are you all right?" Her wary gaze shot to Orville.

"Mr. Morris, you'd best explain yourself. Why are you here, and what is that... that creature?"

Orville opened his mouth to answer, choosing his words carefully. "Mrs. Lynde, I understand this all seems—"

Just then, Thomas stepped in, a dead sheep slung over his shoulder, its smell instantly filling the barn, overpowering the stale scent of blood.

"That wasn't easy. All I had was me penknife," he grunted, letting the sheep drop with a heavy thud near Orville. "Found this one straggling by the fence, thought it'd do for a start."

Sarah's mother whirled around, her face pale, eyes wide with disbelief. She struggled to find her voice, her gaze darting from the sheep to Thomas. "Who...?" she stammered, her fingers tightening on Sarah's hand.

"It's alright, Mum," Sarah squeaked. "That's—"

"Mr. King," Peter chimed in.

"Mr. King! He and Orville came to help," Sarah finished

117

quickly, her voice trembling. She looked at her mother, her wide eyes pleading for her to understand.

Orville cleared his throat and stepped in. "Ah, Mrs. Lynde… this is Thomas. He's here to, er… assist with the situation, you see." He gestured towards the dragon. "The dragon is in need of, well… care, and Thomas is… sorting out its meal."

Orville managed a nervous smile, wiping a hand across his brow. "I know it's rather a lot to take in, but… well." His gaze darted to Thomas, then to the dragon, and back to Mrs. Lynde, his composure teetering. "We came to look into what the children were saying," he explained, a hint of exasperation creeping into his voice. "And, believe me, Mrs. Lynde, I was just as taken aback as you… but I assure you, everything's under control."

"It's okay, Mum," Sarah offered, "they really are here to help."

Peter stepped forward, his tone polite yet earnest. "I'm Peter Clarke, ma'am, and this is my sister, Olivia. We live just up the lane. I know it's a lot to take in, miss, but it was Olivia and me who found Mr. King and Orville, and we brought them here to help with Anselm."

Her mother's gaze darted between Sarah, Peter, the dragon, and the dead sheep. Fear gave way to exasperation. "Help with what, exactly? Sarah, what on earth have you got yourself mixed up in?" Her eyes locked on Anselm, her voice rising with a tremor. "And wh-what is that?"

Sarah took a deep breath, forcing herself to stay calm. "There's been a lot going on, Mum. That's Anselm. He fell through the roof—he's hurt, and we've been looking after him."

Her mind grappled with the situation, her eyes moving from the imposing form of Anselm to the worried faces of her daughter and the strangers, the enormity of it all hit her like a wave—the dragon, the strangers, the danger her daughter might be in. Her breath caught, her chest tight with anxiety and confusion. She managed to whisper hoarsely, "I… I need some air."

Without waiting for a response, she stood and hurried out of the barn leaving an unsettling silence in its wake. Sarah watched her mother go, a knot of worry tightening in her stomach. She knew explaining everything wouldn't be easy, but seeing the fear and confusion in her mom's eyes made it even harder.

Sarah glanced back at Anselm, his form still covered by the blankets. The previous movement reassured her. He was alive, that was all that mattered.

Taking a deep breath, Sarah turned and followed her mother outside. The fresh air hit her, a refreshing change from the stale warmth of the barn. Her mother stood by the fence, her back to Sarah, standing stiffly, arms crossed, trying to calm herself with deep breaths.

Inside the barn, the silence stretched. Orville checked on Anselm while Olivia stroked the dragon's brow. Peter cleared his throat awkwardly

Muffled shouts reached inside the barn. "A dragon!" came the voice, on the verge of hysteria.

Thomas broke the tension, "Alright, then. Where can I clean this sheep? Don't want the flies gathering." Gesturing towards the dead sheep with his chin.

Peter, "Uh… At the pump, I suppose."

Peter led Thomas out of the barn and they slinked past Sarah and her mother. Her mother still taking deep breaths to calm herself.

"This is beyond reckless, Sarah!" Her mother's face was etched with frustration as she reached out and placed her hands firmly on her daughter's shoulders. "A dragon, Sarah? A dragon? How can this be? It's a wonder you weren't killed!"

"I know, mum," Sarah leaned into her mother and embraced her, "But, he's not what you think. He's weak, injured. And... he's intelligent, he wouldn't hurt anyone. He talked to us."

Sarah's mother sighed, pinching the bridge of her nose. "Alright, alright... Start at the beginning. How did this.... creature even end up here? And how did it get hurt?"

Sarah, relieved that her mother was calming down. "It all started a few days ago, Mum. I was getting the eggs, when I saw a hole in the barn roof –"

Her mother's gaze drifted towards the barn, fear replaced by new emotions – a spark of curiosity battling with disbelief. *How could this be real? What HAD her daughter gotten herself into?*

Chapter 18

The sunlight cast long shadows across the dusty floorboards of the barn. Anselm seemed more stable, so Orville left him to sleep and crouched beside the open suitcase, its worn leather displaying the mysterious contents – a movie camera, an amber colored stone, and a stack of papers.

Orville's hands cradled the amber stone, its surface warm and smooth against his skin. The intricate symbols etched into its honeyed depths seemed to pulse with energy. He'd seen markings similar to these before, carved into ancient stones that dotted the countryside, their meaning lost to time. But here, in his hands… they meant something important.

Beside him, Olivia leaned forward, her eyes wide with wonder. 'What is it?' she breathed.

Orville's gaze met hers, a smile on his weathered face. "I don't know, Olivia," he said, his voice low. He extended the stone towards her.

Orville placed the amber stone in Olivia's small hands. Surprised by its unexpected warmth, a gasp escaped her lips. The stone slipped from her grasp and tumbled with a dull thud onto the wooden floor of the barn. The stone lay still, but for a fleeting moment, it seemed to shimmer faintly, as if reacting to the fall.

"Steady on," Orville cautioned patiently. "We oughtn't risk damaging it." With surprising agility for his age, he reached down and scooped up the stone gently. His gaze then shifted towards the doorway, where Sarah and her mother stood.

Sarah's mother's face was wary, her expression clouded with uncertainty over the startling revelations she'd just learned. Her gaze lingered on the glowing stone in Orville's hand before she looked at Olivia, deliberately avoiding glancing in the direction of the dragon. Sarah's account of what had occurred in the barn over the past few days must have seemed like a fever dream, overwhelming and surreal.

Taking a deep breath, Sarah stepped forward, her fingers nervously twisting a strand of hair, though her voice remained firm. "Mum, I'd like to formally introduce you to Orville… Mr. Morris," she said, gesturing toward the wiry man holding the stone. "Orville, this is my mother, Mrs. Lynde."

Orville carefully placed the stone back into the suitcase and offered Sarah's mother a warm smile. "Mrs. Lynde, I do apologise for the awkwardness of our earlier introduction." Straightening, he gave her a polite nod. "Allow me to properly introduce myself—Orville Morris, Home Guard, at your service. Mr. King and I came to look into the discovery your children were so keen to bring to our attention."

He cast a quick glance at the dragon before turning his attention back to Mrs. Lynde. "It's all quite extraordinary, I must say, but rest assured, we'll be notifying the proper authorities. They'll need to be made aware of this discovery." Orville paused, a faint smile playing at the corners of his mouth. "Though, if I'm honest, I've no idea how we're going to convince them it's real."

Mrs. Lynde's posture relaxed slightly, her gaze softening as she absorbed the sincerity in Orville's face. She gave a small, nervous nod, her voice faltering as she stammered, "How… how do you do?"

Sarah took a deep breath, "Mum," she began, "I know this is a lot to take in, but I need you to trust me. That's Anselm there. I would like you to meet him." She gestured towards the back of the barn, where the massive form lay, steeling herself for her mother's reaction.

Fear crossed Mrs. Lynde's face, her grip tightening on Sarah's arm. "Sarah, honey," she said, her voice strained, "I don't know."

She'd handled plenty of horses before but nothing could have prepared her for this. It wasn't a creature she knew. It was a dragon.

Sarah squeezed her mother's hand reassuringly. "It's okay, Mum. He wouldn't hurt anyone, I promise." Sarah knew blind trust was a big ask, but she needed her mum to see that it was safe.

Her mother hesitated, her eyes filled with a mix of apprehension but also a glimmer of curiosity. She glanced back at Orville, who offered her a gentle, understanding smile. Taking a deep breath, she let her apprehension soften just enough to nod slowly. "Alright," she said, her voice still wavering. "Alright."

Sarah led her mother towards the end of the barn. As they moved down the barn, she kept a tight grip on Sarah's arm. Her eyes widened as she took in the sheer size of the creature— bigger than any animal she'd ever worked with. An impossible creature, and yet it was real.

As they drew closer to where Anselm lay, Sarah's mother

123

stopped, her breath shallow. For a long moment, she simply stared, her mind grappling with the impossibility of what stood before her.

There was silence as Sarah's mum took in Anselm's form. Her fear started to melt away, replaced by a sense of wonder. The sight before her was magnificent – shimmering scales catching the last rays of sunlight, powerful claws tucked beneath the massive body, and a noble head resting peacefully.

"It really is a dragon," she whispered, her voice filled with amazement. Disbelief lingered, but awe quickly overshadowed it. This mythical creature, once confined to stories and legends, was real—and it was here, nestled in her barn.

A slit opened, revealing a large, intelligent eye. It blinked open, the golden iris catching the fading light. The dragon, Anselm, looked at Sarah's mother.

Sarah's heart swelled when she realized that Anselm's eyes were open. A warm smile bloomed on her face. "Anselm? Are you feeling better?" she asked, her voice trembling slightly with hope. Anselm purred weakly in response.

The sight of the massive creature stirring, however, sent a jolt of fear through Mrs. Lynde. Seeing him waking brought up a primal urge to protect her daughter. Mrs. Lynde reached for her daughter's arm. "Sarah, get back," she hissed.

"It's okay, Mum" Sarah gently told her mother.

"Anselm, this is my Mum," introducing the dragon.

Anselm's massive head lifted slowly, hinting at the full majesty of his form. His golden eyes watching Sarah's mother, taking in her cautious stance. In a display of surprising courtesy, the dragon dipped his head in a deep bow. A display of respect that seemed almost courtly.

This wasn't just a monstrous beast; there was an intelligence, a nobility. Fascinated, Sarah's mother found herself unable to tear her eyes away from the magnificent creature before her. The fear that had gripped her began to melt away. A tremor ran through her voice, barely audible, as she finally spoke. "How... how do you do... Anselm."

Chapter 19

As the late afternoon French sun cast long shadows across the expansive, weather-beaten farmyard, a group of GIs sought temporary refuge, finding relief from the heat and ongoing series of battles. Their faces etched with fatigue, they slumped against the crumbling stone walls of what was left of a farmhouse. The air was heavy with the scent of sweat, dust, and the lingering acrid tang of their weapons. A quiet settled, punctuated by sporadic conversations, the occasional cough, or the metallic clink of someone adjusting their gear.

Sergeant Levine leaned wearily against a weathered wooden post, his eyes scanning a worn copy of "Popular Mechanics" that lay open on his lap. The magazine offered a semblance of normality. Yet, even the articles within couldn't dispel the monotony that clung to him like the dust on his uniform.

A shadow fell across the page, and Levine glanced up to see Corporal Horowitz approaching. They had known each other since basic training.

"Sarge, you won't believe what I heard!" Horowitz blurted out with barely restrained excitement.

Levine sighed, lowering the magazine with a hint of amusement playing on his lips. "What is it now, Horowitz? A rumor about the Fuhrer having his mustache gold plated?"

Horowitz shifted uncomfortably at the jab, his reputation as the company's rumor mill preceding him. "The fellas down by the southern sector are spooked," he said, his voice tinged with the thrill of shared secrets. "The talk is that the Germans have a wonder weapon. Something fantastic they're using to take out airfields."

Levine's smile faded. "A fantastic wonder weapon, huh? Sounds like another tall tale to me." Despite his dismissal, the idea of airfields being leveled by any weapon made him uneasy.

Horowitz didn't look convinced. "Maybe. But there's somethin' else. Some of the locals... they were talkin' about a 'Feu... something.'"

"Feu...?" Levine trailed off, trying to recall his limited French. Fire?

Horowitz supplied, "Feuerdrachen."

Levine's interest piqued. "Feuerdrachen? What's that supposed to be?"

"A creature straight out'a their old folk tales." Horowitz leaned closer, his voice dropping to a conspiratorial whisper. "They say it can melt entire squads of men with a single breath."

Levine snorted, a laugh escaping his lips. "Hold on. Are you talking about, dragons? You're telling me the Krauts are using fire-breathing dragons now?"

Horowitz squirmed and rubbed the back of his neck, "Well. I don't know... but our airfields are being razed by something."

Levine scoffed. "Look, Horowitz," he said, "fire-breathing dragons? The Germans are probably using incendiary munitions on the airfields."

Horowitz nodded sheepishly. "I know, that makes sense, but… they would've said that, right? I'm just sayin', maybe we should keep an eye out for… unusual activity. Stories can have a sliver of truth to them, you know."

A silence descended upon them. The chirping of birds seemed to grow louder as Horowitz shuffled off to share his rumor with others.

Levine reopened the magazine, the worn paper crinkled in his hand. He couldn't help but glance up at the sky and wonder if there might be a grain of truth to Horowitz's rumor.

Chapter 20

The morning sun cast a gentle glow across the countryside, dappling through the trees and illuminating Sarah's path as she finished her usual morning chores. After gathering the eggs from the chicken coop, she'd stopped by the cottage to drop them off in the kitchen before heading towards the barn. The fresh scent of dew-laden grass mingled with the earthy aromas of the farm, creating a sense of serene normality. Yet, a small knot of anticipation tightened in her stomach as she approached the barn, hoping that Anselm was on the mend. She quickened her pace, her laced boots crunching on the drive.

Her mother had been particularly protective, insisting that Sarah not go into the barn without her. But today, determined to check on Anselm, Sarah had reassured her mother that it was fine as Orville and Mr. King were already in the barn tending to Anselm.

The two men had spent the night roughing it in the barn with Anselm. Although Sarah's mother felt uneasy about having two strangers on the farm, knowing they were there to keep watch over the dragon brought her a measure of comfort and eased her nerves.

With their presence now somewhat reassuring, she offered

to drive Orville and Mr King to the base, so they could inform the authorities about the suitcase—and about Anselm.

Informing the authorities was the right thing to do—Sarah was certain of that. It was the only way to help Anselm fulfill his mission. Yet, a nervous knot twisted in her unease settled low in her belly at the thought. *Would they take Anselm away. Or worse, what if they saw him as a threat and hurt him?*

These fears clung to her as she made her way to the barn. She tried to shake them off, focusing instead on the hope that today would bring good news—that Anselm was well and that everything would work out, somehow.

Inside, Orville and Thomas stood watching Anselm who was slurping up a large pot of lamb broth with surprising gusto. His eyes, though still weary, held a spark that hadn't been there the days before. He seemed less frail.

"Good morning, Sarah," Orville greeted.

Thomas nodded in greeting, "Morning," he said, though his expression was one of mild fascination. "Tried raw lamb earlier, he wouldn't touch it. Orville suggested hot broth, and that seemed to do the trick."

"A raw shank, eh?" Orville grimaced, catching Anselm's eye. "Wouldn't fancy that myself."

Anselm snorted in agreement.

Thomas grunted thoughtfully "Bit odd, isn't it? A dragon so particular about his meals?"

Sarah walked over and gently began stroking Anselm's neck, her fingers brushing over the rough, warm scales. "How is he doing?" she asked.

"Much better," Orville replied. "Getting food in him seems to be helping him regain his strength."

Anselm lifted his head from the pot, his gaze shifting from

Sarah to the two men. There was a softness in his eyes, a silent gratitude for their care. He let out a low rumbling purr, and went back to lapping at the broth.

Sarah smiled at Anselm and hugged him. "I am so glad you're feeling better." Anselm leaned his head into Sarah in response.

Just then, Sarah's mother appeared in the doorway, concern etched across her face as her eyes fell on her daughter, who was crouched so close to the dragon. She forced herself to look instead at Orville and Mr King, offering a small, tentative smile. "Did you both manage to sleep well?"

Orville straightened slowly from where he'd been crouching, wincing as a twinge of pain shot through his back. "We did, ma'am, thank you," he said with a sheepish smile. "The bedding you provided made all the difference—though I'll admit, sleeping on anything other than a proper mattress reminds these old bones just how old they are."

Mr. King chimed in with a polite nod. "Speak for yourself, Orville. I slept like a log. We're most grateful for your kindness."

Mrs. Lynde's smiled slightly. "I'm glad to hear that."

Her gaze shifted to the dragon. "And... is he better?" she asked hesitantly.

Orville looked at the dragon and then back at her with a reassuring nod. "Yes, ma'am. Much better," he said. Glancing at his watch, he added, "We should get ready to leave soon, don't you think?"

Her mother straightened, her relief evident. "Yes. Quite."

They had discussed it the night before and concluded that it was crucial to get the suitcase and its contents into the hands of someone in command without delay. Orville and Mr. King both knew the base commander in town and were hopeful he could ensure the contents reached the right people.

As they were talking, Sarah's classmate, Peter, and his younger sister Olivia, showed up to watch Anselm while the others were away.

"'ello, Sarah," Peter called out.. "How is Anselm?"

Sarah's face lit up at the sight of her friends. "Peter! Olivia! Anselm is doing much better!"

Peter approached the dragon,. "Hey, Anselm! How are you feeling today?" he asked warmly.

Olivia, still slightly behind Peter, added in a gentle voice, "Hello, Anselm."

Anselm bowed his head in response, his large eyes blinking slowly. A soft rumble emanated from his throat.

Sarah's mother's voice cut through their reunion. "Come along, Sarah, it's time we be going."

"But Mum," Sarah protested, torn between her mother's orders and her desire to stay. "Shouldn't I stay with Peter and Olivia to watch over Anselm?"

Her mother shook her head firmly, her tone leaving no room for argument. "No, Sarah. We've already talked about this. I'd rather not drive back on my own—I want you with me."

A wave of disappointment swept over Sarah, her shoulders sagging, she yearned to stay and help nurse Anselm back to health.

She opened her mouth to argue further, but a look from her mother stopped her. She understood. With everything that had happened, her mother's protectiveness had only grown stronger. Her unease about Anselm—and the trouble Sarah might find herself in while she was away—was clear. This wasn't just about the drive; it was her mother's way of keeping Sarah close, of keeping her safe.

"Alright, mum," Sarah conceded, looking back at Anselm, who watched her with a calm understanding gaze.

Peter stepped forward, placing a reassuring hand on Sarah's shoulder. "Don't you worry, we'll take good care of Anselm. You just focus on getting that lot to someone who can do something with it."

Sarah looked up at him, her lips twitching into a faint smile. She gave a small nod, her gaze dropping to the floor for a moment. "Alright," she said softly, her voice steadying as she looked back at him.

With a last look at Anselm and her friends, Sarah reluctantly followed her mother, Orville, and Thomas out of the barn.

Friends, she thought, a warm rush spreading through her chest. She had friends.

But just as quickly, a shadow of insecurity crept in. Would they still be my friends if there was no dragon to bring us together? The thought lingered for a moment before she pushed it aside.

The drive to the base was uneventful, the countryside rolling by in a blur of green and gold. In the back seat, Orville turned the amber stone over in his hands, his brow furrowed in concentration as he traced the intricate markings with a calloused finger. "I wonder if they're Stone Age pictographs," he murmured, his voice almost lost beneath the steady hum of the engine.

Beside him, Sarah leaned against the window, her eyelids growing heavy as the rhythmic vibration of the car and the muted sound of the tires on gravel began to lull her to sleep.

Sarah's breath hitched as she woke, the gate of the base just ahead. Prefabricated buildings painted a dull olive green stretched into the distance, their utilitarian facades a noticeable change from the rolling green hills they had left behind. A constant hum of activity filled the air—the rumble of a Bedford QL's engine as it passed by, the shouts of soldiers, the rhythmic click of boots on gravel. Despite the seriousness of wartime, a faint melody drifted from a nearby building—a gramophone playing a cheerful tune.

"There's a chance it might take several days before the higher-ups realise just how important all this is," Thomas explained. "And when they do, we'll have to… well, we'll have to tell them about Anselm. I can't say for certain how they'll take it."

Sarah's stomach tightened. They were placing precarious trust in strangers.

Orville leaned in toward Sarah, his gaze gentle. "Now listen, Sarah," he said, "he's getting stronger, faster than I'd have thought, but he still needs proper care. Make sure he's fed regularly, and check those bandages every day—you and Peter must keep an eye out for any sign of infection."

Sarah nodded, "I will."

He turned to Mrs. Lynde, offering a respectful nod. "And thank you, ma'am," he added sincerely as he slid out of the car. "What Sarah's done, looking after a dragon like that—it's remarkable. And the dragon… Anselm… well, it's clear as day he cares for her. He wouldn't dream of hurting a single hair on her head."

Thomas echoed Orville's sentiment. "He's not a beast, ma'am. He's a creature with intelligence and heart."

Orville and Thomas stepped away from the car. With a nod,

they turned and headed toward the base entrance.

As the two checked in at the guardhouse, a feeling of unease rose within Sarah. A woman with fiery red hair, a wild mane that defied any attempt at control, stood out from the crowd milling around the base entrance. She was watching them intently. The woman's gaze went from Sarah and her mother to Orville and Thomas, then back, lingering on them for an uncomfortably long time. Dressed in a simple, almost threadbare, country dress. There was something unsettling about her. Her smile was too wide, almost manic, revealing her teeth.

The strange woman approached Sarah and her mother, her gaze continuing to shift from Sarah and her mother to Orville and Thomas.

Sarah's mother asked hesitantly, "Hello, may I help you?"

The red-haired woman's grin widened further, her eyes gleaming with an unsettling amusement. A burst of manic giggling erupted, devoid of humor and laced with madness.

The sound sent shivers down Sarah's spine. It was a laugh that didn't reach the eyes, a laugh that spoke of hidden agendas.

Without engaging the woman further, Sarah's mother engaged the car and pulled away. The red-haired woman watched them leave, her grin never leaving her face. Then she turned and disappeared into the throng of people on the street.

Chapter 21

For the next week, there was no word from the authorities. Thomas and Orville remained in town, waiting for news, while back at the farm, the children cared for Anselm. Peter had learned a lot from Orville and diligently followed his instructions, checking Anselm's bandages, looking for signs of infection, and making sure the dragon was eating well. Sarah and Olivia assisted Peter, each contributing to Anselm's care in their own way.

Anselm's recovery was progressing remarkably well. The gashes across his abdomen, which were initially deep and painful, were healing rapidly. Each time Peter changed the dressings, he was pleased to see the wounds healing. The edges of the gashes were closing, and the risk of infection was decreasing.

One of Anselm's wings had been broken, and Peter had splinted it. Even that showed signs of recovery. Anselm could already move the wing with cautious, deliberate motions.

"You're mending nicely, aren't you?" Peter said one morning as he carefully applied fresh bandages. Anselm winced slightly but nodded, acknowledging the boy's efforts with a gentle rumble.

As Anselm's health steadily improved, his scales gained a sheen, and his eyes sparkled with a renewed vitality. One sunny afternoon, they decided he was well enough to come outside for some fresh air. Along the fence line, patches of wooded areas shielded the yard, offering enough cover to keep him out of sight from the road. It allowed him to stretch his wings and let the warmth sink into him without fear of being seen.

Peter, Sarah, and Olivia watched expectantly as Anselm shakily rose to his feet, stiff after having been sedentary for so long, and made his way out of the barn. The process was slow, but he seemed to savor every movement. When he finally found a comfortable spot beside the barn, Anselm lay down and closed his eyes, basking in the sunlight. He looked content, the fresh country air and warm sun clearly doing wonders for his spirits.

"Look at him," Sarah whispered, not wanting to disturb the peaceful moment. "He's so much stronger. He'll be back to full health soon enough."

Olivia, looked to Sarah and asked, "Do you think he'll fly soon?"

"I think so," Sarah said. "He made it here with an injured wing, and now it looks practically healed."

As they sat in the sun, watching over Anselm, something steady formed between them.

During this time Olivia would bring Anselm wildflowers and sing to him in her sweet, childish voice. Her innocence and warmth brought a unique kind of healing to Anselm, lifting his spirits.

Sarah, who had found Anselm in the barn and grown very

attached to him, spent her days talking to him and reading him stories. Her presence was reassuring to Anselm, providing a sense of connection and family.

Sarah would settle next to him with a well-worn copy of "The Wind in the Willows" and read aloud.

Anselm listened intently, his large, luminous eyes fixed on the distance as Sarah's voice filled the barn.

The weight of his mission bore down on him like a crushing stone, a gnawing fear that everything might unravel. The relentless uncertainty of whether the British could stop Krammer—or worse, if Krammer might come for him—kept his thoughts trapped in an unending loop of anxiety.

And then there was the deeper ache, the one he kept buried: the knowledge that he could never go home again.

But as Sarah's soft voice read the stories, recounting the adventures of Mole, Rat, and Toad, their exploits along the riverbank offered a welcome distraction, drawing Anselm into their world and pulling him away from the dark spiral of his fears.   For a little while, the familiar rhythm of her storytelling soothed him, and the shadows in his mind receded.

As Sarah read, Anselm's breathing would relax, and he would close his eyes, a look of contentment spreading across his face. The bond they shared grew stronger with each story.

She read to him about the picnic on the riverbank, about Toad's wild adventures, and about the warm camaraderie between the animal friends.   These stories of friendship and simple joys rekindled a sense of tranquility in Anselm, a feeling he had known in his youth but had long since forgotten.

When she wasn't reading to him, Sarah would talk about

her own life—the things she enjoyed, her favorite places to explore, and the little things that made her smile. She often spoke of how much she missed her father, sharing her worries and fears about his safety, as well as her hopes for his return. Anselm, though unable to speak, listened with a depth of understanding that surprised her. He would nudge her gently with his snout when she seemed particularly sad, or curl his massive tail protectively around her when she sat close.

Sometimes, Anselm would use his claws to draw simple shapes in the dirt, responding to her stories with a kind of wordless communication that only strengthened their bond. He would tilt his head or blink slowly, his golden eyes reflecting a quiet empathy that made Sarah feel truly heard. Despite the vast differences between them, their friendship blossomed in those shared moments. Sarah found solace in Anselm's presence, and in turn, he found a rare connection in the sincerity of her companionship.

Sarah's mother, initially wary of the dragon, had a moment with Anselm that changed her perspective. She approached cautiously, watching as Anselm lay in the barn, his eyes reflecting a deep sadness.

"What is it, Mum?" Sarah asked, noticing her mother's hesitation.

"He looks… sad," her mother replied, her voice soft.

Anselm, hearing the concern, clumsily picked up one of Sarah's crayons with his claw. With effort, he wrote on a sheet of butcher paper, "**WORRIED FOR FAMILY**"

Sarah's mother stared at the message, her eyes widening in surprise, then looked at Sarah with a newfound understanding.

From that moment on, Sarah's mother was less afraid of Anselm. She even began to bring meals to the dragon, ensuring they were properly prepared lamb dishes. The lamb broth had been a good start, but they decided to try him on more substantial food as he grew stronger.

Sometimes Sarah's mother would sit with Anselm, sharing stories of her own. She spoke of her husband, who was away fighting in the war, and, like Sarah, her fears for his safety. Anselm listened with empathy, his eyes reflecting his own worries. This shared vulnerability created a bond between them.

One evening, as they sat together in the barn, Sarah's mother gently asked, "Anselm, where do you come from?"

Anselm looked at her for a moment, then picked up a crayon with his claw and carefully wrote on a sheet of butcher paper, **"RIENECK"**

Sarah's mother stared at the word, trying to pronounce it. "Rieneck," she repeated softly. "Is that where your family is? In Germany, I mean?"

Anselm nodded solemnly, his gaze fixed on the ground. It was a simple exchange, but it deepened their connection, affirming that Anselm longed for his home and family just like anyone else caught in the turmoil of war.

Curiosity piqued, Sarah's mother retrieved an atlas from inside the cottage. Sitting at the table, she carefully turned page after page until she found a detailed map of Germany. Running her finger over the map, Sarah's mother stopped at a small town nestled along a river.

"Rieneck," she whispered to herself, tracing the name with her fingertip. She paused, feeling a mix of surprise and curiosity. It struck her as odd that a creature of fantasy like

Anselm could hail from a place in the real world. Yet, there it was, marked clearly on the map.

The idea unsettled her, blurring the lines between the fantastical and the real. She couldn't quite reconcile the image of a dragon with that of a town in the heart of Europe, but it also made Anselm seem more grounded, more like someone who belonged here, just as they did.

She closed the atlas quietly, the discovery lingering in her thoughts.

Chapter 22

Back in town, Thomas and Orville continued to wait. The days passed slowly, each one blending into the next as they watched for any sign that their message had been received and acted upon.

At last, they decided to visit the Colonel's office to follow up, hoping for some indication of progress. Colonel Harding, however, did not share their sense of urgency. When they were finally granted an audience, he looked up from his desk with a mixture of annoyance and impatience.

"The matter has been referred to the appropriate channels," he said crisply, his tone carrying an air of finality. "Should there be any developments, you will be informed. Do not waste your time, or mine, with repeated visits."

The dismissal was swift and unmistakable. Thomas and Orville left the office with a growing sense of unease, shaken by the Colonel's noncommittal response.

Orville spent much of his time at the local historical society, poring over dusty volumes and fragile papers in search of meaning. The symbols etched into the amber stone had taken root in his thoughts. The more he studied, the more convinced he became that they were not decorative at all, but deliberate—

part of something far older and far more significant.

Late one afternoon, surrounded by stacks of books, Orville's eyes lit with sudden excitement.

"Look here," he said, tapping a yellowed page in a volume written nearly a century earlier by an eccentric antiquarian. *Mysteries of the Ancients*, by Erasmus Wentworth—a man ridiculed in his time for theories most scholars dismissed outright.

"These markings," Orville continued, his voice quickening, "they're very like the ones on the stone, don't you think?"

Thomas, who had been enjoying a cigarette nearby, leaned in to examine the images in the book, his curiosity now piqued. "What does it say they mean, then?" he asked.

"Well, that is very interesting," Orville began, flipping a few pages, "Wentworth reckoned they were part of some lost language—used by an ancient civilization with knowledge of powerful, mystical forces. He even suggests these symbols opened portals or gateways between worlds."

Thomas raised an eyebrow, skepticism etched on his face. "Gateways? Portals? Are you having me on? You're not saying you believe this, are you?"

Orville nodded, his gaze steady. "I know it sounds barmy, but think it through. Anselm isn't just any creature—he's a dragon, for heaven's sake. He's not from anywhere on Earth that I'm aware of. Perhaps these symbols tell us how he managed to find his way here in the first place—how he crossed over from his world into ours."

As Orville spoke, fragments of old memories surfaced. He remembered his grandmother's stories from his childhood, tales of the little people who used symbols in their magic. The fairy tales were full of mystery, describing doors to the homes

143

of the little people. As an adult, had dismissed those tales as mere folklore, but now they seemed to hold a deeper truth.

"When I was a lad," Orville began, pausing to sift through the memory. "Gran used to tell me stories about doorways of the little people."

Thomas raised an eyebrow. "Folktales, Orville. That's all they are."

"Yes, I know," Orville replied thoughtfully. "But what if, all the same? I'm merely trying to draw a connection between Anselm's being a mythical creature that by all rights shouldn't exist and the items in the suitcase. Why was the stone adorned with such markings? And why did those very same symbols appear in the documents? And why do similar marks appear throughout Europe? They must be connected somehow, mustn't they?"

Thomas exhaled a slow stream of smoke, sitting back in his chair. "I don't know, Orville. It does sound far-fetched. The Nazis dabbling in magic? Come on."

Orville shrugged, his gaze fixed on the book in front of him.

Thomas took another drag from his cigarette and tapped the ash into a tray. "Look, just because the symbols on the stone resemble those on that stone doesn't necessarily mean they're connected to the fairy tales your gran told. Similarity isn't proof."

Orville nodded slowly, absorbing the remark. "You're right, of course. Resemblance doesn't mean relevance. But still... it's fascinating to think about, isn't it? The idea that the symbols represent something we've yet to uncover?"

Thomas flicked the ash off his cigarette and leaned back with a faint smirk. "Intriguing, sure. But don't let your imagination run wild, old man."

As the week dragged on, the lack of communication from the authorities became increasingly frustrating. Thomas and Orville knew they had done their part, but the waiting was unbearable. They could only hope that the information they had delivered was being taken seriously and that the wheels of bureaucracy were turning.

One evening, as the sun dipped below the horizon, casting long shadows across the town, Thomas and Orville sat in the pub, nursing their drinks. The conversation was sparse, both men lost in their thoughts.

"What if we never hear anything back?" Thomas asked, breaking the silence.

"We will," Orville said firmly. "What we've brought them is far too important to be ignored."

As they sat in the fading light, acceptance had settled over them. Now, all they could do was wait and hope that the authorities would recognize the importance and act accordingly.

Chapter 23

Further East, a primeval forest in the heart of Germany that shrouded an ancient castle, SS-Obergruppenführer Rupel was greeted at the entrance by Field Marshal Guilder. As the two men met, Rupel's face was etched with grudging respect. "Ah, Herr Feldmarschall, congratulations are in order," he said, his voice clipped. "The Führer personally approved your projects moving forward."

Guilder forced a smile as they stepped inside the castle. "I'm sure that's not something you're pleased with, Herr Obergruppenführer."

"My concerns remain," Rupel admitted, reaching up to touch a healing cut across his mouth, a reminder of an encounter with another creature from one of Krammer's projects. "But I admit, the dragon's effectiveness surprised me."

A short, elderly gentleman with a surprisingly youthful glint in his eyes met them. "Gentlemen." It was Herr Krammer, the project's lead scientist.

Rupel gave him a begrudging nod. "Herr Krammer, I wholly expected to be escorting you to be executed, but as I was telling Generalfeldmarschall Guilder, I can't deny that your project has successfully proven itself."

A sly smile played on Krammer's lips. "As I told you it

would," he said, his voice tinged with a hint of triumph.

"The Führer wants more. Thousands, as you promised," Rupel dropped his voice, leaning closer. "Three are delaying the enemy, but they still make progress towards us."

"Impossible." Herr Krammer's smile faded. "The stone the traitor stole held the energy we needed. Without it, the process cannot be repeated."

"We can arrange for all the power you require," Rupel pressed.

"It wouldn't be nearly enough," Krammer countered sharply. "I need enriched uranium for the device, without it I cannot create more." "It will be provided," Rupel promised confidently.

Krammer sighed and regarded him with a sardonic gaze. "You do realize, of course, that the Allies captured the facilities in Norway? Even if you could extract enough raw material from the Czech mines, you lack the means to refine it."

Rupel's face flushed red with frustration, his patience snapping. "Find another way, damn it!" he roared.

Field Marshal Guilder stepped in before the exchange could escalate further. His voice was calm. "Has the location of the traitor been identified?" He looked steadily at Rupel.

"No," Rupel replied, his tone betraying his frustration. "He slipped through. He was last seen over France, then disappeared. We assume the enemy has him, but where? We don't know."

A contemplative silence descended upon the room, broken only by the rhythmic dripping of water.

Krammer pursed his lips before finally deciding to speak. "The traitor is in England."

Rupel's eyes narrowed. "How could you possibly know that?"

Krammer's voice was measured and slow, letting the weight of his words sink in. "I have an agent in England."

Both Rupel and Guilder exchanged startled glances, the revelation catching them off guard. "You've had someone there all along?" Rupel asked, his tone a mixture of astonishment and resentment.

Guilder sighed deeply, a furrow forming between his brows. "In England... If that's true, he's out of our reach."

Krammer shook his head, his voice sharp with conviction. "Not at all. We have three dragons. They could eliminate the traitor and retrieve what he stole in one swift, decisive operation."

Rupel was quick to protest. "Impossible! The dragons have already been assigned to the Eastern Front. Their orders are already decided: eliminate the Soviet command—Stalin himself included!"

Krammer's eyes narrowed as he responded. "Surely you can see the bigger picture by now. Killing Stalin won't cripple the Red Army; another will take his place. But recovering the stone? That changes everything. Thousands of dragons tearing through their lines, destroying their industry, overseeing their population—the Soviet Union would collapse in days."

Rupel frowned, irritation etched into his face. He knew Krammer had a point. The dragons, unleashed in great numbers, were the key to turning the tide of the war. But defying direct orders from high command was a gamble fraught with risk. "We would have very little time," he said finally. "If the traitor could be found quickly..."

The silence returned, broken only by the incessant dripping. Could they locate the traitor in time, or would the opportunity slip through their fingers?

Krammer broke the silence. "My agent is very close to both the stone and the traitor, he's waiting for an opportunity. Does that change your calculations?"

Guilder nodded slowly, visibly relieved by the revelation. "That does improve our position," he admitted. "Knowing we have eyes on the traitor changes everything."

Rupel gave a reluctant nod, acknowledging the advantage. With an agent in England, their chances of success increased significantly, offering a faint glimmer of hope.

Guilder made the decision, his voice firm. "Very well, we'll refine our plans. A little more time spent strategizing the Soviet strike will increase its chance of success. In the meantime, we shall prepare the dragons for their retrieval mission to England."

As the meeting concluded, Rupel prepared to depart, his mind racing with the new information. "Gentlemen," he said with a curt nod to both men before swiftly exiting the room, leaving Guilder and Krammer alone.

Guilder lingered, his expression thoughtful as he approached Krammer. "Herr Krammer, a moment, if you will," he said, lowering his voice. "There's more we need to discuss about the agent in England and the implications of this strategy. Can we truly count on this agent's reliability?"

Krammer turned to face him fully, a faint smile playing at the corners of his mouth. "Ah, Guilder, my agent in England is dependable and uniquely suited for such an operation."

"And if he's identified?" Guilder pressed. "Do you have a backup plan?"

Krammer's smile deepened, though his eyes held an enigmatic glint. "His identity is his greatest strength, Field Marshall," he said smoothly, his tone measured. "There's no need to worry."

Guilder regarded him for a moment before shifting the conversation. "One other thing, Herr Krammer. I've been thinking—despite the enormous power requirements, perhaps we should consider attempting to create another dragon using another source. Just one. The potential benefits could outweigh the risks."

Krammer's expression turned contemplative. "It's doubtful it would succeed, my friend. The power requirements are tremendous, and with less energy to fill the new stone, the process is extremely hazardous. The subject might not survive the transformation."

Undeterred, Guilder leaned closer, lowering his voice further. "What if we were to use an American prisoner for the experiment? I have a subject in mind who may be suitable for such a test."

Krammer paused, his expression thoughtful as he considered the implications. "And if it succeeds? Yes, you'd have a dragon, but one that could be a threat to us. A dragon is a dangerous weapon, Guilder—powerful. Is it truly wise to risk using an enemy subject for such an experiment?"

Guilder smiled thinly, the corners of his mouth barely lifting. "This prisoner has voiced disdain for certain American institutions. We would return him to America to wage his own fight. Indirectly, he would serve as our asset."

Krammer contemplated the suggestion, his brow furrowing slightly. "It remains a risky gamble. Even if the transformation succeeds, we must prepare thoroughly to ensure he remains under control."

Guilder nodded, his expression resolute. "Indeed, it is a gamble, Herr Krammer. But if it becomes necessary, we have the other three dragons at our disposal to neutralize the new one should he pose a threat."

Krammer's eyes locked with Guilder's, his gaze sharp and calculating as he weighed the implications. After a moment, he inclined his head slightly. "A prudent backup plan," he conceded. "Very well. Let us discuss what I will need to proceed…"

Chapter 24

Thomas was busy in the butcher shop, helping his son through the day's tasks. The rich aroma of fresh cuts of meat filled the air, and the rhythmic sound of chopping and slicing created a comforting backdrop. Thomas had taken over the shop from his father, though it hadn't been his first choice. He had dreams of something different, something beyond the confines of the butcher's block. But duty and family obligations had kept him here.

His son, on the other hand, had loved working in the shop from a young age. The boy had an innate knack for the business, a sharp eye for quality cuts, and a natural rapport with customers. When he became an adult, Thomas had gladly stepped aside, allowing his son to take over the shop. He figured that it was time to retire soon anyway, and his son had much more business sense than he had ever had. Under his son's stewardship, the shop thrived, attracting a growing stream of loyal customers. Thomas took pride in seeing the family business flourish.

The shop's bell tinkled, signaling a customer. Thomas looked up to see a man in a crisp military uniform enter. The newcomer was tall and well-built, with sharp features and piercing blue eyes that scanned the room before settling on

Thomas.

"Mr. King, is it?" the man asked, stepping forward with an air of authority. His voice carried the refined, polished tones of an upper-class British accent. "I am Captain Linton of the Intelligence Corps. Might I have a moment of your time? It is of utmost urgency."

Thomas felt a jolt of anticipation and nodded. "Yes, that's me."

Captain Linton smiled, his eyes reflecting a sense of relief. "I'm very pleased to have found you, Mr. King," he said, extending his hand. Thomas instinctively reached out, their handshake firm and brief. "Excellent. I also need to speak with your friend Mr. Morris. Where can we find Orville?"

Thomas quickly informed his son that he was leaving and then followed Captain Linton to his car, an olive green Humber Super Snipe. A common vehicle for officers, it served as both a staff car and a command vehicle, blending the elegance of pre-war craftsmanship with the ruggedness required for wartime utility. The car featured a solid, boxy frame with broad fenders and a sturdy front grille, giving it a robust and commanding presence. Its long, sweeping hood housed a powerful engine essential for wartime operations, capable of handling rough terrains and extended journeys.

The interior was spacious and practical, designed for both comfort and efficiency, with wide leather seats and a dashboard equipped with the necessary instruments. Large, round headlights and a prominent chrome bumper added to its distinctive, authoritative appearance.

As they approached, the driver, a young NCO with a crisply pressed uniform and a disciplined demeanor, stepped out and briskly opened the doors for them. His posture was erect, his expression serious and attentive.

Thomas felt a mix of nerves and elation, knowing that he and Orville had succeeded in getting the items from the suitcase to someone who could understand their importance.

Settling into the back seat, Thomas directed the driver through the bustling town towards where Orville's home awaited. As they left the main thoroughfare, the streets gradually gave way to quieter lanes lined with quaint cottages and overgrown gardens. Orville's cottage sat nestled at the edge of town, a place he had shared with his wife until her passing.

The walkway leading to the cottage was lined with neglected flower beds, overrun with weeds that once bloomed under his wife's care. Orville rarely tended to the garden. Gardening was his wife's favorite past time. Despite the wild exterior, the cottage itself was immaculate.

As they approached Orville's home, Thomas's mind was consumed with the gravity of the impending conversation with Captain Linton. Thoughts raced through his mind— about the mysterious items, their potential significance, and what Captain Linton might reveal or request from them. He couldn't shake off the weight of responsibility, knowing that their actions and words could have far-reaching consequences in the current war effort.

Orville, wearing reading spectacles, greeted them at the door, his curiosity piqued by the unexpected visit. "Thomas! What brings you here?" he asked, eyeing Captain Linton.

"This is Captain Linton from the Intelligence Corps," Thomas explained, giving Orville a significant look, "He's here to speak with us. Says it's urgent."

Captain Linton stepped forward, offering his hand. "Good

afternoon, Mr. Morris. We have some matters of great importance to discuss."

"Of course, come in, come in," Orville said, taking the Captains hand then stepping aside to let them enter.

After they entered Orville's home and closed the door, the quiet street outside settled back into stillness. Moments later, a soldier emerged from an alley across the street. His uniform was rumpled, his hair disheveled, and his eyes wide with excitement. A broad grin was spread across his face as he regarded Linton's driver leaning casually against the vehicle. After catching the driver's attention, he began gesturing enthusiastically, his movements sharp and insistent, as if he couldn't contain whatever news or revelation had set him off.

The driver rolled his eyes, crying out, "I'm workin', mate," as he glanced at the soldier's frantic motions. He tried to ignore him, leaning back against the car with feigned indifference. But the soldier's persistence—combined with his infectious, almost childlike grin—finally wore him down.

With a resigned sigh, the driver shoved off the car. "Alright, mate, make it quick then. What's got you so worked up?" he called out, his tone a mix of irritation and curiosity.

The soldier's grin widened as the driver began moving in his direction, and a strange glint in his eye made him all the more compelling to the driver. Without another word, he gestured for the driver to follow him into the alley. The driver hesitated for a moment, glancing over his shoulder to ensure Linton was still inside the cottage. Then, shaking his head, he crossed the street. Within moments, both men had disappeared into the shadows.

Inside Orville's cottage, everything was meticulously arranged—clean and orderly with a touch of lived-in comfort. Not a speck of dust marred the polished furniture, and the shelves displayed neatly stacked books and trinkets. On the table where Orville had been seated, old books lay open, indicating his recent readings.

Captain Linton pulled out a notepad and wasted no time in getting to the heart of the matter. "Right, gentlemen, I'll need you to tell me everything you know about the items you handed over to Colonel Harding. Where did they come from? What do you make of them? And who gave them to you?"

Thomas and Orville exchanged a quick glance, before Thomas spoke up. "The suitcase and its contents turned up on a farm to the west. They were brought over from Germany by someone who was adamant they be handed to the British authorities."

Linton leaned forward. "Do you know where this person is now?"

Orville nodded. "He's still at the farm, convalescing. He was quite badly injured."

Linton asked, "What is the name of this foreign agent?"

"His name is Anselm," Orville replied.

Linton pressed further. "And his surname?"

Orville hesitated, shifting uncomfortably. "Well, I don't know if he has one," he admitted, his tone uncertain.

Linton gave a curt nod. "I understand Colonel Harding informed you that a German aircraft, along with the pilot's body, was discovered not far from here. Am I right in assuming your informant bailed out?"

Thomas shook his head slowly. "No... I mean, yes, he did inform us. But I don't think that's how Anselm arrived." As he spoke, Linton raised an eyebrow, intrigued by Thomas's uncertainty about Anselm's arrival.

Before Thomas could say more, Orville jumped in, keen to steer the conversation away from Anselm's true nature. "We've seen the papers, sir. Whatever this is, it's tied to some sort of device or weapon, and the stone seems to be a key part of it."

Linton's eyes narrowed, his interest clearly piqued. He didn't miss Orville's attempt to deflect but chose to focus on the new information instead. "Do you have any idea what this stone might be, or how it was used?" he asked, his tone sharp with curiosity.

Orville nodded thoughtfully, his fingers brushing his chin as he spoke. "Well, Captain, I've spent a fair bit of time poring over books and documents, comparing those symbols to others I've come across in old texts. Some of the markings match patterns I've seen on standing stones and ancient carvings across Britain—symbols no one's ever quite managed to make sense of. A few resemble designs in a manuscript I found, which theorized they might represent geographical points or cartographic markers. Perhaps, locations."

Linton leaned forward slightly, his brow furrowed. "Locations, you say? Interesting. What sort of places are we dealing with, then?"

Orville tilted his head, looking thoughtful. "If the manuscript's theory holds, perhaps they were places of power or particular significance—sites that time and memory have long since cast aside."

Linton's gaze remained fixed on Orville, his interest keen. "Have you any notion of what those forgotten places might have been?"

Orville hesitated, glancing at Linton before continuing. "You see, when I was a lad, my grandmother would tell us stories—folktales, really. They spoke of mystical creatures dwelling in hidden corners of the world. In the stories they used markings—symbols much like these—to indicate where they could be found, where their treasures lay concealed."

His voice turned wistful. "She'd sit by the fire and speak of doorways—secret passages connecting their world to ours. In her tales, the little folk would use these portals to come and go as they pleased. I always assumed it was mere fancy, but..."

He trailed off, his eyes drifting back to Linton. "The more I study this, the less certain I am that her stories were pure imagination. These symbols—seeing them in those documents—makes me wonder if they have cracked the code to something far older than we can fathom..."

Orville looked at Linton, half-expecting a scoff or dismissal. "I understand how this must sound, Captain," he said, "I do apologize if it sounds... fanciful."

Captain Linton his sharp eyes fixed on Orville. "Not at all," he said firmly. "You may be closer to the truth than you realize."

After a moment of consideration, Captain Linton reached into his case and withdrew a folder, handling it with deliberate care. His tone was low and measured, carrying a weight of authority. "Now, listen carefully. What I'm about to show you is classified—Most Secret. No one outside this room is to know about it. Is that perfectly clear?"

Thomas and Orville nodded as Captain Linton held up a large photograph.

Linton paused, his gaze fixed on the photograph in his hand. "This still image is one frame from the film on the camera you delivered. It shows the device depicted in the blueprints being activated. There was a bright flash, but in a single frame, the light dimmed just enough to reveal something remarkable."

He placed the photograph carefully on the table in front of them. "Tell me, what do you notice?" Linton's tone was probing, his eyes keenly observing their reactions.

Orville leaned forward, studying the photograph intently. "It's blurry," he said slowly, "but I can see it's inside a bunker. And... a dragon—or part of one," he added, his brow furrowing. "And a bright halo of light behind it."

"Within that halo?" Linton prompted, handing Orville a magnifying glass.

Orville adjusted the glass, squinting as he examined the overexposed background. Slowly, faint shapes began to emerge. His breath caught. "Figures," he murmured. "Four of them, standing on a rocky outcropping."

His breath caught as realization dawned. "A doorway...!"

Linton nodded gravely, his voice low. "This is more significant than you might imagine. I can't tell you everything, but it's clear the enemy is dabbling in esoteric practices—things we don't understand. If those symbols hold the key, we need to decipher them. And quickly."

Thomas, his mind racing, leaned forward. "What do you need us to do?"

Linton didn't answer immediately. Instead, he leaned back in his chair, fixing the two men with a penetrating look. "Before we go any further, I need to know something. You've seen this photograph, and neither of you seems particularly surprised by the sight of a dragon. That should've been your first reaction."

Thomas and Orville exchanged uneasy glances.

"Mr. Morris," Linton continued, his tone measured but probing, "Colonel Harding informed me that you reported seeing a dragon while on watch. Meanwhile, Mr. King here stated he saw nothing and thought it might have been a trick of the clouds."

Orville shifted uncomfortably, clearing his throat. "Yes, that's true," he admitted.

Linton's eyes narrowed slightly. "You were quite insistent about what you saw, Orville. Do you still maintain it was a dragon?"

Orville hesitated, clearly apprehensive, his gaze going to Thomas for support.

Linton asked plainly, "Was it a dragon you saw? Have you seen any dragons since?"

Thomas interjected, "Oh, go on, Orville. We were going to tell him anyway."

Orville gave him a slight nod, and Thomas turned back to Linton. "Orville did see a dragon, Captain. And the foreign agent who gave us those items? He's the very same dragon Orville saw that night."

Linton's eyes widened, the color draining from his face as he processed the words. For a moment, he looked as though he might not speak, but then he managed, his voice squeaked, "I see."

Orville hurried to fill the silence. "He's real, Captain. We're not daft, I promise you."

Linton stood, visibly shaken. His voice trembled slightly as he spoke. "I believe you," he said slowly. He paused, running a hand over his mouth, the weight of this revelation pressing heavily on him. "But you must understand… these creatures— they are lethal. Merciless. The reports we've received… they leave nothing but devastation in their wake. If one of them is here, in England—"

Thomas cut him off, his tone firm and steady. "This one's not like that, sir. He's helped us, not harmed us. We're not in any danger from him."

Linton stared at him, disbelief and fear in his eyes. "Not dangerous? Do you have any idea what you're saying, man? The dragons encountered in France are nothing short of harbingers of death," he said, his voice rising slightly. "They've attacked our forces without mercy—raining fire from the skies, wiping out entire battalions in moments. Airfields reduced to smouldering rubble. They bring the very wrath of hell with them."

Thomas and Orville exchanged somber glances, the weight of Linton's words settling heavily between them.

After a moment, Orville spoke, his tone quiet and firm. "Captain, this dragon—the one we've encountered—isn't like that. He's shown no aggression whatsoever. If anything, he's remarkably gentle."

Linton shook his head slowly, his expression a mix of skepticism and unease. "I've read the reports. I've seen the devastation they left in their wake. How can you be so certain this one is any different?"

Thomas leaned forward, his voice steady but insistent. "Because he's being tended by children at the farm—without anything untoward. Because he risked everything to bring us vital information. He is aiding us, Captain. He's on our side."

Linton frowned, the weight of this revelation pressing heavily on him. "If what you're saying is true... a dragon, friendly to our cause..." He took a deep breath, steadying himself as his thoughts raced. "I must see him for myself," he said at last, his tone firm. "You'll take me to meet this dragon."

"Yes, of course." Thomas replied.

Turning to Orville, he added, "And if you're agreeable, Mr. Morris, I'd like you to work for us. We'll have you travel to a laboratory in London, where you can share all you've discovered about the symbols on that stone."

Orville blinked, clearly caught off guard by the request. He glanced nervously at Thomas, seeking reassurance. "Work for you?" he stammered, his uncertainty plain. "Captain, I'm not an expert. I'm no scholar."

Thomas placed a steadying hand on Orville's shoulder. "You've been studying those symbols night and day, man. You've got more insight than anyone else. Give yourself a bit of credit—you've earned it."

Linton's expression eased slightly, though the urgency in his voice remained unmistakable. "We haven't the luxury of time, Orville. I need someone who can grasp the significance of these symbols, and—if I'm honest—your understanding already surpasses that of my current team. Your insights could prove vital in deciphering their meaning and appreciating the full extent of what we're dealing with."

Orville took a steadying breath. "If I can be of any help," he said at last, nodding, "then yes. I shall do it."

"Good man," Linton replied briskly. "Pack a bag; we'll get you to the station immediately."

Orville his mind swirling with a mix of excitement and apprehension. "Right away," he replied before leaving the room to fetch his suitcase.

Reaching into his case, Linton pulled out a piece of paper and quickly scribbled a message before sealing it in an envelope.

Linton turned to Thomas. "And you, Mr. King," he said, his tone taking on a nervous edge. "Will you introduce me to this dragon?"

Thomas nodded firmly.

Once Orville had a bag packed the three headed outside to the car where the driver was waiting, his mouth stretched in an enormous grin.

As the driver opened the door for the Captain and Orville, the Captain handed Orville an envelope. "This contains your authorisation to join our task force. They'll see to your accommodations."

He then passed Orville a slip of paper bearing an address. "This is where the London laboratory is located—where the team working with the stone is based."

Orville regarded the address, then slipped it into his coat pocket.

Neither of them noticed the driver covertly taking note of the address.

Chapter 25

The car rolled to a gentle stop outside the station in town, its engine settling into silence as Orville reached for his case. He adjusted his coat and glanced at Thomas, offering a wry smile.

"Well then," Orville said, his tone light but warm. "Looks like the two musketeers go their separate ways.

"Thomas nodded, his weathered face softening with a smile. "You'll send word once you've made a mess of things, won't you?"

Orville chuckled, shaking his head. "No chance of that. It never seems to happen without you."

Thomas reached out, briefly gripping Orville's shoulder. "Look after yourself, old chap."

"And you," Orville replied, his voice steady but fond. He adjusted his case, then turned his attention to Linton.

Linton leaned slightly forward, his tone formal yet courteous. "Safe travels, Mr. Morris."

With that, Orville stepped out of the car, suitcase in hand. He paused for a moment, turning back to tip his hat before heading toward the platform.

The driver sat unmoving, his hands gripping the steering

wheel as though weighing a plan. The grin tugged at his lips, but it betrayed nothing of its nature. His gaze lingered on Orville's retreating figure, watching as he disappeared into the station.

From the back seat, Linton's voice cut through the hesitation, sharp and commanding. "Driver, let's be on our way. No delays."

The driver hesitated, his hand lingering on the gear lever as if considering a different plan, as though he were piecing together a puzzle. His eyes still betraying nothing, before he gave a curt nod and shifted the car into motion, whatever thought had crossed his mind seemingly dismissed.

In the spacious back seat of the Humber Super Snipe, Captain Linton turned toward Thomas, his expression marked with quiet curiosity. "Would you be so kind as to tell me about how you first came to meet your dragon?"

"Indeed," Thomas began, his voice thoughtful as the car hummed steadily along the country road. "Anselm was in a bad way when he arrived—injured quite severely. Orville, with his experience in the Great War—he worked at Casualty Clearing Stations, you know—managed to see him through. Stabilized him, at least." He paused, a faint smile touching his lips. "And the children—Sarah, Olivia, and Peter—they've been looking after him ever since. Remarkable, really. They've taken to him like nothing I'd have expected. Quite a bond they've formed."

Linton listened intently, "Extraordinary," his curiosity growing. "And you said earlier that the creature can communicate?" he asked.

Thomas smiled, "In subtle ways, mostly. Anselm has ways of

conveying his needs and feelings without words. He gestures, sometimes even makes sounds that seem purposeful. But the most remarkable thing is that he can write."

Linton nodded thoughtfully, absorbing the details. "It's quite extraordinary," he remarked. "He's intelligent. Truly intelligent. And you say he's never shown any aggression?"

"Not once," Thomas said firmly. "He's gentle, especially with the children. They've grown quite fond of him, and he reciprocates that affection."

As the Humber Super Snipe continued its journey towards the farm, Thomas glanced in the rearview mirror. He caught a glimpse of the driver's reflection. Something about the man's constant smiling struck him as familiar as it was disturbing.

They soon arrived at the farm. Peter and Olivia hurried out to the driveway to see the car arrive, their eyes widening at the sight of the robust auto in its drab military green. Its imposing silhouette and rumbling engine drew their immediate attention. Sarah emerged from the barn to join them, her expression curious and expectant.

The driver stepped out and opened the door for Thomas, while Captain Linton gracefully exited the car from the other side. Thomas took the lead and introduced him to the children.

"Captain Linton, meet Sarah, Olivia, and Peter," Thomas said warmly. Peter stepped forward and extended his hand to the officer with a polite nod. "How do you do, sir?" he said with formality.

Sarah followed suit, curtsying slightly as she offered her hand. "How do you do, Captain Linton." she said politely.

Olivia, the youngest, managed a shy smile and a quick bob

of her head, murmuring a soft, "Pleased to meet you, sir."

Linton returned their greetings with a nod, his eyes briefly studying each of them, as if trying to gauge their mettle. "A pleasure," he said simply.

Thomas turned his attention to Sarah. "Sarah, is your mum about?" he asked gently..

Sarah shook her head. "No, sir. She's not back yet, but she'll be home soon."

"And Anselm?" Thomas asked, shifting his gaze to Peter. He noticed Linton stiffen slightly at the name, clearly bracing himself for the inevitable encounter.

Peter straightened, his response crisp. "He's quite well, sir. Mending quickly."

Sarah added eagerly, "He's moving about now. Came outside for some fresh air earlier."

Olivia added with a hopeful smile, "He'll be well enough to fly again soon."

Linton's face betrayed a hint of unease at the thought, though he quickly composed himself. The weight of what he was about to face clearly sinking in. Taking a steadying breath, he crouched down to the children's level, his tone soft yet probing as he addressed them.

"Sarah," he began, his voice measured and calm, though nervousness lingered beneath the surface, "Mr. Morris tells me you're the one who found Anselm. Could you tell me what happened?"

Sarah nodded. "Yes, sir. I found him in our barn. There was a hole in the roof, so I knew someone must've been in there. Peter went in first, but he didn't know what Anselm was—he thought he might've been a dinosaur. But when I went in, I saw him lying there. He was hurt, so we gave him water."

"And then what happened?" Linton prompted.

Sarah continued, her eyes bright with the memory. "Well, sir, we fed him and nursed him. He couldn't speak, but when Peter asked his name, he scratched it in the barn floor. That's how we learned his name is, Anselm."

Even though Thomas had already recounted the story, Captain Linton's face betrayed genuine surprise. For a moment, his nervousness gave way to fascination. "Remarkable," he murmured.

Peter, eager to contribute, spoke up. "Anselm told us to take the suitcase to someone in authority, sir. He said it was important."

Linton nodded thoughtfully, his composure returning as he absorbed the information. "He was right—it was very important. Tell me, has Anselm ever shown any signs of aggression?"

Sarah shook her head firmly. "Oh no, sir. Never. He's always been gentle with us. He even let Peter put a splint on his wing."

Turning to Peter, Linton asked, "You've been treating his injuries?"

Peter straightened slightly, his tone matter-of-fact. "I splinted his wing, sir, but it was Mr. Morris who did the proper bandaging. I just help change them."

Olivia chimed in, her voice bright. "And he likes lamb, sir— but only if it's cooked!"

Captain Linton couldn't help but chuckle softly at her earnestness. "That's very good to know, thank you."

His expression turned more serious as he addressed the children, his nerves still simmering beneath his outward calm. "Do you think Anselm would be willing to meet me? It's very important that I speak with him."

Sarah and Peter exchanged a glance, a silent agreement passing between them, before Sarah replied earnestly, "Yes, sir. I know he would."

Linton straightened, the weight of what lay ahead settling on him. "Very well, then. Lead the way."

Just as they were headed to the barn, Sarah's mother, Mrs. Lynde, arrived home from her shift at the factory. Riding up on her bicycle, she slowed abruptly, her eyes narrowing as she took in the unfamiliar military vehicle parked in her driveway. Dismounting quickly, she pushed her bike toward the cottage, glancing warily at the driver who watched her intently, his grin unnervingly wide. A chill ran down her spine as she recalled seeing the same unnerving expression on a strange red-headed woman in town just days earlier.

Thomas noticed her approach and stepped forward, offering a warm smile. "Mrs. Lynde, it's good to see you."

She nodded, "Yes. Hello, Mr. King," she said. She glanced back at the driver's unsettling grin again before turning back to Thomas. "What's going on?"

"This is Captain Linton from the Intelligence Corps," Thomas replied smoothly, gesturing toward the officer.

Captain Linton stepped forward, extending his hand. "Mrs. Lynde, a pleasure to meet you."

Her gaze shifted to him, taking in his posture, his uniform, and his demeanor. "Captain Linton," she said formally, shaking his hand briefly. Her tone was polite, but there was a guarded edge to it. She wasn't about to let her guard down with a stranger, especially one showing up unannounced in military uniform.

"Mrs. Lynde, I understand this is an unusual situation," Linton said, his voice measured and professional. "But I assure you, the information we've received from your daughter is proving invaluable."

"Have you seen anything like it before?" she asked pointedly.

Linton gave a small, carefully neutral smile. "No, not quite like this. I really can't speak on it. My role here is to ensure this situation is understood and managed properly."

"Mum!" Sarah interrupted, wrapping her in a quick embrace. "We're going to talk to Anselm!"

Mrs. Lynde's expression softened slightly at her daughter's enthusiasm, but the unease in her eyes didn't fade entirely.

"I see," she said, her eyes shifted between the children and the adults, and her protective instincts flared anew

"Perhaps it's best if the children don't join us while you speak to Anslem," she said firmly, her tone leaving no room for debate. "There's no need for them to be involved in the questioning."

Sarah's eyes widened in protest. "But Mum—!"

Peter added quickly, "Anselm knows us. He'll be more comfortable if we're there."

Mrs. Lynde's lips thinned into a determined line. "That may be, but this is official business. It's not something children should be part of."

Captain Linton raised a hand gently, offering a reassuring smile to the children. "I understand you're disappointed," he said, his tone calm and kind. "And I do appreciate everything you've done so far."

Sarah and Peter exchanged glances, their protests lingering in their eyes.

Linton crouched slightly to meet their gazes. "Right now, I

need to speak with Anselm in an official capacity. It's part of my responsibility to understand this situation properly. I may still need your help." he added, "You've been closer to him than anyone else, and your insights could be very important."

Peter relaxed, taking the words to heart, while Sarah's lips pressed into a reluctant line.

"You've already done so much," Linton continued. "And if I need more, I'll come to you straightaway, I promise."

Sarah hesitated, then nodded reluctantly. "Alright, Captain," she said quietly.

"Thank you," Linton replied with a warm smile before standing and turning back to Mrs. Lynde. "Shall we, then?" he asked, his voice regaining its professional edge.

Mrs. Lynde gave the children one last glance. "Stay near the house," she reminded them, "don't go wandering."

Linton nodded at Thomas and Sarah's mother.

Mrs. Lynde looked again to where the children were, before following Captain Linton and Thomas toward the barn.

As she walked, a wave of relief washed over her, knowing that someone from the military was now involved. It felt like a weight lifted, however slight, to have an official presence to finally resolve to what had been an overwhelming and surreal situation.

While she had grown to like Anselm—his gentle nature and the way the children had bonded with him—it didn't erase the stark truth that he was a dragon. A creature that simply shouldn't exist. The thought of her daughter being so close to something so potentially dangerous, still made her stomach knot. She longed for the days when her biggest concerns were rationing and factory shifts, not mythical creatures. All she wanted was for Sarah to be safe—and for life to go back to normal. But deep down, she feared that "normal" was something they might never see again.

Thomas led Captain Linton into the dimly lit barn, the air thick with the scent of oil and aged wood. Sarah's mother lingered by the door, her arms crossed as she kept a wary eye on the scene.

The shadows at the far end of the barn shifted, and the outline of a large form gradually came into focus—a dragon. Majestic yet grounded, Anselm's intelligent eyes glimmered faintly in the dim light. He sat calmly, his posture neither threatening nor submissive, though a flicker of apprehension crossed his gaze as he studied Captain Linton.

Thomas approached Anselm. "Anselm, this is Captain Linton from the Intelligence Corps. They've got the items you brought and are having a look at them. He'd like to ask you a few questions, if that's alright with you."

Anselm nodded in a gesture of acknowledgment and readiness to communicate as his gaze shifted from Thomas to Linton, his golden eyes steady and unblinking.

Thomas turned to Linton. "Captain, this is Anselm."

For a moment, Captain Linton simply stared, his composure faltering as the reality of the situation settled in. The sheer presence of the creature before him—a living dragon—was something no amount of training or preparation could have equipped him for. Gathering himself, he stepped forward cautiously and was momentarily at a loss for words, struck by the presence of the dragon before him.

Sensing the Captain's hesitation, Thomas put a hand on Linton's shoulder reassuringly. "It's alright, Captain. Anselm wants to answer your questions."

"Anselm," Linton said, his voice measured and formal, though tinged with an unmistakable awe. "It's an honor to meet you. I understand you've already gone to great lengths to help us. I hope we can speak freely and... begin to understand each other."

Anselm inclined his head in a slow, deliberate nod, his intelligent eyes briefly meeting Captain Linton's before shifting downward. His gaze settled on a freshly spread sheet of butcher paper laid out neatly in front of him. With an almost delicate movement for a creature of his size, he reached out and grasped a crayon in his clawed hand, the action practiced though awkward.

He paused, his grip adjusting slightly as if ensuring he could write clearly, then looked back up, waiting silently for Captain Linton's first question.

Captain Linton watched, astonished. He cleared his throat softly, stepping forward to close the distance between himself and the dragon, careful to keep his tone measured. "Anselm," he began, "Can you tell me about yourself... why you came here? What led you here?"

All eyes in the barn were fixed on the dragon as Anselm lowered his gaze back to the paper, the crayon poised to write. The silence was heavy with anticipation, broken only by the faint scrape of crayon against paper as Anselm began to answer. "**ANSELM BAUER. I WAS TECHNICIAN FOR PROJECT THAT MADE ME THIS.**"

Captain Linton, filled with fascination cautiously approached to sit on a crate where he could better see what Anselm wrote, his eyes scanning Anselm's message intently. The realization that he was communicating with a dragon was both surreal and profoundly intriguing.

Linton's eyes widened slightly, his professional composure cracking just enough to reveal the astonishment beneath. He stared at the dragon before him, the weight of Anselm's previous words—or rather, his written answer—hanging heavily in the air.

"Are you telling me that you're a man?" Linton asked, his voice tinged with disbelief.

Anselm's golden eyes met Linton's with quiet intensity. Slowly, he nodded, the motion deliberate and unambiguous. Then, with measured movements, he picked up the crayon again and wrote with surprising clarity on the butcher paper: **I WAS**.

Anselm's mind drifted to the oppressive atmosphere of the underground facility, the memory so vivid it felt as if he were there again. The air had been heavy with the acrid tang of metal and chemicals, the flicker of dim lights casting long, unnatural shadows on the walls. He remembered weaving through the labyrinthine corridors, determined to uncover the truth of Krammer's ambitions.

He had heard whispers—terrible rumors of experiments that combined science and arcane practices, of monstrous creations meant to turn the tide of war. He hadn't believed such things could be possible, not in the age of reason and machines, but strange occurrences had begun to add weight to those rumors.

There was one colleague—a rational, level-headed man— now grinning constantly, a hollow and unsettling expression that never left his face. He was always at Krammer's side, his eyes vacant, his presence unnerving.

Then there was the SS officer, sent to oversee the project,

who had burst from Krammer's office one day with his face streaked with blood. He was shouting for something to be taken away and destroyed, something that had been kept locked in a small metal box. From the lab, Anselm and the others couldn't see what had transpired, but they had heard the high-pitched squeal of whatever it was, a sound that sent chills down their spines.

Anselm had been assigned to a team assembling a part of a larger device—a bomb, or so he had been told. But the design document they working from wasn't complete. He was curious and managed to sneak into Krammer's office. There, amidst scattered blueprints and schematics, he had seen more complete plans. It was then he realized he didn't truly understand what he had been working on. It wasn't just a bomb. What it was, he didn't know.

And then, he overheard. Krammer's voice, calm and confident, speaking to a German officer about dragons. Dragons to be unleashed upon the world. And later, Krammer's chilling promise to the Field Officer—"the power of the gods."

Anselm's curiosity had driven him deeper into the facility, to the heart of the operation, a vast chamber that felt more like a cathedral. At one end of the room stood the device. It was a strange fusion of machinery and a stone.

Anselm had hidden among the shadows, his heart pounding, knowing that he was in an area that he wasn't allowed to be in. But he couldn't resist a closer look at what he'd been contributing to.

The symmetric shell he had worked on had a lens and a stone attached to it. An amber-like stone about the size of an ostrich egg. The stone, with its ominous depths, was etched with swirling glyphs. *Why was it there? What role did it serve?*

What purpose could justify such a strange addition?

He understood the science of the shell they had assembled. Its intent was to direct symmetrical shockwaves from explosives inward to compress a mass of plutonium into a smaller mass resulting in an atomic explosion. What he didn't understand was the purpose of the stone nor why the blast would be directed towards it. The detonation should by all rights consume the stone, the device, the entire facility. *What was the point of this entire experiment?*

As he pondered this, the chamber began to hum with activity. He hadn't realized that a test was scheduled. Panic set in as he saw three soldiers enter the chamber and take positions near the center of the room. Anselm slipped behind some equipment, searching frantically for an exit.

The soldiers spoke in hushed tones, apprehension in their eyes, their voices tinged with uncertainty and nervous bravado. They had volunteered for the glory of serving their country.

A series of clicks from the machine and then a sudden burst of energy filled the chamber, and Anselm felt a searing pain rip through his body. He screamed along with the other men, the agony unbearable as his mind fractured.

The sensation was indescribable, as if his very essence was being torn away.

As the unbearable wave of pain reached its crescendo, he felt his humanity, replaced by something... other. Something primal and bound to unnatural forces.

Anselm's gaze met Linton's, a silent understanding passing between them. The revelation that Anselm was not just a dragon but a transformed human being was staggering.

176

As Captain Linton's mind raced with questions about Anselm's story, the project that had altered him, and what significance this revelation might hold, he felt a mix of awe and concern. The implications of transforming a man into a dragon were staggering, both scientifically and morally. *What had driven such a drastic experiment? And what did it mean for the war effort, knowing the Nazis had delved into such forbidden realms of science?*

Captain Linton then asked, "Who was in charge of this project?"

Anselm carefully wrote, "**KRAMMER**"

Linton's mind was racing to recall if he'd ever heard of Krammer, "What was the goal of the experiment?"

Anselm hesitated, his memories swirling. When the torment had subsided, Anselm looked down at a body he didn't recognize. When he looked up there were three dragons where the soldiers had stood. His mind clouded with confusion and horror as he realized what Krammer had succeeded in doing.

Anselm's response came slowly as he struggled to write, but with clear intent, "**TO CREATE THOUSANDS OF DRAGONS, DOMINATE EARTH. WHY I STOLE STONE AND BROUGHT HERE.**"

Captain Linton, knowing all too well the devastation that the other dragons had wreaked on the battlefields of Europe, found this revelation chilling. The thought of thousands of such creatures, bred for world domination, sent a shiver down his spine.

Linton continued, "How many other dragons were created?" He feared the answer, imagining the implications of a vast number of dragons unleashed upon the world.

Anselm's claw moved deliberately across the paper, "**3**"

Linton grew quiet, contemplating the realization that it had only taken three to bring down an entire formation of American bombers. "Four, in all then," he muttered, the implications of what could happen if there were thousands of them terrified him, "You took the stone before more dragons could be created?"

Anselm nodded. Then he wrote, "**OTHERS TRIED TO STOP ME**", then he gestured to his splinted wing and the bandages around his torso.

Linton's curiosity deepened. "Were the other three technicians as well?"

Anselm shook his head slightly before writing, "**LOYAL SS SOLDIERS**."

Linton hesitated for a moment before asking, "Anselm, I need to ask. Are you loyal to the Nazis?"

Anselm paused, his claw hovering over the paper. Anselm's mind was a whirlwind of disjointed memories, his thoughts scattered like fragments of a broken dream. Yet one thing remained clear: he had to stop Krammer, no matter the cost.

After a moment of contemplation, he wrote, "**NO. I LOVE FATHERLAND, LOVE GERMANY. DON'T SUPPORT NAZIS. KRAMMER CANNOT SUCCEED!**" Then he scrawled a line under the word, "**CANNOT**".

Linton drew a steadying breath. "Anselm," he began, his tone careful but direct, "I need to ask you about the stone. The one you stole. What is it, exactly?"

Anselm tilted his head slightly, a flicker of frustration crossing his features. He hesitated, his claw hovering over the paper before he began to write with slow, deliberate strokes:

I DON'T KNOW.

Linton frowned, leaning in. "You don't know? Why was it so important to take?"

Anselm nodded again, his expression grim. He scrawled his next words with deliberate emphasis: **MACHINE BUILT AROUND IT**.

Linton's frown deepened as he read the words. "The device you worked on—it depended on the stone?"

Anselm nodded his head slowly.

Linton felt a chill creep through him as the pieces began to align. "So, without the stone, they can't create more like you?"

Anselm shook his head slowly, then added: **NOT WITH-OUT STONE.**

As Captain Linton mulled over Anselm's answers, trying to grasp the full scale of what Anselm was sharing with him, Anselm glanced out a small window and noticed the children outside.

Sarah, Olivia, and Peter had gathered around the Humber Super Snipe. The driver was allowing them to sit in the enormous automobile. The children took turns sitting in the driver's seat and pretending to steer. Their excitement was palpable as they explored the interior of the military vehicle. By then, Sarah and Olivia were sitting in the back seat, laughing, while Peter stood outside, waiting his turn.

Anselm's eyes fixed on the driver, who was now turning towards the barn. His gaze sharpened as he saw the unnatural grin on the man's face.

Anselm rose in a panic. That smile! Somehow Krammer had found him. Unsure what to do Anselm began scraping his claws across the floor and swinging his tail in agitation knocking over tools and equipment, crashing into barrels and crates. Captain Linton and Thomas scrambled back in alarm

"Anselm! What is it?" Thomas's voice cut through the commotion as he stepped forward cautiously.

Sarah's mother, alarmed by the dragon's sudden outburst, moved closer, her face filled with concern. "What's wrong with him?" she pleaded, looking to Thomas, then Captain Linton for answers.

Anselm scooped up the crayon and wrote urgently, "**KRAMMER MAN**" then motioned for Linton to look out the window.

Linton looked out the window confused. His brow furrowed. "What am I looking for?" he asked.

Anselm underlined the words he had written and added, "**SMILE**" then jabbed the crayon toward the writing for emphasis. His tail lashed again, narrowly missing Thomas, who stepped back quickly.

"My driver?" Linton had noticed that his driver was smiling, which was out of character, but he'd known the young man long enough to know he wasn't a spy.

Anselm, still agitated, kept underlining, "**KRAMMER MAN**" and "**SMILE**" Then he wrote, "**DANGER**" grunting for emphasis and slapping his tail down as he underlined which upended a workbench sending boxes and tools crashing.

The driver, hearing the commotion coming from inside the barn quickly realized Anselm had identified him. His eyes darted towards the girls in the car. Without hesitation he shoved Peter out of the way. Peter stumbled back with a startled shout. The driver yanked the door open, leaped into the driver's seat, shoving Sarah roughly aside, ignoring her cry of protest.

Peter saw Sarah's face flash past the window—surprise, then fear—before the door slammed and the car tore away.

"Oi!" Peter yelled, scrambling to his feet, but the driver was already gunning the engine.

The car roared to life, its tires spinning on the gravel before catching. With a violent lurch, the car sped out of the drive and onto the road, a cloud of dust trailing in its wake.

Peter's voice rang out, sharp and panicked. "Olivia!" as Captain Linton's car raced away.

With a guttural growl, Anselm surged past Linton and Thomas, sending them stumbling back into a stack of crates. The dragon burst from the barn, claws tearing into the dirt as he charged toward the fleeing car.

Sarah's mother hurried behind him, her expression shifting from confusion to alarm as they watched Anselm's frantic pursuit of the vehicle.

Peter stumbled toward them visibly shaken. "He took them!" he gasped, pointing down the road where the car's taillights were vanishing into the distance. "He took them, he drove off with Olivia and Sarah!"

Sarah's mother clutched Peter's arm, her voice shaking. "Took them?"

Peter turned to her, trembling, his words tumbling out in a rush. "The driver!—he's taken Sarah and Olivia!"

For a moment, Sarah's mother stood frozen, her eyes wide with disbelief. "No!" she cried, her voice breaking as the faint roar of the car's engine faded into the distance. Her hands flew to her mouth as if trying to stifle the wave of panic threatening to overwhelm her.

Thomas and Captain Linton staggered out of the barn, brushing themselves off.

Captain Linton's expression was tense, his mind racing to make sense of what had just happened. Why? he thought. Why would my driver—someone I've trusted implicitly—do this? But there was no time for reflection.

Anselm, having chased the car to the road, stopped abruptly, realizing it already had too much of a head start—especially with his wing still bound. He clawed at the ground in frustration, his tail lashing violently. His sharp gaze swung back to the group, locking onto Linton's with a burning urgency. The dragon let out a deep, guttural growl that resonated through the air.

Linton met Anselm's eyes, understanding the silent plea. Turning to Thomas. Despite not understanding the reasons, Linton knew enough to recognize that something critical was unfolding, something that needed to be stopped immediately.

His voice cut through the chaos. "We need to get after them. Now!"

Thomas led the way to the Morris Eight. Linton jumped in the passenger seat. Sarah's mother rushed over. Before Thomas could suggest she stay, "It's my daughter!"

Peter, started to get in the car as well. Thomas told him, "Stay here, son."

Peter said, "It's my sister!"

"I know, lad," Thomas placed a hand on Peter's shoulder gently, "I need you to stay here and find out everything you can from Anselm. If we can't catch them, it's possible he knows something that might help us figure out where they're heading."

Peter's eyes, betraying a glimmer of fear, as he nodded

reluctantly. "Alright. Just get her back."

Thomas squeezed his shoulder reassuringly before jumping into the car. The engine roared to life, and the Morris Eight sped down the lane in pursuit.

Chapter 26

There was no sight of the Humber Super Snipe. Thomas gripped the steering wheel of the Morris Eight, his knuckles white as he pushed the car to its limits. The Morris Eight, while sturdy, couldn't match the raw power and speed of the Super Snipe. He drove as fast as he could handle while navigating the narrow, winding country road.

Captain Linton sat in the passenger seat, his mind racing as he tried to piece together the driver's motives. His thoughts kept circling back to the driver's sudden, inexplicable behavior. The driver's eerie smile.

"He's headed somewhere," Linton muttered, half to himself. "Somewhere important. If he's tied to Krammer—if he's connected to what Anselm warned us about—we have to stop him."

Thomas, eyes fixed on the road, spared a quick glance at Linton. "Krammer? Who's that?"

Linton turned to him briefly, his voice grim. "From what I gather from your dragon, Krammer is the one he was running from. The one behind all of this."

Sarah's mother, sitting in the back seat, leaned forward, her face a mask of worry and determination. "Do you have any idea where he might be taking them?" she asked, her voice strained with fear for her daughter.

Linton turned slightly, his eyes meeting hers in the rearview mirror. "The stone," he said simply. "That's what Krammer needs. That's what this is all about. Anselm said it was the key to their entire plan."

The road blurred past as Thomas maneuvered the Morris Eight through the countryside. Each minute felt like an eternity. The urgency in Linton's voice echoed in Thomas's mind, pushing him to coax more speed from the car.

Linton hesitated, a question cutting through the noise in his mind. He frowned, his gaze narrowing, "Why didn't the driver just go for the stone? Why wait around while I was questioning Anselm? If the stone is so important, why didn't he take off after it when he had the chance? Why wait?"

Thomas piped up, his voice tight as he swerved to avoid a pothole. "Maybe he was stalling—for something or someone."

Linton's jaw tightened. He didn't answer at once, his thoughts turning over the possibilities. "That's possible. He might've been waiting for orders—or for someone else to make their move."

Mrs. Lynde, her face tense as she considered his words. "Who?" she asked, her voice low and strained.

Linton shook his head, his voice grave. "I haven't the faintest idea. But whatever it is, it bodes ill." He straightened, his tone turning resolute. "If he's making for the London laboratory, I must warn them. We need to locate a telephone at once."

Thomas nodded, focusing intently on the road while processing Linton's strategy. "The next village ought to have one at their post office," he suggested.

Linton turned in his seat, addressing Sarah's mother in the

back. "I'll see to it that we get help to search for the girls as well," he said, his tone reassuring.

Mrs. Lynde's hands gripped the edge of her seat as though holding on for dear life. Her voice trembled slightly as she whispered, "Please… bring her back to me. Safe." Her gaze remained fixed on the horizon, scanning the landscape for any sign of the Humber Super Snipe.

The Morris Eight sped onward, its small engine straining as it raced through the winding English countryside, the tension in the car as thick as the low-hanging clouds above.

Chapter 27

The driver giggled incessantly as he raced the car down the winding country lane, his laughter sending shivers down Sarah's spine. She was squeezed against the passenger door, trying to put as much distance between herself and the crazed soldier as possible. Every sharp turn of the car made it a struggle to keep from sliding towards him. Her knuckles whitened as she held herself in place. Her mind raced with strategies for escape, the driver's unnerving grin and the unsettling speed of their escape had her pulse pounding. She imagined throwing open the door and jumping out, but the thought of hitting the hard road, rolling and scraping her skin raw, bones possibly breaking, flashed through her mind. Even more painful was the idea of leaving Olivia behind.

In the back seat, Olivia huddled in a full-blown panic, her fear manifesting in screams that pierced the air. Her cries were frantic, her face streaked with tears, her body trembling uncontrollably. The car's interior felt suffocatingly unfamiliar, the sense of claustrophobia causing her chest to tighten, making it hard to breathe. She stole a glance at Sarah in the front seat, but the driver's unnerving grin and the unsettling speed forced her to squeeze her eyes shut.

The driver paid no heed to their terror, his maniacal giggles continuing unabated as if their suffering were an amusing sideshow.

They drove for miles through the undulating country-side, the landscape unfolding in a patchwork of fields and woodlands growing increasingly unfamiliar to the girls. The narrow, twisting roads wound their way between rolling hills adorned with clusters of ancient oaks and beech trees. Where quaint villages nestled in valleys and hedgerows lined the roadside, casting flickering shadows in sunlight. As they ascended and descended the hills, panoramic vistas opened up, revealing distant farmsteads, and glimpses of winding streams cutting through verdant meadows. The air carried the scent of earth and wildflowers.

The driver seemed to be searching for something, his maniacal eyes scanning the countryside. His giggles becoming laughter. He would drive up one road, then abruptly turn the car around, retracing their path only to veer off onto another road. Frequently, he would stop, peering intensely at the surroundings before continuing his erratic route.

Eventually, they came to a secluded dirt track nestled beside a lonely hill. The driver slammed on the brakes, jolting Sarah towards the windshield, his eyes blazing with a manic intensity. Without a word, he reached down and pulled a revolver from his holster, the cold metal glinting in the light. He motioned for the girls to exit the car and marched them up the hill, brandishing the gun menacingly.

At the summit, there were three small granite stones arranged in a circle. Under the driver's watchful gaze, the girls gathered wood from the sparse woods dotting the hillside, their fear mounting with each twig and branch they collected.

Once satisfied with their haul, he escorted them back to the top, where they dropped the wood near the center.

While the driver stacked wood to build a fire, his back turned to them, Sarah saw their opportunity. She glanced at Olivia, her heart pounding, and took her hand. With slow, deliberate movements, the two began to slowly back away, inch by inch, their footsteps as quiet as they could manage on the uneven ground.

As they edged further away, Sarah focused on getting to the car. The driver had left the keys in the ignition. Her mind raced. If they could reach it, she was fairly confident she could get it moving before the driver made it down the hill to stop them. She tightened her grip on Olivia's hand, willing her to stay calm.

A loud crack shattered the silence.

Both girls froze, their eyes snapping to the driver. He stood rigid, his arm extended, a thin wisp of smoke curling from the barrel of his standard-issue Webley revolver. Slowly, his grin twisted into a menacing sneer as he lowered the barrel toward them.

Sarah's jaw clenched with overwhelming frustration as her mind raced desperately for a way to outwit their captor. Tears welled in her eyes, threatening to spill as the crushing weight of hopelessness bore down on her. It was too much. A sob escaped her lips, and soon the tears came freely. Beside her, Olivia began to cry as well, their shared fear spilling into the heavy silence.

The driver ignored their fearful sobs, his expression unchanged as he gestured sharply, directing them back toward the hilltop. Once there, he resumed his work at the fire, meticulously stoking it. Each movement was deliberate and precise, his unnerving calm giving the impression that he had all the time in the world.

As the flames intensified, he retrieved a palm-sized granite stone from his pocket, engraved with three intricate grooves and shallow cup marks. Placing it in the fire's center, he pulled out a scrap of paper and swiftly penned an address and a cryptic message.

Sarah scanned their surroundings, searching for any sign of help or escape. She knew they had to remain vigilant, their hopes pinned on finding a way to get away and bring an end to their terrifying ordeal. Sarah whispered urgently to Olivia, "If we get the chance, can you open the door and make a run for it when I tell you? Head to the back of the car and don't stop—just keep going. Think you can manage that?"

Olivia, her eyes red from tears, whispered back, "What about you?"

Just then, the driver glanced up, catching their whispers. He gave them a sharp look, his grin unreadable, before returning his attention to the fire.

Sarah, trying to sound braver than she felt, whispered, "I'll slow him down. Just be ready to run."

The heat intensified, causing the coals to glow a fierce red. The driver poured water from his canteen over the scrap of paper, soaking it thoroughly. With deliberate care, he brushed the glowing stone from the fire, letting it roll onto the cool ground where it hissed softly against the dirt.

Sarah watched in wide-eyed silence as he placed the damp paper over the heated stone. A faint hiss rose, and then, to her astonishment, ghostly wisps of steam curled upward, carrying faint traces of ink into the air.

At first, it seemed like nothing—just vapors twisting and rising. But as Sarah stared, the shapes sharpened, and ghostly letters began to form within the smoke. Her breath caught, her fear momentarily forgotten. Was she imagining it? Were her eyes playing tricks in the dim light?

But no—Olivia's gasp confirmed she wasn't alone.

The letters floated for only a moment before dissipating, but Sarah leaned forward, squinting to catch the fleeting words. The phrases danced just beyond her grasp, fragments forming and vanishing like a fleeting mirage.

The driver's smirk widened, clearly enjoying their reaction. He adjusted the paper and stone, and another plume of smoke rose. Sarah strained to read the next fragment, catching glimpses of words—numbers, locations, and, finally, an address. An address in London.

The paper began to curl at the edges, thin wisps of smoke rising as the ink bled into the stone. A new plume twisted upward, and this time, Sarah's heart raced as she read the words: "Signal vom Dach für die Drachen."

Her stomach lurched. The last word was unmistakable. Dragons!

The driver brushed off the stone and returned it to his coat pocket, his eyes narrowing as he looked at Sarah and Olivia. He turned sharply, the gun in his hand pointing directly at them. Sarah's breath caught in her throat.

His gaze shifted between the two girls, his grin unreadable, his thoughts turning toward a decision.

Chapter 28

P eter approached Anselm cautiously, unsure of what to ask the dragon. Anselm had been an enigmatic presence since their first encounter, and Peter realized he still knew very little about him.

"I'm not sure what to ask that will help get Olivia and Sarah back," Peter pleaded, desperation in his voice. "I need your help."

Anselm let out a frustrated snort and began pulling at the bandages on his injured wing with his teeth, trying to loosen the splint. Peter rushed up to him, alarmed. "What are you doing? You'll hurt yourself!"

The dragon ignored him completely, pulling and tearing at the splint until it fell away in pieces. He stretched his wing gingerly, unfurling it with slow, deliberate movements. Peter stared, dumbfounded, as Anselm flexed the limb, shaking it out as if testing it for flight.

"Anselm!" Peter said, stepping in front of the dragon to get his full attention. "Hang on! Your wing—it's only just healed!"

The dragon eyed Peter disapprovingly, his massive eyes narrowing slightly. Peter felt his nerves wobble but pressed on, determined. "Anselm, you can't just fly off. I need you to tell me something… Anything that will help."

Anselm finally grunted softly, acknowledging Peter's concern but clearly intent on taking action. He scratched into the dirt, "**SEE SARAH FROM AIR.**" Then he tested the range of motion of his wings again. Anselm knew Peter was right about the potential risks, but time was of the essence.

As Anselm readied himself to launch, Peter scrambled onto his back.

"Oi, Anselm, hang on!" Peter pleaded, his voice cracking. "You can't leave me behind!" His tone grew more urgent. "It's my sister who's out there!"

Anselm snorted dismissively, shaking his head and motioning for Peter to get off.

But Peter clung on stubbornly, moving closer to Anselm's neck where he could get a firm grip. "You need me to come with you!" he argued, his words coming fast. "What if you've got to land? You can't exactly explain yourself to people, can you? And what if the RAF shows up, eh? They're not going to shoot at me, are they? I'll wave them off!"

Anselm regarded Peter with a mix of exasperation and begrudging respect. Peter had a point, despite the risks involved. With a resigned huff, he gave in, stretching his wings wide

"Right, then!" Peter called, tightening his hold as Anselm crouched.

The dragon's wings beat powerfully, each stroke sending a rush of wind and dust across the ground. Peter gripped harder as they rose, the earth falling away beneath them. His heart raced, a mix of terror and exhilaration flooding his senses.

Together, dragon and boy soared into the sky, the wind whipping through Peter's hair as they climbed higher and higher.

Peter had never been this high off the ground before—he'd never even been in an aeroplane. The altitude made his head spin, and the chill of the cooler air was creeping onto his skin. He shivered, tightening his grip on Anselm's scales, wishing he'd thought to grab a coat.

As they climbed higher, Peter forced himself to focus. *Anselm wouldn't let me fall*, he thought, trying to calm his racing heart. The breathtaking view below began to distract him from the cold and the height. The fields and forests stretched out like a patchwork quilt, and the villages looked like dollhouse models with tiny ribbons of rivers winding between them.

Anselm banked slightly, heading in the direction the automobiles had gone. Peter held on tightly, determined to find Olivia and Sarah, and nothing—not the height, the cold, or the fear—was going to stop him.

After several minutes that felt like an eternity, Anselm let out a low rumble and nodded toward the road below. Peter followed his gaze and spotted the Morris Eight, trundling along like a toy car. Relief mixed with frustration as he searched desperately for the Super Snipe, but there was no sign of it.

Anselm surged forward, increasing his speed to catch up with the car below. Peter held on tightly, the wind whipping past them as they soared over the countryside. They searched desperately, eyes scanning the roads and fields for any sign of the car that carried Sarah and Olivia.

Before too long, the Morris Eight headed towards a nearby village and stopped near the town square. Anselm circled above.

Captain Linton exited the car and quickly ran to a telephone booth. He lifted the receiver and spoke to the operator, his voice insistent.

"Operator, get me LAM1212 at once, please. It's an urgent matter. Yes, that's correct." There was a brief pause as the operator connected him. Linton glanced back at the Morris Eight, where Thomas and Mrs. Lynde waited anxiously.

Once connected, Linton wasted no time. "This is Captain Linton speaking. Security is to be heightened immediately. Be on the lookout for a soldier with a... peculiar grin. Yes, you heard me—a man who won't stop smiling. Under no circumstances is he to be allowed into the premises. If he attempts to gain entry, you are to shoot on sight. Do you understand?"

He paused for confirmation before continuing. "Also, inform the constabulary. The same man has abducted two young girls. They're traveling in an olive green Humber Super Snipe, military issue. Get word out as quickly as you can."

As they waited, Sarah's mother stepped out of the car, her anxiety spilling over into restless pacing. She wrung her hands tightly, her gaze darting up the road every so often. Thomas exited as well, striking a match and lighting a cigarette, his mind clearly working through the situation.

"I just don't understand it," Mrs. Lynde said, her voice trembling. "Why take the girls? He could've gotten away without them."

Thomas exhaled a long plume of smoke, his brow furrowed. "I can't say, Mrs. Lynde. Doesn't add up, does it? Maybe... maybe he plans to use them as some kind of leverage."

Mrs. Lynde stopped in her tracks, her brow knitting as she

struggled to make sense of it. "That driver… when I dropped you and Mr. Morris at the base, I saw a woman in town with the same awful grin. It was… unnatural, Thomas. Do you think they're connected?"

Thomas hesitated, taking another drag from his cigarette. Her words stirred a memory, something unsettling. He met her gaze, his voice low and measured.

"Yes. That grin," he said slowly. "I've seen it too. There was a woman—same unnatural grin—when Peter first met me and Orville. Gave me the creeps, if I'm honest."

He rubbed his chin thoughtfully, the memory becoming sharper. "She was in the pub. Shocking red hair. Her grin stretched wide, like it was glued on. But her eyes—they didn't match. Cold as ice."

Mrs. Lynde's face drained of color. "Yes! Red hair! That's the same woman! She was outside the base. She came right up to the car. Didn't say a word, just stood there grinning at us, like she knew something I didn't."

She hugged herself tightly, her voice cracking. "I drove away as quickly as I could."

Thomas took another drag from his cigarette, the ember flaring briefly in the dim light. "And now this—taking the girls. It's all connected, Mrs. Lynde. That driver, the woman… they're connected. Have to be."

Mrs. Lynde shook her head, her worry spilling over. "But why? Why the girls? What could they possibly want with them?" She stopped pacing and turned to Thomas, her eyes wide with desperation. "We have to find them. We have to get them back."

Thomas nodded resolutely. "We will, Mrs. Lynde. We'll get them back."

Captain Linton returned from the phone booth, his expression serious. "Security is being heightened at the lab. They've been instructed to be on the lookout for the driver and the girls. The constabulary has been informed and are coordinating a search with the surrounding villages. They're doing everything they can."

He paused, glancing between Thomas and Mrs. Lynde. "We can continue searching the countryside, but I believe our best lead to finding the girls lies in London."

Mrs. Lynde nodded, struggling to steady her breathing. "Then let's not waste time," she said, her voice trembling. But as the gravity of the situation overwhelmed her, the tears she'd been holding back began to fall. She wiped at her face quickly, ashamed of breaking in front of the others, but unable to stop the flood of fear and helplessness.

Thomas stepped closer, resting a steadying hand on her shoulder. "We'll find them" he said softly.

Meanwhile, high above, Peter and Anselm circled, their eyes scanning the endless patchwork of fields and hedgerows below for any sign of the Super Snipe. The landscape stretched on relentlessly, offering little in the way of clues. With no other options, Peter urged Anselm to follow the direction of the Morris Eight.

"Stay with them," Peter said, his voice barely audible over the rush of wind. It was all they could do—follow and hope. His eyes stayed locked on the ground below, his chest tightening as he desperately searched for any sign of Sarah and Olivia.

Chapter 29

Miles to the east, at a hidden site in France, the dragon eyed the V-1 pulse-jet engine securely mounted on the makeshift launch ramp. This was Field Marshal Guilder's idea—using the V-1 engines to give the dragons a swift and powerful start. The Germans had repurposed the weapon, adding special handholds and footholds to assist the dragons. He climbed up the launch ramp and positioned himself carefully on the V-1, his claws gripping the added fixtures attached to the rocket.

A bell called out to let the dragons know that the first launch was eminent.

With a deafening roar, the pulse-jet ignited, its violent buzzing shaking the launch ramp as the catapult hurled the V-1 forward. In an instant the rocket surged past 300 kilometers per hour, yanking the dragon hard against his own grip. The sudden acceleration tore the breath from him, a sharp, involuntary gasp swallowed by the howl of the engine.

The countryside became a smear of green and brown beneath him as the engine's relentless hammering drove them higher and faster. Wind tore at his scales, rattling his bones, the sound of the pulse-jet vibrating through his chest like a second, savage heartbeat. The speed climbed past 600 kilometers per hour, faster than any living thing was meant to travel.

Exhilaration became something intoxicating. His heart thundered as the rocket clawed skyward, carrying him toward England on a column of noise, fire, and stolen momentum.

After about five minutes the engine cut out and the dragon disengaged from the V-1, letting the engine fall away as he unfurled his wings. The initial boost had given him the momentum needed for the journey across the Channel. With powerful strokes, he raced towards England.

As the first dragon raced into the distance, the second V-1 was prepped and launched, followed by the third. Each dragon repeating the process, gripping the specially added fixtures on the rockets, feeling the surge of power, and soaring into the sky. Following the path of the first, ensuring their coordinated arrival in England.

As they settled into their cruising altitude, the dragons couldn't help but marvel at their own transformation. Once men, they had been promised by Krammer that they could be restored to their human forms. But now, soaring above the earth, they felt a thrill unlike any other. The wind rushing past their scales, the vast expanse of land and sea below—it was exhilarating.

They allowed themselves to revel in their newfound power and freedom. The sky was theirs, an endless domain where they could soar and dive, unfettered by the constraints of their previous lives. The feeling was intoxicating, a heady mix of power and liberation.

When the dragons finally crossed over the English coast, they scanned the landscape below for landmarks. The journey had been swift, thanks to the boost from the V-1, taking little more than half an hour. Now it was time to focus on making their way to London. However, the dragon's keen eyesight detected something approaching rapidly from the west.

Two Spitfires, on patrol, zoomed into view. The pilots had been briefed about the possibility of new German technology, but they weren't informed of its nature. Even if they had, nothing could have prepared them for the sight of dragons in the sky.

"Control, this is Red Leader. I have visual on... three.... dragons?" the lead pilot radioed in disbelief. He blinked hard and shook his head, taking a second, more focused look to confirm what he was seeing. "I repeat, dragons," he affirmed, his voice steadying.

"Red Leader, confirm your last transmission. Did you say dragons?" Control responded, equally stunned.

"Affirmative, Control. Engaging now."

The Spitfires roared towards the dragons, their engines screaming.

The dragons, realizing they had been spotted, veered off in different directions with practiced precision. They had trained for engagements like this, their maneuvers honed to deadly effectiveness. The first dragon, still exhilarated from the launch, felt a fresh surge of adrenaline as it banked sharply, ready to outmaneuver the incoming fighters. Its sharp instincts, combined with its rigorous training, made it a truly formidable target.

The pilots opened fire with their plane's four 7.7 mm Browning machine guns, tracer rounds streaking through the sky. The first dragon flew directly towards the fighter, twisting and turning with surprising agility. A round from the guns managed to graze its flank, but the dragon pressed on, focused on its prey.

The second dragon, initially seizing upon the pilots' shock and bewilderment at encountering dragons for the first time, dove towards the ground. After allowing the second Spitfire pilot to maneuver behind him, he began dodging and weaving, cleverly using the rolling hills and forests as cover.

Meanwhile, the third dragon ascended sharply to exploit the open sky for his attack

"Red One, I can't keep up with this one! Blimey! It's like nothing I've ever seen!" the second pilot called out, struggling to line up a shot.

"Stay on 'im, Red Two." Red Leader responded, his voice tense as he focused on his target.

The first dragon executed a sharp flip that no aircraft could match. It twisted its body mid-air and spewed a torrent of flame at the first Spitfire. The fiery breath engulfed the Spitfire, melting the acrylic plastic canopy protecting the pilot, before the plane exploded in a ball of fire.

"Control, Red Leader is down! He's down!" Red Two's panicked voice crackled over the radio before it, too, was silenced by the third dragon's flame as it raced at him from above. The pilot saw him at the last moment, tried to veer away, but it was too late A burst of flame shot through the air, and consumed the aircraft, sending it plummeting to the ground.

The air was thick with the scent of smoke and burning fuel as the dragons regrouped and continued their flight to London, their minds again focused on their ultimate goal.

Chapter 30

Sarah's forehead was pressed against the passenger window, the world outside a blur of green fields and distant trees. Fatigue weighed heavily on her, her eyelids drooping despite her best efforts to stay awake. Each time her eyes began to close, she dug her nails into her arm, the small sting snapping her back to alertness.

She tried to think of where she might be able to give Olivia a chance to escape. Peering around the edge of the seat, she could see that Olivia had fallen asleep from exhaustion, her small form curled up and temporarily oblivious to their predicament. Sarah felt hot tears filling her eyes as the responsibility pressed down on her—she was the only one who could get them out of this. She pushed the tears back. She had to force herself to be brave; there wasn't room for anything else.

Sarah noticed that the scenery was changing, the landscape becoming less rural. The green fields and open spaces giving way to more buildings and fully paved roads. They were approaching a city. London. It had to be. She glanced at the driver from the corner of her eye, noting his unwavering grin. A sinister expression that never faltered. He'll have to slow down, she thought. In a city like London, there will be more traffic, more stops. There will be lots of people, witnesses, and places to hide. She mentally mapped out possible escape routes, imagining the crowded streets and bustling sidewalks.

Soon they were in the thick of the city, the driver glancing at a map he was holding up on the steering wheel. The once smooth ride turned jerky as he navigated the crowded streets, swerving around pedestrians at crossings, and as he passed other vehicles. Sarah's pulse quickened. This was it. She knew her chance was approaching. The increased traffic and frequent stops would give her the opportunity she needed. The driver's eyes flickered between the road and the map, his focus divided. She could sense his distraction.

She leaned back slightly, taking a deep breath to steady her nerves. The air in the car felt charged, as she mentally rehearsed her escape. In her mind, she planned her move, timing it with the ebb and flow of the city streets. She would wait for the right moment, the perfect distraction. She had to be ready at any moment. Her hands were sweaty, and she discreetly wiped them on her dress, willing herself to stay calm.

The driver glanced at her. Did he suspect what she was planning? Sarah forced a neutral expression, her heart hammering in her chest. His eyes were cold, unnervingly so, and his grin looked glued to his face. There was something about him that didn't seem human. She shuddered inwardly, trying to shake off the chill that ran down her spine.

The driver put aside the map seemingly satisfied that he knew where he was and where he was heading. Without the map, he grew more alert, his eyes scanning the surroundings with a predatory intensity. Sarah peeked back at Olivia, who was awake now. Olivia caught her eye, fear evident in her expression, but she nodded subtly, indicating she was ready. The trust in Olivia's eyes steeled Sarah's resolve.

Traffic wasn't heavy, but it was busy enough that it might provide Olivia a good chance to get away. A bus crossed in front of the Super Snipe, causing the driver to brake suddenly, nearly stopping. Sarah seized the opportunity and shifted, pressing her back against the passenger door to brace herself. "NOW, Olivia!" she yelled, her voice piercing the silence of the car.

In a swift motion, Sarah kicked her legs hard at the driver, striking him in the face. A surge of adrenaline coursed through her as she kicked again and again. Olivia, reacting instantly, yanked hard on the door handle and shoved the heavy door open. She rolled out of the car as Sarah had instructed, tumbling onto the pavement before scrambling to her feet and sprinting in the opposite direction. Sarah caught a glimpse of Olivia running away just as the car suddenly lurched forward.

The driver, caught off guard, slammed his foot down - too hard, the wrong pedal. The Super Snipe lurched forward and swerved into oncoming traffic. With a violent jolt, the car collided with an oncoming vehicle, wedging the driver side against it. Although the impact was jarring, it created a critical opportunity for Sarah to act.

Sarah seized the moment, kicking at the driver even harder as her hands frantically searched for the door handle. Her fingers fumbled, slipping off the smooth metal, but sheer desperation drove her. Finally, her trembling hand found purchase, and with all her strength, she pushed the door open. She tumbled out of the car, hitting the ground hard. Pain shot through her knees and palms, but she barely noticed. She scrambled to her feet and bolted in the opposite direction from Olivia. He couldn't catch them both, and she meant to make sure he didn't catch her sister.

The outside air hit her face as she burst into the open street, the solid ground beneath her feet was a welcome reality, her breath coming in ragged gasps. Each step hammered in her chest, but she couldn't stop. People on the street turned, startled by the sight of the frantic, disheveled girl barreling past them—but Sarah didn't dare slow down. Her only thought was to put as much distance as possible between herself and the driver.

Her eyes scanned ahead, searching for an alley, a doorway— anything that could hide her. The driver's face haunted her mind, that terrible grin burned into her memory. The fear that he might be chasing her, closing the gap with each second, gnawed at her. Her ears strained for the sound of pounding footsteps or the sharp crack of a gunshot, but all she could hear was the thunderous beat of her own heart and the rasp of her breath.

People parted as she ran, their gazes fixed on her with concern and curiosity. She barely registered their stares, her focus singular: escape.

Sarah's legs burned, her muscles screaming in protest, but she pushed herself harder. The city around her became a blur of brick walls, lampposts, and the startled faces of strangers as she pushed past them. Her mind screamed at her to keep moving. Don't stop. Don't let him catch you.

She spotted a street sign. The address from the smoke came rushing back. She was on the very street the driver had been searching for. Looking at the building numbers, she knew she wasn't far from the address. Her mind raced. She needed to find help, find safety. She searched the numbers for the address, hoping it was a place where she'd find refuge. And she could warn them about the man who kidnapped them.

As Sarah fled, the driver struggled to get out of the car. The driver's side of the car was jammed against another vehicle, forcing him to clamber across the seat and exit through the passenger side—a delay that cost him precious time. His plan had hinged on using one of the girls as a disguise to get into the lab. The man, Orville, wouldn't have suspected either of them. Now, he'd have to adapt. His grin never faltered, but his eyes hardened, his mind recalculating.

Ignoring the gathering crowd drawn by the commotion, he moved to the back of the car and popped open the boot. From within, he retrieved a pilot's survival pouch, slinging it over his shoulder. Then, with unnerving composure, he turned in the direction Sarah had fled. His grin remained fixed, his eyes cold and focused. Each step he took was deliberate, his gait precise and unyielding as he wove through the curious onlookers and concerned citizens.

Sarah's legs burned as she sprinted down the street, her surroundings a blur of stone facades and shop windows. The building numbers flashed by. She clenched her teeth, forcing herself to keep running, even as the pounding of her heart and her labored breath threatened to overwhelm her. She knew she was close—so close—to the address she'd seen in the smoke. Her eyes darted frantically, searching for any sign of help, a door left ajar, a sympathetic face. Anything.

Behind her, the driver strode with quiet determination, the

survival pouch swaying with his steps. He scanned the street methodically, his cold gaze dissecting every corner and alley for a trace of Sarah. His pace quickened. The lab was near, and he was closing the gap.

Sarah's breath came in ragged gasps as her eyes locked onto the building. Her pulse quickened as she recognized the address. Relief surged, mingled with a fresh wave of dread. The building was here—but he was coming. She hurled herself toward the door, her hands trembling as she grasped the knob. With one final, desperate shove, she stumbled inside, slamming the door behind her.

Inside, a soldier stationed at the entrance turned at the commotion. His stern expression shifted to one of alarm as he took in the sight of the terrified girl. Sarah's words tumbled out between gasps. "Please, sir… there's a man coming… he kidnapped us. He's looking for this place."

The soldier's eyes widened. Captain Linton had called earlier, warning them about two girls kidnapped by a soldier who might be heading for the lab. He leaned out the door and glanced down the street, ready to confront whoever might follow.

Chapter 31

The streets of London were bustling with activity as the Morris Eight weaved through the traffic. Inside, Sarah's mother sat anxiously in the back seat, her eyes tiredly scanning the scene outside, searching for any sign of her daughter. Thomas gripped the steering wheel tightly, his attention fixed on navigating the crowded streets. Beside him, Captain Linton meticulously scanned the surrounding vehicles, his eyes darting in search of the Super Snipe.

Captain Linton directed Thomas, "Left at the next intersection. The lab will be up the street"

Linton turned to address Sarah's mother in the rear seat, "Ma'am, As soon as we reach the lab I'll be able to organize a larger search for your daughter." She nodded weakly, continuing to stare out the window.

As they continued down the street, Sarah's mother suddenly spotted a familiar figure. "Stop the car!" she shouted. "I see Olivia!"

Thomas's heart skipped a beat as he quickly stopped in the middle of the street. Sarah's mother didn't wait for the car to come to a complete halt before she opened the door and climbed out.

Thomas called after her, "We'll swing around at the next

intersection." She waved her hand to acknowledge she'd heard.

He turned to Captain Linton. "If that's alright with you?"

Linton nodded. "Of course," he replied, his eyes sweeping over the traffic in search of the Supersnipe and Sarah.

"Olivia!" Sarah's mother called urgently as she navigated through the lanes of traffic, heading back to where she had last caught a glimpse of the little girl. "Sarah!" she called again, her voice growing desperate as she clung to the hope that the girls were together.

Alone in the vast, bustling city of London, Olivia felt the panic covering her like a suffocating blanket. The sounds of the city were overwhelming—the rumble of passing buses, the clatter of footsteps on the pavement. Every face in the crowd was unfamiliar. She was lost. She was alone. The busy sidewalks felt impersonal, people brushing past her as though she didn't exist. Her chest tightened, and her breaths came in shallow gasps.

She couldn't shake the thought that she hadn't run far enough. The man with the smile—he could be anywhere. Was he searching for her now, blending seamlessly into the crowd? The fear chewed at her, urging her to keep moving, to find a safe place to hide. But where? The city stretched endlessly around her, its labyrinth of streets more daunting than reassuring.

Her thoughts turned to Peter, her brother. Olivia wished desperately that he were here with her. She clung to thoughts of him like a lifeline. They'd always been together—exploring woods, climbing trees, or daring each other to cross the creek without falling in. Peter was always there, steady and brave, pulling her out of trouble or encouraging her to try something new. He'd know what to do now. He'd be clever, coming up with a plan.

Tears pricked her eyes, but she blinked them back. You have to be brave, Olivia, she told herself, repeating the words Peter always said when she was scared. "You're braver than you think," he'd say. But it didn't feel true now. Every shadow seemed menacing, every sudden movement a threat. She imagined the driver appearing around every corner, that fixed grin and those cold eyes locking onto her.

She clutched her hands tightly together, trying to steady her trembling fingers. Olivia's eyes darted from one street corner to the next, scanning for help. The busy sidewalks felt impersonal, the people brushing past her as though she didn't exist. It wasn't like the quiet village streets she knew—here, everything was cold, vast, and unyielding.

You have to be brave, Olivia, she told herself.

Olivia considered ducking into one of the narrow alleyways branching off the street. They seemed quieter, less exposed. But the thought of being cornered in the shadows by the driver froze her in place. She hesitated, her breathing ragged, trying to think clearly. *What would Peter do?* she asked herself, summoning her brother's steadying presence in her mind. Peter always had a plan. He wouldn't just run aimlessly—he'd stop, look around, and figure out the best plan.

She took a deep breath, forcing herself to think past the fear. *Stay where there are people.* That's what he'd say. *The driver won't do anything with so many eyes on him.* She nodded to herself, clutching her hands tightly together as if holding onto Peter's advice. She turned back to the street, her eyes scanning the moving crowd, the buses trundling past, the doors of shops and pubs that might offer a refuge.

Keep moving, she told herself. *Stay in the open,* her steps more deliberate now. *Look for somewhere safe. Somewhere he can't follow.* Her heart still pounded, and every shadow still felt like a threat, but Peter's imagined voice kept her calm, helping her hold onto just enough courage to keep going.

The fear of being found propelled her feet forward, though her legs felt heavy with exhaustion. Olivia wasn't sure where she was going, only that she needed to put as much distance as possible between herself and the nightmare she had escaped.

Every step she took felt like a gamble, but she had no choice but to keep going, her small figure weaving through the bustling crowd, her heart pounding in time with her hurried footsteps.

When she heard her name, Olivia froze, her heart skipping a beat. The voice was unmistakable—Sarah's mother, calling out to her. Relief washed over her, overwhelming and unstoppable. She turned, her small frame trembling, and saw Sarah's mother hurrying toward her, her face a mixture of worry and relief.

"Olivia!" Mrs. Lynde cried out, her voice breaking as she rushed forward. They collided in a fierce embrace, Olivia clinging tightly to her as though letting go might make the nightmare return. Tears streamed down her cheeks, her sobs mingling with shaky breaths of relief.

"I was so scared!" Olivia sobbed, burying her face in Mrs. Lynde's blouse.

Mrs. Lynde held her close, stroking Olivia's hair and murmuring softly, "It's alright, darling. You're safe now. I've got you." Her own voice was thick with emotion, though her focus remained on finding Sarah. "Where's Sarah?"

Olivia pulled back just enough to look up at her, her voice trembling. "She… she was still in the car," she stammered, pointing shakily in the direction she had run from. "That way."

Mrs. Lynde's heart sank, dread gripping her as she followed Olivia's gaze. The realization hit her like a blow: he still had Sarah. But she couldn't allow her fear to show, not now. Taking a deep breath to steady herself, she cupped Olivia's face in her hands, forcing a reassuring smile. "You've done so well, sweetheart. So very brave," She straightened, taking Olivia's hand firmly in hers. "Come on," she said, her tone resolute. "Let's find Sarah."

Olivia nodded, her small hand gripping tightly as they began walking in the direction Olivia had pointed. Mrs. Lynde's eyes darted around constantly, scanning the streets for any sign of Sarah—or the man who had taken her. Her heart hammered in her chest, but she pressed on, her steps quick and determined, fueled by equal parts fear and hope.

As Thomas approached the intersection, the unmistakable sight of the olive green Super Snipe loomed ahead, its crumpled form resting against an oncoming car. The scene was chaos—bystanders gathered in clusters, murmuring and gesturing toward the wreckage. Some pointed animatedly, recounting what they had witnessed, while others stood back, their faces etched with bewilderment.

Captain Linton's eyes narrowed as they drew closer. "Pull in there," he ordered.

Thomas nodded and steered the Morris Eight to the side of the road, bringing it to a halt. Linton was out of the car in an instant, striding purposefully toward the crash. The Super

Snipe's driver's side was mangled, the door jammed shut from the impact. He leaned down, peering into the interior. Broken glass littered the seats, and the smell of burnt oil lingered in the air, but there was no sign of Sarah—or the driver.

"She's not here," Captain Linton told Thomas as he returned to the Morris Eight. His expression was tense. "Go back to Mrs. Lynde. Hopefully the girls are together. I'll continue on foot, it's not far from here."

Thomas gave a curt nod. "Be careful," he said.

Without another word, Linton turned and began weaving through the crowd, his steps brisk and purposeful. Thomas lingered for a moment, watching as the captain disappeared into the throng, then turned his attention back to the car. He pulled away from the curb and into traffic, heading toward the next intersection to turn around. He whispered a silent prayer that Mrs. Lynde had found Sarah and Olivia safe.

Captain Linton moved swiftly along the sidewalk, his senses sharp, scanning for any sign of the grinning driver or Sarah. The driver's destination was clear: the lab and the stone. Linton was certain of his objective now, and if the driver got away with the stone, it could spell catastrophe.

The distant wail of air raid sirens suddenly cut through the city's clamor, halting Linton in his tracks. He looked upwards, the sound chilling. The Germans had increased their V-1 attacks since D-Day. Around him, people on the street, their faces etched with unease as they looked toward the sky listening for the signature sound of buzz bombs as they rushed for shelter.

Linton quickened his pace, determination driving him forward. Whatever was happening, the stone had to be secured.

Chapter 32

The driver was near the lab, mulling his options, when he spied Captain Linton coming up the sidewalk. This was a serious complication, Linton would identify him instantly. He quickly crossed to the other side of the street and stood behind a light pole to cover himself while Linton continued into the lab.

He needed a new disguise, someone who could get into the building, but no one he saw on the street seemed like they would be allowed in. It started to seem impossible until it occurred to him that if Captain Linton were here so could the others from the farm. Perhaps Orville's friend, or the girls' mother. They would be searching for the girls. A plan started to form when he glanced up and saw three recognizable black shapes in the distant sky.

Krammer had sent the dragons to collect the stone, and they were here. Perfect!

Double-checking to see that all was clear, the driver crossed back and carefully approached the building. Careful to avoid exposing his face to anyone within, he slipped around the side of the building while pulling a flare gun from the pilot bag slung over his shoulder. He paused, scanning the area to ensure no pedestrians were in sight, then quickly fired it into the air. The brilliant streak of light appeared in the sky. The dragons would see it. They would retrieve the stone and deal with whoever was inside.

He slipped away, his steps quickening toward the Super Snipe, intent on finding Mr. King or the girls. Taking the dragon had been his plan—the ultimate prize that would have guaranteed his triumphant return to Krammer with the stone. But being recognized at the farm had shattered that possibility, forcing him to recalibrate. At this juncture, any victim would do, but taking one of them would be far more satisfying.

A maniacal laugh bubbled in his throat as he strode purposefully up the sidewalk, his eyes darting wildly, scouring the area for his quarry. Nearing the crashed Super Snipe, his sharp gaze locked onto the mother and the little girl approaching. A wicked giggle escaped him as his fingers brushed over the revolver at his side. With calculated precision, he crept in their direction, his movements eerily silent, his intent chillingly clear.

As traffic began to move again, Thomas craned his neck from the Morris, his eyes sweeping the bustling sidewalk. He scanned the faces in the crowd, searching for Sarah's mother and Olivia. At last, he spotted them, weaving through the throng as they made their way up the pavement.

Walking briskly toward the Super Snipe, Sarah's mother held Olivia's hand firmly. Looking down she instructed her,"Stay close, and keep an eye out for Sarah." But the moment she looked up, her gaze landed on the grinning driver weaving through the crowd towards them, her heart jolted. "Olivia, this way—quickly!" she gasped, pulling Olivia into a sudden dash in the opposite direction.

From the car, Thomas saw the grinning driver moving up the sidewalk towards Olivia and Mrs. Lynde. He saw the fear in their movements as she and Olivia turned and went in the opposite direction. He swerved the Morris Eight, cutting through traffic in a desperate bid to catch up.

Panic rising, Sarah's mother scanned the buildings lining the street, her mind racing for a place to hide. Her eyes landed on a recessed doorway partly obscured by a corner lamppost. "There!" she exclaimed urgently, gripping Olivia's hand and pushing her forward as they made a desperate dash for cover. The crowd on the sidewalk blurred around them as they sprinted, Olivia struggling to keep pace.

Behind them, the driver skidded to a stop, thrown off by their sudden disappearance. His eyes narrowed as he scanned the area, his mouth still locked in that unnatural smile. Then, movement—a door on a three-story building of flats—caught his attention. Its motion subtle, it had to be them. His grin widening into something both gleeful and more menacing. He adjusted his stride, angling toward the building with purposeful intent.

Thomas tailed the driver, urgency propelling him into action. Afraid of losing sight of him from the car, he yanked the Morris to a halt at the curb, ignoring the honk of passing vehicles. Flinging the door open, he climbed out, keeping his eyes fixed on the driver weaving through the crowd up the sidewalk. Slamming the door shut behind him, he hurried after the grinning man, his boots pounding against the pavement.

Ahead, he caught a glimpse of the driver slipping into a recessed doorway. Thomas's heart thundered in his chest, the danger to Mrs. Lynde and Olivia pushing him forward. His breath came in sharp bursts. Clenching his fists, he quickened his pace, adrenaline surging as he prepared to intervene.

Chapter 33

Captain Linton entered the lab building and was immediately confronted by two soldiers at the door. The soldier's eyes scrutinized him, then recognition flashed, and they snapped to attention, saluting sharply. Linton returned the salutes and proceeded to the soldier stationed behind a desk at the back of the lobby.

"All clear, sir. No sign of the fella you told us to watch for. You'll be glad to hear, though, we've got ourselves a visitor," the soldier reported.

From behind the soldier, a familiar face caught Linton's attention. His eyes lit up as he recognized her. "Sarah! Thank heavens, you're safe!" he exclaimed, the relief clear in his voice.

"Yes, sir. Olivia is still out there..." Sarah's voice trembled slightly.

Linton's expression softened, his tone steady and reassuring. "It's all right. Your mother's with her, and Mr. King is on his way to collect them. They'll be over the moon to know you're safe." He paused, a sudden thought crossing his mind. "Blast, I forgot to give Mr. King this address." He frowned briefly but refocused on Sarah. "We'll find them, no doubt about it. But tell me, how did you manage to get away? What happened to the man who took you?"

Sarah, her eyes welling up from both relief and the memory of the ordeal, stammered, "I—I waited until the car slowed down and then I kicked him, kicked him hard, until Olivia got away. Then when he was trying to grab me, he crashed the car and I got away."

"You're safe here," Linton assured her. "These soldiers are top-notch; if he shows, he won't get past them. Now, I need to check on the lab upstairs. You know Mr. Morris, don't you?"

"Orville is here?" Sarah brightened, following Linton as they began ascending the stairs.

Suddenly, the sharp pop and whiz of a flare gun cut through the air outside, drawing their attention. The soldier nearest the door peered outside.

The few people still outside stared upward at the flare. Whoever launched it had slipped away, but their attention was soon diverted as they began pointing frantically towards the sky. Panic quickly set in, and the crowd scattered.

The soldier at the door stepped outside for a clearer view, but the sight above him froze him in place. His wide eyes locked onto enormous shapes swooping down towards the building, their fiery forms dark against the sky. Heart pounding, he turned and sprinted back inside, his voice laced with disbelief. "Sir, you won't believe this—dragons! Actual dragons!"

His outburst was met with skeptical glances from the two other soldiers. "Dragons? Are you loopy, mate?" one scoffed, his tone laced with doubt.

"Look!" the first soldier hissed, his trembling hand pointing toward the window.

The other soldiers crowded cautiously toward the window.

Their expressions shifted from skepticism to sheer terror as a colossal creature landed heavily in front of the building. Its fiery scales shimmered in the light. Wings spread wide, casting a massive shadow that swallowed the street below.

"It's... a bloody dragon!" one of the soldiers stammered, his voice breaking with panic.

The soldiers moved on instinct, their training battling against the surreal terror of the moment. Rifles were raised and they began firing through the window. Bullets ricocheted harmlessly off the dragon's impenetrable scales, their metallic pings swallowed by the chaos. The beast responded with a deafening roar, a sound so fierce it seemed to shake the very foundation of the building.

"Get back!" Captain Linton's bark cut through their rising panic like a whip. His voice carried the unmistakable authority of someone who knew what they were up against. "You can't fight it! Everyone, upstairs, NOW!"

The soldiers scrambled to obey as a thunderous crash echoed through the building. The main doors exploded inward, sending splinters flying in all directions. A desk flipped violently across the room as the massive head of an enormous red dragon forced its way inside. Its molten eyes glared menacingly, smoke curling from its nostrils in thick, lazy tendrils.

"Move! Get upstairs!" Linton roared again, his voice edged with urgency as he herded Sarah up the staircase. The dragon's jaws snapped at the air, splintering another desk with terrifying ease as it clawed its way further into the building.

The soldiers reached the second floor, their breaths ragged, pressing themselves against the far wall in wide-eyed terror.

Captain Linton stood resolute at the top of the staircase, his gaze darting between the beast and the soldiers.

"It wants the stone!" he bellowed. "Sarah, get yourself to the roof! Go!" His words carried the weight of a command, leaving no room for argument.

Suddenly, from outside, a concussive cracking sound pierced the chaos. It was followed by a deep, resonating boom that echoed across the streets. The dragon roared in fury, its bellow shaking the building to its core. Linton's heart surged with both fear and a spark of hope. Had reinforcements arrived?

Chapter 34

They had fled to the second floor of the flats, panic gripping Sarah's mother as she frantically tried each door, hoping to find one unlocked. Her hands trembled as she twisted knob after knob, each door locked. Olivia clung to her, eyes wide with fear, repeating, "He's coming, he's coming," over and over. The driver's slow, deliberate footsteps echoed ominously as he ascended the stairs, growing louder with each passing second. She glanced over her shoulder and caught sight of his grinning face turning her way as he approached the top step.

Desperation surged through her as she fumbled with yet another doorknob. Finally, the next one turned. Relief surged—then died instantly. The door didn't open. She twisted the knob again, harder. Nothing. She twisted the knob back as hard as she could and put her shoulder into the door and it popped open. She yanked Olivia into the flat, turning to slam the door behind them. But it was too late. The driver was there, he lunged forward, forcing himself against the door.

Sarah's mother threw herself against the other side, her breath coming in short, ragged gasps, as she fought to keep him out. But he managed to inch the door wide enough to get his fingers in, then forced his arm through to grab at her. Olivia put her hands against the door trying to help, but it wasn't enough. He was getting in.

Sarah's mother realized they needed to find another way out, a place to hide. With a sudden burst of determination, she released the door, scooped up Olivia, and dashed to the other end of the flat. The driver, caught off guard by the abrupt movement, lunged after them but misjudged his step. He stumbled into the room, his momentum carrying him forward uncontrollably. His foot caught on the edge of a rug, sending him crashing headlong into a chair. The impact was brutal; he toppled over it, his body twisting awkwardly as he fell, landing with a heavy thud, his grinning face smashing into the floor. The room seemed to reverberate with the sound of the collision.

They dashed down the hallway, the bathroom at the end their only hope. It had to have a lock. Sarah's mother hurriedly pushed through the door with Olivia, frantically scanning the small room for any means of escape. There were no windows, only the solid walls closing in around them. Desperately, she glanced down the hallway as she struggled to shut the door, but what she saw made her blood run cold: the driver was coming, but vines were bursting from his chest and abdomen, writhing like living tendrils.

In a panic, she slammed the door shut and engaged the lock just as his body crashed into it, the impact rattling the frame. She felt his weight slide down the door, but the bathroom offered no other way out. With no windows and no ventilation shaft, the reality of their situation closed in— trapped, with only the thin barrier of the door between them and the horror outside.

Suddenly, Olivia let out a piercing scream. Sarah's mother looked down to see the writhing vines creeping under the door.

Thomas raced into the building, his voice echoing as he called out for them. He frantically searched the first floor, finding no sign of them, and then bolted upstairs. Spotting an open door, he sprinted toward it, still shouting their names. Sarah's mother heard Thomas and yelled back, "We're here!!"

Thomas burst into the flat and was immediately greeted by a horrifying sight—the driver's lifeless body sprawled on the floor, thick vines twisting out of it. He froze for a moment, his stomach churning at the unnatural scene before him. The shock of it all nearly made him falter, but the sound of Mrs. Lynde's voice snapped him back to reality.

"Mrs. Lynde, where are you?" he called, his voice tinged with urgency as he pulled his eyes away from the grotesque figure.

"In here!" Sarah's mother shouted back, panic clear in her voice. "Hurry!"

He saw the door where Sarah's mother and Olivia were trapped and cautiously approached the vines. A sickeningly sweet odor caught him off guard, and he watched in fascination as they moved on their own. Some of the vines began to stretch toward him. The way they moved, with a life of their own, was unnerving.

"Thomas! Hurry! They're coming under the door!" she called out again, her voice filled with fear.

He could feel his pulse pounding in his ears as he realized he needed to act. "Okay, hold on!" Thomas called out, his eyes darted around the room, searching for something—

anything—that could help.

He spotted a broom leaning against the wall and quickly grabbed it. With the broom in hand, he began to prod at the vines, trying to push them back. But as soon as the broom made contact, the vines reacted with terrifying speed. They wrapped themselves around the broom's handle, tightening their grip with unnatural strength. Thomas yanked on the broom, trying to pull it free, but the vines held fast, twisting and curling around the wood like constricting snakes. No matter how hard he pulled, the vines refused to let go, their tendrils coiling tighter and tighter, pulling the broom toward them with a relentless force.

Realizing that the broom was a lost cause, Thomas released his grip and took a step back, his mind racing for another solution. The vines, now fully in control of the broom, dragged it down to the floor, leaving Thomas empty-handed and more desperate than ever.

Thinking quickly, "Okay, hold on" Thomas scanned the flat for anything else he might use to get past the vines.

Spotting a knocked-over chair in the living area, Thomas grabbed it and set it in the writhing vines, planing to use it as a makeshift bridge to reach the door. He hopped onto the chair, but soon realized that he was still too far from the door. He would have to step into the vines to get the rest of the way. As he turned to step off, the chair shifted violently. Vines had coiled around the legs and were rocking it.

Thomas struggled to maintain his balance, but managed to step off the chair to safety. He grabbed the chair's backrest to move it out of the way. The vines resisted, tightening their grip.

He began smashing the chair against the vines on the floor,

trying to crush them. Each time the vines pulled, he swung the chair down hard on them. Suddenly, the vines released their hold, and Thomas was thrown backward with the chair. A vine reached for him but he was out of its reach.

Breathing heavily, he realized how dangerous the vines were.

Thomas dashed to the kitchen, frantically rummaging for a knife—anything he could use against the vines. His hand brushed against bottles of liquor in one cabinet, and a desperate idea sparked.

Grabbing a whiskey bottle, he smashed it against the wall near the vines, then struck a match and tossed it. The flames ignited quickly, spreading along the floor as the vines recoiled from the heat. Smoke began to fill the flat, and the fire in the hallway started to spread rapidly.

He pulled a mattress from the small bed in the flat and threw it over the burning vines. "Mrs. Lynde, open the door and leap across! Now!" he shouted. The door creaked open, and Sarah's mother appeared, coughing from the thickening smoke. Her eyes widened at the sight of the smoldering mattress and flames licking the walls. "You can't be serious," she cried in disbelief.

"Come on!!" Thomas urged, his voice rising in desperation.

Sarah's mother knelt beside Olivia. "I want you to run and jump as far as you can. Mr. King will catch you!" she instructed gently.

Olivia hesitated, her wide, fearful eyes locked on the flames. "It's okay, Olivia." Sarah's mother encouraged.

With a deep breath, Olivia took a few steps back, then sprinted forward and jumped. She landed near the end of the mattress, tumbling into Mr. King's waiting arms. He held her tightly.

"You're okay," he reassured her.

Thomas reached out his hand to Sarah's mother. "Your turn, Mrs. Lynde."

She looked warily at the mattress, noticing that the flames had been snuffed out and the vines were beginning to stir, reaching out from underneath in search of a victim. "Come on, I'm here!" Thomas urged.

Taking a few steps back into the bathroom, she rushed forward and leaped. She landed in the middle of the mattress, too far to step off without risking contact with the vines. They immediately began snaking around the edges, reaching for her legs. Thomas lunged forward, grabbed her hand, and pulled her the rest of the way to safety. But as he did, he found himself too close to the advancing vines. They coiled around his ankle, tightening their grip as he tried to backpedal. The vines pulled, knocking him down to the ground, dragging him toward them as he struggled to break free.

Thomas struggled desperately against the tightening vines, their grip relentless as they wound further up his legs, pulling him into their writhing mass.

"Get more liquor!" Thomas shouted, his voice strained. "The kitchen!!"

Sarah's mother ducked low to avoid the thick smoke filling the flat, making her way to the kitchen as quickly as she could. She grabbed two bottles of alcohol, the glass cool against her trembling hands, and raced back to the mattress. Without hesitation, she poured the contents of one over the smoldering fabric.

The vines tightened mercilessly around Thomas's legs, dragging him closer to the heart of the mass. His hands fumbled for the matchbook in his pocket, desperate to get it to Sarah's mother. He managed to retrieve it, but just as he was about to throw it, a vine lashed out, snagging his arm, and the matchbook slipped from his grasp, falling to the floor.

Before anyone could react, Olivia darted forward, her small frame moving swiftly. She snatched up the matchbox and scrambled back, her eyes wide with fear. Sarah's mother grabbed the matchbox from Olivia, quickly pulling out a match and striking it. She threw it onto the soaked mattress, but it fizzled out immediately.

"Olivia! The other bottle!" she called urgently. Olivia fumbled with the bottle, her small hands shaking, but managed to pass it to Sarah's mother. She yanked off the cap and drenched the mattress with the remaining alcohol. With a quick motion, she struck another match and tossed it onto the mattress.

This time, the mattress erupted into flames, the fire roaring to life with intense heat. She immediately began pulling on Thomas's free arm, trying to drag him away from the vines that still held his legs in their tightening grip.

The heat was overwhelming, the flames roaring louder, and the smoke thickened, making it nearly impossible to see or breathe.

The vines, now smoldering and burning, began to lose their hold, loosening slightly as the fire consumed them. But they were still strong, biting into Thomas's flesh, pulling him ever closer to the flames. He could feel the intense heat searing his legs, the pain unbearable. He cried out as the fire licked at him, burning his skin. His vision blurred from the smoke and pain, but he fought to stay conscious, knowing that if he passed out, it would be the end.

Finally, the vines, weakened by the heat, released their grip and fell away from him. Sarah's mother, coughing and eyes stinging from the smoke, pulled with all her might. The vines started to loosen their hold, and she felt a surge of hope. "Come on!" Thomas, his body trembling with pain and exhaustion, scrambled free from the last tendrils, collapsing onto the floor away from the flames.

"We need to get out!" Sarah's mother coughed, her voice hoarse and strained from the smoke. Nearly overcome, they stumbled through the thick, acrid haze, their lungs burning with each desperate breath.

The flat was becoming a blazing inferno, flames hungrily consuming everything in their path. Thomas, Sarah's mother, and Olivia pushed through the suffocating smoke, their movements sluggish as the heat and fumes overwhelmed them. They found their way out of the burning flat and into the hallway, where the air was slightly clearer but still thick with smoke.

As the flames engulfed the vine creature, its final thoughts were of the pleasure it had found in feeding on humans—a delicious change from its usual, mindless prey.

Through the haze of its last moment, the creature clung to one thought above all: Krammer's promise. The doors would open, he had said. All the doors. The vine creature's existence had been small, but Krammer had offered its kind something much more vast.

The three of them stumbled out of the building, coughing violently, gasping for fresh air. The cool outside air hit them like a balm against their smoke filled lungs and Thomas's singed skin. They collapsed onto the ground outside, exhausted and shaken, but alive. The fire roared behind them, consuming the building, but they had survived, Olivia clinging to Thomas in the aftermath of the horror they had just escaped. But where was Sarah?

Chapter 35

In the laboratory, the faint hum of machinery blended with the rhythmic ticking of a wall-mounted clock. The air carried the sharp tang of chemicals and a trace of dust. Secured firmly in a vice at the center of the workbench was the amber stone, roughly the size of an ostrich egg. Its golden hues shimmered under the bright overhead light, almost mesmerizing in their intensity.

Grumby, an older technician with a head of thick, silver-streaked hair, had been found by Captain Linton to assess the stone's properties. His expertise in geology and mineralogy had proven valuable in other wartime investigations, and he now leaned over the workbench with practiced precision. His civilian clothes—a practical shirt and trousers—were hidden beneath a well-worn lab coat, its pockets stuffed with pens and small tools. His weathered hands, steady from years of precise work, carefully held a piece of calcite from his hardness testing kit. Pressing it gently against the stone's surface, he drew it along the surface, his brow furrowing as he inspected the result. Nothing—not even a faint scratch. Setting the calcite aside, he selected the next mineral in the scale, a sample of quartz.

"Amber's typically much softer than this," he muttered,

positioning the quartz and repeating the test. Still, the stone remained unmarked, its surface as smooth and unmarred as before.

Orville stood a few paces away. His arms were crossed as he watched intently, his sharp gaze flicking between Grumby and the stone. Though he was there to interpret the strange runes etched into it, Orville couldn't help feeling drawn to the stone itself.

"What's that you're doing?" Orville asked, breaking the silence.

"Testing the hardness," Grumby replied, his tone calm but focused. "Amber falls around 2.5 on the Mohs scale. This..." He trailed off, pressing the quartz firmly against the stone's surface. Nothing. Not a scratch. "...this is harder."

He frowned, leaning closer as he selected a piece of feldspar from the kit, its hardness rated at 6. Carefully, he repeated the test, drawing the mineral along the stone's surface. Still, the amber-like material remained unmarred, its smooth surface defying expectations.

"This doesn't make sense," Grumby muttered, his voice tinged with intrigue and frustration. He reached for a steel file—rated even higher on the scale—and scraped it lightly across the stone. Again, nothing. "Not a mark,"

Orville frowned, leaning slightly closer. "So it's not amber?"

Grumby straightened slightly, setting the file down and rubbing the back of his neck. "No." he said slowly, his voice carrying a hint of disbelief, "this stone isn't just harder than amber—it's harder than most minerals."

He leaned closer again, angling the light over the stone, as if hoping to glimpse some explanation in its glowing depths. "I've never seen anything like it." The faint golden sheen seemed to mock him, offering no answers.

Next, Grumby brought a small ultraviolet lamp to the stone. As he switched it on, the amber glowed faintly, a soft bluish hue shimmering on its surface. "That's something," he murmured. "Amber fluoresces under UV, but this is... brighter. Purer."

Orville shifted his stance, watching intently. "What does that mean?"

"It means that it's unusual," the technician replied, reaching for a pipette filled with diluted hydrochloric acid. Carefully, he applied a single drop to the stone. Both men waited, watching for a reaction.

"Nothing," the technician said, tilting his head. "No fizz. Not a carbonate."

Grumby adjusted the vice, ensuring the ostrich-egg-sized stone was securely clamped. He then reached for a Bunsen burner, striking a match to light it. The soft hiss of the flame filled the room as he carefully positioned it beneath the stone.

Orville flinched as the flame licked against the stone's surface, but instead of the expected reaction—discoloration, melting, or even a faint scorch—the flame itself seemed to falter. The technician's brow furrowed as he leaned closer. The fire dimmed slightly, the heat seemingly drawn into the stone, which began to glow faintly at its core, a pulsating golden light.

"What on earth...?" the technician muttered, pulling the flame away and watching as the glow within the stone slowly faded. He waved his hand near the surface then touched it, eyes widening. "The stone was warm before, now it's cold."

Orville stepped closer, his arms still crossed, "That's not normal," he said, his voice low.

The technician didn't respond immediately. Instead, he adjusted the burner and tried again, angling the flame toward a different part of the stone. Once more, the heat seemed to vanish, absorbed by the strange artifact. The glow returned, more pronounced this time, flickering faintly like a heartbeat.

"It's doing something," the technician said at last, his voice barely above a whisper. "It's not... natural"

Straightening, he stared at the stone, the faint glow within its core seeming to mock his inability to categorize it. He turned toward a cupboard, retrieving a refractometer. "If heat won't tell us what it is, maybe light can."

He carefully positioned the refractometer on the workbench. "This will measure how light bends when it passes through the material. Should give us a clue about its composition—assuming it behaves like anything on Earth."

Orville frowned. "And if it doesn't?"

Grumby chuckled softly. "Then we're in for an even bigger mystery."

He squinted at the stone through his magnifying glass, tilting it this way and that under the lamp's glow. He leaned in, inspecting it closely, his breath fogging the cool, amber-like surface for a moment "See how it catches the light? This isn't just a pretty bauble—it's a treasure trove of information, if you know what to look for."

"Subtle variations in the refractive index might give us clues about where this little beauty came from. Different regions, different resins, different conditions of formation—they all leave their mark, like fingerprints. Imagine being able to tell whether this stone formed in the Baltic, the Caribbean, or somewhere else entirely. It's like tracing the history of an ancient world trapped inside this golden droplet."

"We know this isn't amber," he said, his voice carrying the weight of certainty. "It looks like Amber, but Amber doesn't behave like this. It's too hard—harder than quartz. You'd never see that in natural resin. And the way it reacted to the flame earlier…" He shook his head, a mix of fascination and wariness in his expression. "Amber would burn sweetly, like a forest after a rain. This thing practically recoiled, as if it knew it was under attack. That's not normal."

Grumby stood back, gesturing to the vice. "Still, whatever it is, it plays with light in an interesting way. That tells me it has a refractive index—a measurable way of bending light. If we take a small sample, we might learn something about its structure, its origins. Maybe even why it's so peculiar."

Grumby stepped back from the workbench, rubbing his chin thoughtfully as his eyes scanned through his tool chest. After a moment's consideration, he reached for a small, precision chisel and a lightweight hammer. His movements were deliberate, the faint clinking of metal filling the room as he tested the heft of each tool in his hands.

"Right, then" he muttered, turning back to the stone secured in the vice. He positioned the chisel carefully against the surface, just above a faint, tree-like rune etched into its side. The runes seemed to catch the light differently than the rest of the stone, as if they were carved with a purpose yet unknown.

"I'll try here," Grumby murmured, almost to himself. "The runes seem to radiate outward from this spot. Could be coincidence, but… let's find out."

He raised the hammer, pausing for a moment to glance at Orville. "Stand back, just in case it fractures."

Orville's eyes narrowed as he stepped back cautiously, his posture tense. "You're sure about this?"

Grumby's faint grin didn't reach his eyes. "No. But we're not getting any answers just staring at it." He adjusted his grip, positioned the chisel carefully and gave a cautious tap.

A soft tink echoed in the quiet room, sharp yet inconsequential. Nothing happened. He frowned, repositioning the chisel and striking again with increased force. The tool produced a crisp ping against the stone, the sound resonating briefly before fading into silence. Still, the stone remained stubbornly intact, its surface unmarred.

Determined, Grumby adjusted his stance, gripping the hammer tightly. With a deep breath, he delivered another, much more forceful blow. The chisel struck true, biting into the stone's surface with a sharp crack that echoed through the room. Tiny fragments skittered across the lab bench as long, jagged cracks branched outward like the veins of a leaf.

For a brief moment, everything seemed still, the air thick with anticipation. Grumby froze, his hand hovering over the chisel as both men regarded the fractured surface of the stone.

Then, from the point of impact, a burst of rainbow-colored energy erupted, spreading like liquid light across the fracture. The vibrant hues danced and shimmered, casting fragmented reflections onto the walls and ceiling. A faint hum accompanied the display, low and resonant, growing louder as the energy unfurled, enveloping the stone in a shimmering, translucent bubble.

Grumby staggered back, his eyes wide as the bubble pulsed outward, its edges shimmering with an otherworldly glow. "What—?" he muttered, the words barely audible over the rising hum.

Orville's face was pale. "Grumby, what in the blazes have we done?"

237

Both men watched, their eyes widening in astonishment as the shimmering bubble expanded, revealing an outdoor scene as vivid and tangible as reality itself. The air that wafted through the bubble was crisp and invigorating, carrying the scent of damp earth, fresh grass, and the faint sweetness of wildflowers. The faint hum of laboratory equipment and the ever-present tang of chemicals were replaced by the rustling of plants in a gentle breeze. It was as if the bubble had opened a window to a pristine, untouched world—starkly contrasting with the industrial hum and faint coal smoke that defined the London streets outside.

The bubble continued to swell, its swirling colors coalescing into an almost hypnotic kaleidoscope. Orville and Grumby instinctively stepped back, the glow reflecting off their stunned faces. The boundary stretched outward with relentless momentum, revealing more of the otherworldly landscape. A wide plain unfolded before them, stretching endlessly under a vast sky painted in hues of blue and silver. The expanse of grassland was dotted with scattered forests, clusters of greenery that added texture to the rolling fields. In the distance, towering mountains rose against the horizon, their jagged peaks partially obscured by wisps of mist. It was breathtaking. Beautiful.

A loud thump echoed above them, rattling the ceiling. Both men flinched, their eyes darting upward. But as the bubble expanded further, the sounds of London abruptly vanished, replaced by the soft, natural symphony of an outdoor world— birds calling faintly in the distance, the whisper of the breeze through the grass, and the rustle of unseen creatures moving through the forests. The shift was so sudden and complete that it felt disorienting, as though the fabric of reality itself had been rewritten.

Suddenly, the door burst open with a loud bang, and Captain Linton stormed in, flanked by three soldiers. All were breathless, their expressions a mix of alarm and urgency. "We need to get to the roof, now! Where's the stone? " Linton barked, his voice sharp and commanding.

The soldiers hovered near the doorway, their wide eyes fixed on the expanding bubble.

Linton's steps faltered as his eyes caught sight of the glowing, expanding bubble. His expression shifted from urgency to sheer bewilderment. The prismatic light reflected in his wide eyes, and he stumbled to a halt, transfixed by the spectacle before him. "What... what in God's name is this?" he asked, his voice trembling.

Before Orville could answer, the bubble surged forward, enveloping Linton and the others in its shimmering glow. They stiffened, momentarily frozen, as the strange light played across their features. When it passed, Linton turned to Orville, his voice tight with confusion. "What just happened?"

"That..." Orville began, swallowing hard as he struggled to put his thoughts into words.

He trailed off, his gaze fixed on the shimmering light that pulsed and expanded, casting the room in its surreal glow. For a moment, he seemed lost, grappling with the enormity of what had just occurred. Then, like a spark igniting a long-forgotten memory, his eyes widened with sudden clarity.

"The doorway..." he whispered, his voice trembling with a mix of wonder and dread. He looked to Linton and Grumby, his expression shifting as the pieces began to fall into place. "The little people's doorways," he said, his words quickening, his tone urgent. "The old stories—myths about the fair folk, about how they'd slip between our world and theirs. They spoke of gates, thresholds hidden in the woods or among the stones."

"We opened a gateway to another world." He gestured to the bubble, his voice steadier now as understanding overtook his initial shock.

Linton's face darkened, his skepticism battling with the undeniable evidence before him. "So you're saying we've been pulled into... what? Some other world?"

Grumby, still standing near the vice, peered out the window, his voice a mix of wonder and disbelief. "Good heavens... How do we stop it?"

Orville's heart sank. The boundary of the bubble was still expanding, a living force with no regard for the destruction it might cause. His mind raced, calculating the implications. If the portal was uncontrollable, the damage could be catastrophic—not just to London, but perhaps to their entire world.

"I don't know if we can," Orville admitted, his voice steadier now as duty overtook his initial shock. He glanced at Captain Linton, his expression grim. "We've already passed from our world."

The world outside the windows continued to shift. The urban sprawl of London, with its familiar rooftops and smoky haze, had melted away like watercolors running under rain. In its place, a vivid outdoor scene emerged, impossibly clear and startlingly real. The light filtering through the windows now carried the golden warmth of an untouched sun, casting shadows of leaves that hadn't been there moments ago.

The laboratory now stood in the midst of a vast plain. Rolling grasslands stretched endlessly in every direction, broken only by scattered clusters of trees. Beyond, a range of towering mountains loomed, their peaks softened by distant mist. A gentle breeze rippled the grass outside, its motion reflected in the golden light dancing on the walls of the lab.

The hum in the air faded into the rustling of leaves and the faint, melodic call of unseen birds. The tiled floor beneath their feet remained solid, but the sense of being indoors now felt absurd against the backdrop of this alien wilderness.

Chapter 36

Anselm and Peter had seen the bright flare shoot into the sky, followed not soon after by the terrifying sight of three red dragons diving toward its source. One of the massive beasts landed heavily on the roof, shaking the building under its tremendous weight, while the other two descended to the ground—one smashing through the front door, the other scaling the building floor by floor with methodical precision, its sinister eyes scanning each window.

Anselm's heart pounded with dread when his sharp eyes spotted Sarah emerging onto the roof, panic etched across her face. She was seeking refuge from the dragon invading the building from below. Her presence on the roof put her in immediate, lethal danger.

For an instant, his wings faltered, the air bucking beneath him. Instinct screamed to dive—to save Sarah before the other dragon saw her—but the boy on his back was fragile. His talons flexed, the sinews of his chest quivering as he hung suspended between mercy and fear. For that heartbeat, he hovered, torn between the two lives depending on him.

Peter saw Sarah as well and noticed Anselms hesitation. "No time to let me off! I'll hang on tight — I promise!" he shouted over the wind, his knuckles white as he held tight to

Anselm.

Anselm dipped his left wing to keep Peter from being whipped free, then struck.

Sarah, unaware of the dragon already stalking the rooftop, looked up. Her breath caught in her throat as she saw Anselm cutting through the sky toward her. For a fleeting moment, relief softened her fear. Then she saw the small figure clinging to his neck. Peter. The sight froze her where she stood, confusion flooding in as her mind struggled to grasp how they were there, together, in this impossible moment.

But her relief was short-lived. A deafening roar erupted behind her, loud enough to rattle the rooftop tiles. She spun around, her eyes widening in horror. The dragon on the roof had noticed her. Its massive wings unfurled, casting a shadow over her as it let out a low, menacing growl. Its golden eyes locked onto her, gleaming with predatory intent.

Above, Anselm surged forward, his instincts driving him to act. With the element of surprise on his side, he hurtled through the air like a living missile, his focus locked on the dragon threatening Sarah. The red beast barely had time to turn its head, its eyes widening in shock as Anselm's claws slashed deep into its wing.

Blood sprayed into the air as he tore through flesh and sinew, the force of his attack driving him past the dragon in a blur of speed. As he soared past, he manage to rake claws across the dragon's neck, leaving a jagged, bleeding gash that sent the beast reeling.

The dragon's agonized screech tore through the air, a harrowing sound that echoed across the rooftops. Its massive, thrashing body sent tremors through the building, the roof beneath it shuddering under the immense force.

One of its wings, now partially shredded, whipped across the rooftop with terrifying speed. The sheer force of the movement nearly caught Sarah as the wing whipped toward her. She barely managed to dive out of the way, her hands scraping against the rough surface as she hit the ground.

Adrenaline surged through Sarah as she scrambled to her feet and bolted for the doorway, throwing herself through the rooftop door and down into the stairwell just as another deafening crash sounded behind her. The force of the impact shook the building, and she slammed the door shut with shaking hands, muffling the chaos outside.

Sarah froze, gripping the rail tightly as her chest heaved and heart pounded. The overwhelming events of the day pressed down on her, the sheer impossibility of it all nearly suffocating. Her legs felt weak beneath her, and her mind raced. She wanted to help—to do something, anything—but the fear and uncertainty held her back.

Her thoughts were a jumble of panic and worry. Anselm, Peter... The image of Anselm battling the enemy dragon flashed in her mind, followed by Peter's terrified face as he clung to Anselm.

Her mind raced. *What can I do? What if they don't make it?* She couldn't bear the thoughts as they curled around her like a vice.

She looked to the door she had just slammed shut, muffling the chaos outside. She edged closer, her small hands trembling as she pressed herself against the wall beside it. Peering through a crack in the frame, her heart wrenched at the sight of Anselm locked in a deadly struggle with the enemy dragon. Peter clung to Anselm's back, a tiny figure amidst the chaos, his face strained and pale.

Sarah's hands balled into fists as frustration and helplessness welled up inside her. She wanted to scream, to burst out onto the rooftop and fight alongside them, but what could she do? No answers came. Her reason and instincts urged her to stay hidden, but every fiber of her being rebelled against doing nothing.

She sank to her knees behind the door, pressing her forehead against the wood. Her small shoulders shook as she tried to suppress the frustration that threatened to escape. "Please, please be okay," she whispered, the words a desperate prayer. As the sounds of the battle raged on, each roar and crash making her flinch. Still, she remained frozen, torn between her helplessness and the burning desire to do something.

Outside, Anselm pressed his advantage. As a man he had never faced a situation that demanded violence. He had always avoided conflict. But now, after seeing Sarah in mortal danger, something deep within him shifted. His gentle nature had no place here.

The sight of the massive dragon looming over her awakened something primal inside him. It surged to the surface, unrelenting and instinctive. Without hesitation, he acted with a ferocity he never knew he possessed.

With a guttural roar, he lunged at the enemy dragon once more. This time, his powerful jaws clamped down on the exposed wound along its neck. The sickening crunch of scales giving way beneath his teeth reverberated through the air, followed by a wet, choking sound. Blood sprayed staining the rooftop as the dragon flailed in desperation. Its cries were desperate and ragged as it struggled to draw breath.

The enemy dragon, though weakened, was not yet defeated. It lashed out in a last, frenzied bid for survival, its claws slicing through the air with deadly force. But Anselm, now fully committed to the fight, was relentless. Anticipating the counterattack, he released his grip and twisted his body, narrowly avoiding the snapping jaws and swiping claws of his opponent.

With a swift, calculated movement, Anselm launched himself onto the dragon's back, his claws sinking deep into the thick, armored scales. The beast bucked violently, its body twisting and jerking as it tried to shake him off. Each thrash threatened to dislodge him, but Anselm clung on with unyielding determination. His muscles strained, every sinew taut as he held firm, his mind singularly focused on ending the threat.

For a brief moment, the chaos of the rooftop faded. Anselm's mind was clear, his purpose undeniable. This wasn't about survival or instinct—it was about protecting Sarah and Peter, and all the ones he loved.

He thought of his family in Germany—faces now only flickers of memory through the haze of war. He had left them behind to stop Krammer's madness. The memory of them steadied him, sharpened his will. In his mind he could still see Sarah's terrified face, the way she had stood frozen in fear as the dragon loomed over her. That image joined the others, fueling his resolve as he tightened his grip on the thrashing beast beneath him.

Meanwhile, Peter, clinging to Anselm's scales, felt the world spin around him in a dizzying blur. Each powerful jerk and whip of the dragon's body threatened to hurl him into the void below. His fingers dug into the rough texture of Anselm's scales, his knuckles white with the effort of holding on. The roar of blood in his ears drowned out the sounds of the battle, adrenaline surging through him as he fought to stay anchored.

Across the street, a French 75mm field gun had been stationed on the roof of a building, repurposed as an anti-aircraft weapon. It was a relic of the Great War, brought out of storage and adapted for the defense of London during the Blitz. The gun crew of six men, a mix of Home Guard volunteers and members of the Anti-Aircraft Brigade, had taken their post when the air raid sirens first sounded, expecting the roar of Luftwaffe bombers overhead.

They hadn't expected dragons.

The red beasts had descended from the sky with terrifying speed, their massive wings slicing through the air like scythes. The gun crew froze at the sight of mythical creatures.

Unbeknownst to the crew, the dragons had proven impervious to smaller arms—machine gun rounds ricocheted off their thick scales, and even the heavier .50-caliber bullets that found their mark failed to penetrate deeply enough to cause meaningful harm.

But the French 75 was no machine gun.

Designed before the First World War, it had been built as a rapid-fire field artillery piece, intended to break infantry formations and smash unfortified positions. Its revolutionary hydro-pneumatic recoil system allowed for quick, accurate successive shots, keeping the gun steady even under sustained fire.

Though never intended as an anti-armor weapon, its high-velocity shells carried far more energy than anything a machine gun could deliver. The rounds were nearly ten times the mass of a .50-caliber bullet, combining raw kinetic power with explosive force enough to tear through fortifications—and in the right conditions, even pierce armor.

The dragons had proven impervious to small arms. Rifle fire sparked uselessly off their scales. Machine-gun rounds ricocheted or embedded too shallowly to matter. But this was something else entirely.

When they spied the dragon attempting to force its way through the front entrance of the nearby building, the gun crew shook off their shock and acted swiftly. The beast's agility and speed in the air had made it nearly untouchable, but now, grounded and focused away from the gun, it had exposed its flank—a perfect target.

The loader hefted a high-explosive shell and slid it into the breech with practiced efficiency, the breech operator snapping it shut with a metallic clack. The Gun Layer, trying to remain calm, reached for the firing cord, attaching it to the trigger mechanism.

The gun commander scanned the target and shouted, "Hold steady—wait for the shot!"

The gunner exhaled slowly, checking that the sights were aligned with the beast's broad, scaled torso. The commander barked, "Fire!"

The gun let out a sharp crack as the shell shot toward its target, the hydro-pneumatic system ensuring the weapon stayed rock steady. The explosive round struck the dragon with a deafening impact, punching through the scales and into softer flesh with devastating force. The creature let out a bellowing roar as it struggled to pull itself free from the building, its massive form still shaking from the impact.

The crew wasted no time. The breech operator yanked open

the breech, the spent casing ejecting with a sharp metallic clang before clattering to the ground. The ammunition handler was already there, passing the next shell with practiced efficiency. The loader hefted the round and slid it smoothly into the breech. "Ready!" he called, stepping back to clear the way for the Gun Layer.

The dragon let out a guttural roar as it tore itself free from the shattered building, debris cascading from its bloodied hide. Its wings snapped wide, beating the air as it wheeled, eyes blazing in search of the source of the strike. It spotted the rooftop gun and prepared to attack, but before it could, the crew fired a second round.

The shell hurtled through the air with a deafening crack. This time striking below the creature's shoulder, driving into its scales. The dragon's massive form shuddered violently under the impact, its wings faltering as it let out another anguished cry and staggered backward.

Rumbling with pain, the dragon began to crawl, dragging his wounded form toward the side of the building. He moved with deliberate effort, his claws gouging into the ground as he sought cover around the corner. Reaching the relative safety of the building's shadow, the dragon groaned with pain and frustration, his once formidable presence now a desperate figure. His lips curled back, revealing jagged fangs, and he let out a guttural snarl, his mind racing with options.

Instinct urged him to unleash his flames, to scorch the gun crew and force them into retreat. He knew the heat might not reach them from his current position, but it would be enough to make them scatter, buying him the chance to charge and attack. He inhaled sharply, his chest expanding in preparation—but the effort sent a searing pain ripping through his chest. His breath faltered, caught in his throat. The wounds he had sustained had weakened him far more than he wanted to admit. Even drawing breath was a struggle; summoning the fire within was impossible.

With labored movements, the dragon tucked himself deeper into the building's shadow, his glowing eyes flickering with pain. He could only hope that his companions would succeed in finding the stone.

Above him the second dragon was scaling the building, moving with relentless purpose, his razor-sharp claws gouging deep to hold onto the stone facade as he peered into windows. His glowing eyes scanned each room with unsettling focus, hunting for the stone. Herr Krammer and Field Marshal Guilder had given explicit orders: recover the stone at all costs. Ignore all else until the objective was achieved.

He crawled steadily upward, his massive frame an unsettling sight against the crumbling stone and mortar of the building. Behind his glowing eyes burned an intelligence sharpened by single-minded determination. The stone was the objective. Failure was not an option.

The British had offered no resistance thus far. On the battlefield, their mere presence had been enough to scatter soldiers, their thunderous roars shattering enemy ranks long before claws or fire were needed. Their impervious scales rendered gunfire useless, reinforcing their dominance. There was no reason to believe London would be any different.

But the sharp cracks of the 75mm gun shattered that assumption. The creature froze, his massive head turning toward the sound. From below came the whimper of his wounded compatriot, and from above, he could hear a fight on the roof. For the first time, he hesitated, his spiked tail lashing against the side of the building, dislodging chunks of masonry that crashed to the streets below.

He let out a low growl, battling against a growing awareness that these enemies might pose a threat. With a determined grunt, he dug its claws deeper into the stone. Dust and debris cascaded in its wake as it surged upward, muscles rippling beneath its shimmering scales. He would assess the threat, and eliminate it.

He slowly tilted its long neck and head, peering cautiously around the side of the building,

His golden eyes scanned the rooftop across the street, where the artillery crew scrambled to reload the 75mm gun. His slit pupils narrowing as it studied the gun position.

Confident in his size, strength, and unmatched speed, he surged toward the top of the building. His impervious scales and raw power had made him unstoppable in every battle so far, and he saw no reason why this encounter would be any different.

He readied himself, and crouched back, his muscles coiling in preparation for flight. His wings unfurled, their immense span casting deep shadows over the facade. He leapt. For a breathless instant he hung exposed, wings still finding purchase, leaving him exposed for a critical moment.

The gun crew seized the opportunity. A thunderous crack split the sky as the 75mm cannon fired, its shell streaking through the air with devastating precision. A lucky shot. The impact was immediate and catastrophic. The explosion ripped into his abdomen. Shards of scale and flesh scattered like shrapnel, and he roared in pain—a deafening, guttural cry of fury and disbelief.

The force of the blast knocked him sideways, his body twisting violently. His claws scraped desperately against the building, leaving gouges as he struggled to gain a hold on the building.

Wings reflexively flapping in a desperate attempt to stabilize. Blood poured from the wound in his abdomen, staining the building.

For the first time since his transformation, he felt something unfamiliar: fear. His assumption of dominance was shattered, and the realization was as sharp as the pain searing through his side. Vulnerability crept into his thoughts, a foreign and unwelcome feeling. Die Engländer, whom he had regarded as insignificant pests, had somehow struck him down.

Realizing the danger too late, his confidence gave way. They had been caught unaware, their arrogance shattered by the unexpected success of the resistance. The sharp, searing pain from his wounds reminded him of his own mortality, and survival now took precedence over their mission.

Anger and frustration churned within him, but he was no reckless beast. He was a soldier, trained to adapt. They needed to regroup, reassess, and plan before they could achieve their objective. With a labored but determined effort, the dragon let out a resonant, guttural call. It was not a cry of defeat but a command, urging its companions to abandon the fight and fall back.

His powerful wings unfurled, trembling under the strain of his injuries as he prepared to take flight. Each beat sent a fresh surge of pain through his body, but he ignored it, his focus locked on survival. Before he released his hold on the building, he cast a final, glance at his wounded comrade sprawled on the ground below. His movements were sluggish, blood pooling beneath its battered frame.

His eyes narrowed, willing his comrade below to rise. He had made the call, and time was running out. With a guttural snarl, he pushed himself into the air.

Below, the second dragon hesitated as he watched the other take wing, his fury warring with his instinct to survive. The burning pain from his wounds was undeniable, but retreat? That was unthinkable. He was an elite soldier, trained to press forward no matter the cost. Failure wasn't just unacceptable— it was inconceivable.

Hubris clawed at him while the bitter realization of their foolish mistakes creeping in. They had overestimated themselves, assuming enemy weapons would be insignificant. If they had been human themselves, they would have cleared the area of resistance before assaulting the building. But as dragons they had believed themselves invincible.

For a moment, he snarled, half-ready to charge at the artillery piece despite his wounds. But even his fanatical resolve could not ignore the stinging truth: the enemy had the upper hand. Survival wasn't cowardice; it was necessity. With a guttural roar, he managed to launched himself into the air, his wings straining against the weight of his injuries, vowing this defeat would not go unanswered.

Another shell from the 75 flew past him.

The two roared in unison as they climbed past the third dragon on the roof, urging him to join them. Anselm rolled off his opponent, his limbs braced for the others to attack. While the dragon he had been fighting, struggled to rise. Its movements sluggish, every motion labored and pained. Blood oozed from deep wounds along its side and neck, pooling on the rooftop beneath it. Clawing to upright himself, he fought for the strength to take flight. With a final, desperate surge of effort, he pulled himself upright, and unfurled his wings unsteadily. He staggered for a moment, then leapt into the air, wings flapping unevenly as he pushed through the pain to join his companions.

Meanwhile, the shimmering bubble that had erupted from the stone in the lab had continued its relentless expansion. It had now engulfed the entire building, its edges radiating an otherworldly light. The once-solid structure dissolved into the swirling colors of the portal, its walls and roof melting away like sand swept by the tide. The shimmering barrier pulsed and shifted, its outline refracting like light through a prism. Above the building, the sky itself seemed to dissolve, London's smoky haze giving way to the swirling, kaleidoscopic glow of the portal, then clear blue sky.

Unbeknownst to Peter, Anselm, and the red dragons, the portal passed over them in its inexorable expansion. The strange energy pulsed beyond the rooftop, brushing unnoticed over scales, skin, and stone alike. In the intensity of the fight none of them noticed the transformation happening around them.

The world around them had faded seamlessly into a new reality. The jagged cityscape blurred and melted into rolling hills and endless plains. The gritty smoke of the city vanished, replaced by fresh, crisp air carrying the scent of wildflowers and damp earth.

The dragons, now in full retreat, climbed into the new sky, their roars tinged with frustration. As they gained altitude, the strange world below them revealed itself—not the streets of London, but another landscape that stretched endlessly in every direction. The dense urban sprawl and expected skyline were gone, replaced by rolling hills blanketed in lush greenery, winding rivers that glittered in the golden light, and dense forests that formed dark patches across the vast expanse. The twilight sky painted the world in hues of purple and gold, casting long shadows across this strange and unsettling terrain.

Whatever this place was, it was not London.

The dragons faltered, confusion rippling through their ranks as they realized something was terribly wrong. Below them, the lab building stood alone in tall grass. Then, as the bubble's edge rolled onward, the neighboring flats and shopfronts *appeared into place* beside it, as if the world were being laid down like a map. The dragons circled, their golden eyes narrowing as they observed the strange phenomenon unfolding beneath them.

As the shimmering edge of the bubble expanded further, more of the London neighborhood began to appear. With a faint shimmer, the entirety of neighboring buildings appeared beside the structure they had assaulted. A moment later, the sidewalk emerged, terminating abruptly where it met the boundary of the bubble.

Slowly but relentlessly, the bubble passed over more of the area surrounding the building. The street and the cars along it, materializing in the pristine plain. Anyone unfortunate enough to have been near the bubble's edge was swept into its shimmering embrace and appeared out of nowhere.

The dragons roared, their guttural cries echoing across the shifting landscape as they struggled to comprehend the scene below. The bubble's relentless expansion continued, casting prismatic hues across the twilight sky as it pulled more and more of the London neighborhood leaving it to stand incongruously surrounded by the tall grass. The stark contrast between the remnants of the city and the untouched beauty of the rolling hills painted a jarring picture of two worlds colliding.

The lead dragon's wings trembled as he struggled to stay aloft, each beat a painful reminder of the human artillery that had pierced his side. With a guttural snarl, he turned his head westward, the direction from which they had come. Germany—their point of origin—logic drove him to seek safety in that direction. Yet, confusion gnawed at him; the world below was no longer familiar. *Was it still there?*

The other two dragons followed, their flight uneven and labored. Blood dripped from the third dragon's flank as it limped through the air, its wings faltering with every beat. The second dragon roared in short bursts, the sound raw and strained, as if willing himself onward despite the growing uncertainty. Each struggled against their injuries, their shared desperation propelling them away.

As they climbed higher into the twilight sky, their eyes continued to scan the horizon, searching for landmarks or signs of their home. But the unknown landscape stretched endlessly below them—rolling hills, dense forests, and shimmering rivers unfamiliar and unsettling. There were no familiar landmarks, no signs of human habitation, nothing to anchor them.

Gradually, their massive forms disappeared into the western horizon.

As the three dragons disappeared into the distance, Anselm, with Peter, still clinging to his back, realized the change as well. The familiar sights of London were gone, replaced by a vast expanse of rolling hills. Moments later, nearby buildings began appearing from nowhere.

"Oi! Anselm, what's happening?" Peter called out, his voice unsteady, still trembling from the violent ride.

Anselm's eyes narrowed as he surveyed the alien terrain. The realization struck them both at once—they were no longer in London.

Chapter 37

In the sky, three Hawker Hurricanes scrambled to intercept what was reported as dragons by the Observer Corps, approached the expanding anomaly, its shimmering surface rising high into the sky. The pilots, trained for combat but unprepared for the supernatural, communicated their astonishment over their radios.

"Charlie Flight, do you see that?" the lead pilot broadcast. Ahead of them, a massive, translucent bubble stretched skyward, its shimmering surface resembling a window suspended in the sky.

Driven by curiosity, they aligned their aircraft with the sky showing within the growing portal. As they flew closer, the view through the window sharpened—vast grasslands, sprawling forests, and towering mountains unlike any terrain they had ever flown over.

The pilots steered their fighters directly through. As they emerged on the other side, the landscape below stretched endlessly, vibrant and untouched. Looking back, the portal from which they had come had vanished; there was no sign of London except for a small section sitting on the grassy plain, which seemed to be growing. There was no trace of their entry point. They were not just observers now; they were part of this new and uncharted world.

"Flight, report," crackled the radio, the connection fuzzy and distant.

"Where are we?" Asked the lead pilot, his voice a mix of awe and apprehension.

In London, the sphere slowed, its relentless expansion halting as if it had reached its limit. For a moment, it hung suspended, shimmering with an otherworldly light. Its translucent surface rippled like water, those watching saw the world within. Rolling hills stretched into a horizon painted with unfamiliar colors, their vibrant hues unlike anything on Earth. Towering, jagged mountains loomed in the distance behind a broad grassy plain.

The sphere held the image for a heartbeat longer, enough for awe to mingle with dread. Then, without warning, it pulsed one final time before vanishing with an ear-splitting snap. A sudden, violent vacuum followed, the air rushing in to fill the void left behind. The force of its closure sent a shock wave rippling through the air, scattering debris and knocking people off their feet.

As the dust began to settle, the enormity of what had happened became clear. The vast area once encompassed by the sphere was gone—erased as if it had never existed. In its place lay a crater, carved with surgical precision into the earth. The edges of the chasm were jagged and unstable. Buildings that had been on the bubble's perimeter now teetered dangerously close to the brink, their foundations weakened by the sudden displacement.

The collapse began slowly. A few bricks tumbled into the abyss, their descent eerily silent until they struck the debris below. Then, whole walls and facades gave way, collapsing with a deafening roar. Severed water mains and sewage lines added to the destruction, spewing torrents of water into the void, where it churned with rubble and debris.

The ground trembled as the remaining structures succumbed, tilting precariously before plunging into the crater. Each collapse sent up a plume of dust and smoke, shrouding the scene in a choking haze. The air was thick with the acrid metallic stench of destruction. Inside, desperate screams of those who had fallen in pierced the air, only to be drowned out by the cacophony of buildings and cars sliding into the crater.

Panic spread through the crowds as those near the edge scrambled to safety. Emergency services, already stretched thin by the war, rushed to the scene. Sirens blared in the distance, their wails rising in urgency as fire engines, ambulances, and military vehicles tried to navigate their way to the chasm. Authorities shouted orders to evacuate the area, their voices barely audible .

Observers at a safe distance stood rooted in place, their faces pale and slack with disbelief. They could only stare at the abyss in mute horror, their minds grappling with the impossibility of what had just occurred.

Thomas, Sarah's mother, and Olivia stood just blocks away from where the city had been abruptly severed. They had fled the expanding portal while it devoured the neighborhood, the ground beneath their feet vibrating with the aftershocks of the catastrophe.

The scene before them was surreal, too horrific to comprehend. A jagged, yawning chasm now replaced the streets.

Smoke and dust billowed upward, mingling with the acrid stench of ruptured gas lines and burning debris. Thomas and Mrs. Lynde stared in stunned silence, their faces pale with shock as the magnitude of the devastation sank in.

Olivia clung tightly to Sarah's mother, her small frame trembling. Too young to fully grasp the enormity of what had happened, but still terrified, she buried her face against Mrs. Lynde's side, seeking comfort in her presence. The quiet sobs she tried to suppress only added to the heavy atmosphere.

Thomas scanned the area, his eyes darting between the rising smoke and the panicked movements of emergency services rushing toward the site. Their efforts, though valiant, were minuscule in the face of such overwhelming destruction. For a moment, he was frozen, unable to tear his gaze from the chasm.

"We need to get further away," he said, his voice cutting through the activity. His arm around Mrs. Lynde's shoulder, steadying her as they began to move.

Mrs. Lynde didn't respond at first, her wide eyes fixed on the devastation. Her mind was consumed by a single thought: Sarah. She had fled in the direction of the vanished streets, and now... *Where was her daughter?*

Chapter 38

Upstairs, Sarah pressed her ear to the door, straining to catch any sounds from outside. The deafening roars had stopped, leaving an eerie silence that only deepened her fear. She hesitated, her breath shallow, and then cautiously pushed the door open to peer out onto the roof.

Her heart leaped with relief as her eyes found Anselm and Peter. Fear still clung to her, but they were alive. And that was enough. The weight of her terror eased, replaced by a flood of gratitude and a sense of belonging she craved.

She stepped onto the roof, her knees weak but steady enough to carry her toward them. Anselm and Peter stood motionless, their gazes locked on the horizon. Towering, jagged mountains loomed in the distance, their sharp peaks cutting into a sky painted with unfamiliar hues. Rolling plains stretched endlessly below, the tall grass swaying gently in a breeze that seemed almost too pure to be real.

For a long moment, none of them spoke. The reality of their situation hung heavy in the air, unspoken. Sarah took a tentative step forward, her hands trembling as her eyes tried to take in every detail of the surreal landscape. "Where are we?" she whispered, her voice barely audible.

Peter turned to her, his face a mixture of awe and unease.

"We're not in London anymore," he said softly, his words underscoring the unshakable truth of what they all could see.

Anselm let out a low, rumbling growl, his eyes scanning the horizon with a mixture of wariness.

Sarah glanced up at Anselm, comforted by his presence. He had fought for her, risked everything to save her. Just like Peter had. These two—so different and yet so loyal—were her friends now. Her strange, wonderful, brave friends. The realization was almost too much to process. Not long ago, she had been alone, wishing for connection, someone who cared. Now, she stood with a boy and a dragon who had risked their lives to find her and protect her. The loneliness that had once defined her life was gone, replaced by the unshakable bond they now shared.

But as the moment of relief passed, the weight of their new reality pressed down on her. Sarah's chest tightened. "What do we do now?" she asked, her voice small and uncertain. She looked at Peter, hoping for guidance.

Peter's jaw tightened as he scanned the strange horizon, the colors and shapes unfamiliar and surreal. His hands gripped Anselm's scales for balance, though the massive dragon beneath him remained steady and watchful. The landscape before them was nothing like home, and the weight of that truth pressed down on him, heavier with each passing second.

But it wasn't just the alien terrain that unsettled him. It was Olivia. His little sister, his constant shadow, his best friend. She wasn't here, and he didn't know where she was.

Peter swallowed hard, forcing himself to focus on the moment. She's okay. She has to be. He repeated the thought like a mantra, trying to quell the rising panic in his chest. But the not knowing was unbearable. Had she made it out of the chaos in London? Had she found someone to help her? The questions spiraled in his mind, each one more suffocating than the last.

His thoughts drifted to the adventures they'd shared—the hikes through the countryside, sneaking into old ruins, claiming secret kingdoms. Olivia had always been there, her small hand slipping into his, her bright eyes looking up to him with trust and admiration. He'd promised her, silently and aloud, to always protect her. And now… she was gone.

Peter took a deep breath, steadying himself. He had to focus. For Sarah, for Anselm, for whatever came next. "We'll figure this out," Peter said, his voice soft but resolute. He wasn't sure who he was reassuring more—Sarah, Anselm, or himself. His voice wavered, but his jaw tightened, determination setting in. He couldn't afford to fall apart.

Sarah stepped closer, her small hand reaching out to rest on his leg. "Together," she said, to Peter and Anselm, her voice steady despite the fear glinting in her eyes.

Anselm shifted, his massive head dipping slightly toward them. He let out a low growl, soft and contemplative, as his thoughts turned inward. His life as a man felt like a distant memory now, a past he could never return to. Krammer's machine had turned him into this, a dragon, severing him from his previous life. His goal had been to stop Krammer, to keep the stone out of his hands, to prevent an army of dragons from enslaving the world.

He had run, fleeing across Europe to find safety among Germany's enemies. There were times when the shame of it had overwhelmed him. He wondered if he was a coward.

And yet, what choice had he had? He told himself again and again that his mission was greater, that keeping the stone out of Krammer's hands mattered more than any personal battle. But the doubts lingered, gnawing at him in the quiet moments. Was he truly fighting a greater fight, or was he simply running?

And then, to find himself here, relying on children to tend his wounds, to be his protector—that had been its own agony. The thought had threatened to unravel him. To have lain helpless while two children had nursed him back to strength.

Still, he had succeeded in his goal. The stone was far away, beyond Krammer's reach. Its power was rendered useless, no longer a tool to fulfill the madman's dark ambitions. That thought, at least, brought him solace. The realization sparked a flicker of triumph deep within him. For now, at least, he had won.

But that wasn't all. The three other dragons that Krammer had created were here, too, trapped in this new world alongside him. That meant they couldn't be used as weapons in the war. Krammer's dreams of unleashing his monstrous army to dominate Europe had been thwarted, the creatures he controlled now as far from his grasp as the stone itself. Anselm felt a grim sense of satisfaction at this. Krammer's plans lay in ruins.

Even so, the victory didn't erase the ache in his chest when he thought of his family in Germany. His wife, his children— their faces haunted his dreams. Did they think him dead? Had they mourned him? The longing to see them, to hold them again, was a sharp and unrelenting pain. Yet that pain was tempered now by the bond he had found with Sarah and Peter.

When the moment had come, when Sarah's life had hung in the balance, he had not hesitated. He had fought for her, fought with everything he had, and it was no longer possible to question his courage. He had risked everything to protect her, just as Peter had. And now, these children—so small and yet so brave—had given him something he had thought lost: a purpose, a family.

Anselm glanced at Sarah and Peter, the warmth of their bond settling over him. His eyes softened as he looked at Sarah, who had cared for him with her gentle kindness, and Peter, whose determination and loyalty reminded him of the man he wanted to be. They were his family now. For now, at least, he could rest in the knowledge that the stone was safe, Krammer's plans thwarted, and he had not fled in vain.

Whatever lay ahead, he would face it with them. Together, they would navigate this vast, uncharted world, and in doing so, perhaps they could find a way back.

Chapter 39

In the aftermath, the vanished section of London was officially reported as the result of a German bombing raid—a carefully crafted cover story meant to conceal the inexplicable. The explanation, however, struggled to withstand scrutiny. There was no rubble, no scattered wreckage, and no evidence of enemy aircraft or munitions consistent with a daylight attack.

Those who had stood just outside the affected area were unconvinced. They had seen it happen. One moment, buildings and streets stood firm; the next, they were gone, leaving behind a sharp, unnatural boundary where part of the city had once existed. All told the same story: an expanding bubble of energy, its shimmering surface reflecting the image of another place—a wide field of rolling hills and distant mountains—before everything within it vanished.

And then there were the dragons.

Witnesses, including Civil Defense Volunteers and members of the Royal Observer Corps, claimed they saw winged beasts silhouetted against the sky, their movements unlike any bird, soaring over the city not long before the phenomenon. However, the authorities were quick to dismiss these accounts, attributing them to mistaken identifications. Official statements suggested the sightings were likely misidentified large birds, such as herons or swans.

Newspapers echoed the official narrative, dismissing the sightings as the result of overzealous spotters and the heightened stress of wartime.

But many in London had seen the creatures with their own eyes. Conversations in pubs and bomb shelters throughout London kept the story alive—talk of threats far stranger and more dangerous than Luftwaffe bombers.

British command, privy to the mysterious circumstances, had to acknowledge that the Germans were delving into supernatural forces—a realization that sent waves of panic through the upper echelons of military strategy. They already knew of the creatures attacking and decimating Allied forces in Europe, but now it seemed the Germans had developed even more fearsome weapons.

"If the enemy could summon dragons and make entire sections of cities vanish, what else might they unleash? How could their forces hope to compete against enemies wielding powers that defied comprehension? Captain Linton, the officer leading the investigation into the strange German activities, was lost in the event, along with the building where his team had been operating, creating a critical void in intelligence.

Urgency gripped the decision-makers, spurring covert efforts to investigate and counter these otherworldly threats. Desperate to maintain morale and control, the government doubled down on its cover story while quietly mobilizing covert teams to unravel the event and its implications.

In the village of Wooton, under the somber canopy of a small churchyard, a gentle rain pattered on the array of umbrellas as friends and family gathered to bid farewell to Sarah and Peter. The steady rhythm of the rain, each drop a tactile reminder of the sorrow bringing them all together.

Olivia stood next to her mother, her face pale and drawn with the weight of unimaginable loss. Her mother kept a steady hand on Olivia's shoulder, as much for her own grounding as for her daughter's comfort. Her grief was quiet, restrained, but the tremble in her lips and the glistening tears that clung to her lashes betrayed the depth of her sorrow. Olivia leaned into her, her small hand clutching her mother's for reassurance.

Neither Peter nor Anselm was on the farm when they returned. Anselm's message, scrawled in the drive, suggested that they had taken to the skies in search of Sarah and had made it as far as London. It was assumed they, too, had been caught in the mysterious event that had claimed her.

The thought of Peter venturing into the unknown, riding Anselm to come to her rescue, was a comfort to Olivia. He would never have allowed himself to stay behind—not while she needed him.

As for Anselm, his friendship with Olivia was unwavering. Beyond that, to the few who knew of him, he remained an enigma—a creature whose very existence defied explanation— yet whose actions had undeniably saved the world. He had confronted an unimaginable threat, shouldering the burden of a fight that was not his own. In doing so, he became a hero in their eyes, his story forever etched in their memories.

Next to Olivia, Sarah's mother clutched a bouquet of wildflowers—Sarah's favorites. Tears streamed down her face, but it was the hollowness in her eyes that spoke the loudest, a profound sorrow that seemed to drain the color from her world. She stood stiffly, as though the weight of her grief had turned her to stone, yet her shoulders occasionally shook with quiet sobs that she fought to suppress.

Her daughter—the girl who had filled the cottage with laughter and the barn with mischief—was gone, leaving an emptiness so vast it felt impossible to cross.

She had chosen the wildflowers herself that morning, picking them from the fields Sarah had loved to wander. It was a small act, but one that connected her to the daughter she could no longer hold.

Her free hand rose to clutch the locket at her neck, its tiny photograph of Sarah now a bittersweet treasure. She whispered under her breath, words meant only for her daughter. "I tried to protected you… I should've kept you safe." The words cracked as they left her lips, and her resolve crumbled for a moment, a sob breaking free despite her best efforts to stay composed.

Thomas stood with the others gathered behind them, his expression somber. Though the service was not for Orville, Thomas felt the loss of his closest friend like a fresh wound, layered atop the grief for the children. His hands were clasped tightly before him, the fingers knotted, bracing against the emotional storm within.

The absence of Orville felt like a missing anchor in Thomas's life—his lifelong friend now gone, leaving him adrift amidst the sea of sorrow. His mind wandered back to the last time they had spoken, the day Orville left for London.

He shifted his weight slightly. The grief for Sarah and Peter mingled with his memories of Orville, the losses intertwining in his heart. The children had been so full of promise and bravery, and Orville had admired them deeply. Thomas straightened his back slightly, his jaw tightening. If Orville were here, Thomas thought, he'd crack some wry remark to lighten the mood. Thomas let out a slow breath, his chest heavy. Orville had a way of making the unbearable feel just a little more bearable.

The pastor stepped forward, his presence calm and steady as he prepared to address the mourners. His eyes, filled with a compassionate understanding of the grief that enveloped the group, slowly scanned the faces before him.

"No parent expects to bid a final farewell to their child—to mark the end of a life that had scarcely begun. Yet here we stand, gathered in the shadow of such an untimely loss, saying goodbye to a vibrant and curious young girl and a brave, adventurous young man," the pastor began, his voice soft but steady, carrying across the hushed churchyard.

He paused, glancing at the mourners, their tear-streaked faces etched with grief. "Sarah was a light in the lives of all who knew her. Her inquisitive nature and joyful spirit were a blessing, touching each of us with her laughter and relentless youthful energy. She saw the world not just as it was, but as it could be—filled with wonder, waiting to be discovered."

The pastor's gaze shifted, softening as he continued. "And Peter, bold and daring, with a heart as big as his imagination. He was the kind of boy who couldn't resist an adventure, especially when his sister, Olivia, was at his side. Together, they explored the world with an unquenchable curiosity, finding excitement and magic in places most of us would overlook. Peter, ever a Boy Scout, brought bravery and loyalty to everything he did, always stepping forward when someone needed him."

A gentle rain fell, its patter softening as if to make room for the pastor's words. "Though their lives were far too short, Sarah and Peter shared a bond with each other—and with those around them—that will never fade. They taught us to seek out beauty in the everyday, to embrace the unknown with courage, and to hold onto hope even in the darkest moments."

He gestured toward the small, simple markers that would stand as their memorials. "Today, we remember not only what we've lost but also what they gave us—their laughter, their kindness, and their unwavering spirit. Let us honor their memory by carrying forward the light they brought into the world."

The rain tapered off, leaving the mourners in a poignant stillness. As the pastor's words lingered, the gathered family and friends clung to the stories of Sarah and Peter, finding solace in the bond they shared and the way they had touched so many lives.

Later, as the reception continued in subdued murmurs and clinking cups, Sarah's mother, Thomas, and Olivia found themselves standing together in a quiet corner of the gathering. The others drifted around them, their voices a distant hum, but the three of them shared a silence that felt comforting.

Sarah's mother held her teacup with both hands, her grip tight as if the warmth could steady her. Her eyes, rimmed red from tears, flicked briefly to Olivia. "You're such a brave little girl," she said softly, her voice faltering. "Sarah always said so."

Olivia looked up at her, her small hands clutching the edge of her cardigan. She didn't speak, but she nodded, her lips pressed tightly together. There was a flicker of guilt in her eyes, as if her bravery hadn't been enough.

Thomas shifted uncomfortably beside them, his hands shoved deep into his pockets. "He was proud of you, you know," he said to Olivia, his gravelly voice quiet but firm. "said you could keep up with him better than anyone."

Olivia's chin quivered slightly, but she held back her tears. "I miss him," she whispered.

"I know, lass." Thomas put a gentle arm around her. "Bravery comes in different shapes. Sometimes it's how you carry on afterward."

Sarah's mother looked at him then, her expression one of quiet gratitude and exhaustion. "Thank you, Thomas," she said, her voice barely above a whisper. "For being here."

He gave her a small nod, his jaw tightening. "They were good kids," he said simply, his voice rough with emotion.

For a moment, the three of them stood quietly together.

Thomas broke the heavy silence. "You know. Orville talked about his theory before he left for London. He believed the stone and the runes—they were keys. Keys to doors that opened to other worlds."

Sarah's mother, looked up at him, her tear-streaked face reflecting yearning. "And you think... they might still be alive?"

Thomas nodded, his brow furrowed in thought. "I do. Orville was convinced the runes on those stones signified doorways to places beyond our world. The stone was in London. What we saw in London—the bubble, the landscape we glimpsed inside it—that wasn't an illusion. That was a doorway if I ever saw one.'"

Mrs. Lynde's eyes welled with fresh tears, but they carried

something new: a faint spark. "Can it be possible?"

Olivia, standing silently beside them, her voice small but filled with a desperate hope. "Do you think we can bring Peter back?"

Thomas crouched slightly to meet her eyes, his expression softening. "I don't know, lass," he admitted gently. "I hope so."

The three stood together, their grief tempered by the glimmer of something to hold onto. The thought of Sarah, Peter, Orville, and Anselm alive—even in a world beyond their understanding—became a lifeline.

Olivia's eyes had lit up. Her brother was still alive, and she would find him.

Epilogue

As the auditorium filled with the gentle hum of an anticipating crowd, Olivia stood backstage, her hands trembling slightly as she gripped the edge of her speech notes. Over sixty years had passed since the day her world had changed forever—when she'd lost her brother, Peter. Today, she was being honored for her groundbreaking work in physics, celebrated for her pioneering research into alternate dimensions and the tantalizing possibilities of doorways between them.

Stepping up to the podium with her granddaughter's steadying arm for support, Olivia was met with a wave of applause. The sound swelled, filling the grand hall, a warm embrace that momentarily quieted her anxieties. She took a deep breath, smiling as her gaze swept across the faces before her.

"Thank you," she began, her voice steady and measured, tinged with the polished elegance of age. "This award isn't simply a recognition of my work; it's a testament to the unyielding pursuit of knowledge—to our shared drive to understand what lies beyond." She paused, a faint, wistful smile playing on her lips as her gaze softened. "I'd like to dedicate this to my older brother, Peter. Though he's been gone for many years now, he's never truly left me. Every theory I've dared to explore can be traced back to the adventures we shared as children. We were inseparable—always exploring, imagining, dreaming of what might be possible."

Her voice wavered ever so slightly, but she pressed on, the emotion lending her words an unvarnished sincerity. "Peter taught me that exploration is about stepping boldly into the unknown, however daunting that may be. So, while this award bears my name, it belongs every bit as much to him—my brother, my first partner in adventure."

A hush settled over the room, broken only by the occasional sniffle. Olivia wiped a tear from her cheek with the edge of her finger and gave a small, wry smile. "Thank you, Peter," she said, her voice quiet but resolute. "Wherever you are, this is for you."

The audience rose to their feet, their applause cascading around her—a poignant tribute to a lifetime of dedication, love, and unrelenting curiosity.

Meanwhile, the physics lab at Cambridge was silent, bathed in the soft glow of monitors and the low, steady hum of machinery. Rows of polished equipment stood in precise alignment, their blinking lights casting faint reflections on the tiled floor like scattered constellations.

Above one of the experiments, a faint flicker disturbed the stillness. A delicate spark, barely perceptible, danced briefly in the air. Another followed. The flickers grew closer together, each one brighter than the last, until a soft crackle heralded the formation of a small bubble—a shimmering sphere no larger than a coin.

It hovered there, spinning lazily, its edges glinting with an ethereal light. Within, the air shimmered, bending and warping like the haze over sunbaked asphalt. Slowly, the bubble expanded, stretching outward until it reached the size of a car windscreen. Its surface rippled like liquid glass, revealing a glimpse into another world.

Beyond the bubble lay a sprawling field of vibrant green vines, their tendrils coiling endlessly across the ground. Small orange pumpkins dotted the landscape, their skins gleaming under a sunlight that was warm and alien. The sky above the field was impossibly blue, unmarred by clouds, and carried the serene stillness.

The lab remained frozen, the only sound the gentle hum of the machines. Then, with a sudden, deafening snap the bubble collapsed, vanishing in an instant. The room quaked briefly as a rush of air swept through, filling the void left behind. Loose papers fluttered to the floor, and the equipment rattled softly, as though exhaling after a held breath.

Once more, the room returned to silence, its stillness heavy and charged. A faint, sweet earthy scent hung in the air.

Lost City of Man Preview

T he following chapters are a preview of *The Lost City of Man*, the first novel in the **Dragon World War** series.

What began in the shadow of World War II becomes a struggle to survive, as an entire world is revealed — one shaped by conflicts far more ancient and less forgiving.

Preview Chapter 1

High above the plain, two Hawker Hurricanes circled in wide, steady arcs. Their engines hummed evenly, the sound fragile against the immensity of the wilderness below.

From his cockpit, Squadron Leader Reynolds could see it all: a perfect circle of city pressed into the earth. The air above that section of London hung in a faint, lingering haze, drifting upward in tatters and thinning as it met the clean sky, until the last traces vanished into the blue. Along the city's edge, the grass bent outward, flattened where the strange light had swept over it. Beyond that, there was nothing but the open wild—rolling fields, dark forests, and the faint glimmer of a river far to the north.

He leaned forward in his harness, the control column steady beneath his gloved hand. The cockpit smelled of hot oil and glycol, the sharp tang of aviation fuel still thick in the air. It was the familiar scent of flight. Sweat beaded beneath his helmet despite the altitude.

He flicked his radio switch.

"Jones, are you seeing this?"

A pause. Then Flight Lieutenant Jones's voice crackled through the static, calm but strained.

"Aye, sir. Looks like London's gone and found itself a meadow."

Reynolds's mouth twitched into a thin smile.

They circled lazily, engines a subdued hum against the vastness below. From this height the world appeared impossibly broad, its contours stretching outward in every direction. The circle of London beneath them—sharp-edged, incongruous, and startlingly small—lay like an island set into an endless sea of green.

Even at this distance Reynolds could make out herds of cattle moving through the grass, their slow, deliberate motion almost ceremonial in the open land. And farther off, along the river—half-buried in shadow and overgrown with moss— the ruins rose, enormous and solemn, their colossal outlines suggesting halls and towers untouched by human feet for longer than history cared to remember.

The sight struck Reynolds with a force quieter and deeper than fear—an inward jolt, a realization that the world beneath them was foreign. For a moment he simply watched, the aircraft banking gently beneath him, the wind brushing the canopy, the sun laying long strokes of gold across broken towers and the river's winding course. It all felt too vast, too untouched, too ancient—ancient in a way that made even London's thousand-year streets seem newly built. He felt as though he were staring into something primordial, some forgotten expanse the world had long tucked away at its edges.

A slow breath escaped him. He hadn't realized he'd been holding it.

Jones kept pace beside him, his Hurricane tracing the same slow arc. Neither man felt a need to speak; awe had rendered the radio unnecessary. For all their hours in the air—for all the dogfights, scrambles, and patrols over Europe—neither had ever flown above anything that inspired such still, bewildered wonder.

Then, as they banked gently westward, Reynolds saw how low the sun had dipped, spilling its last golden light across the plain. The spell loosened. Practicality reasserted itself. There were limits to fuel and to daylight, and dusk would overtake them long before their tanks ran dry.

He thumbed the radio switch.

"Jones," he said, his voice steady but not untouched by what they'd just seen, "no airfields—just grass and God knows what else. We'll have to find somewhere to put down before the light goes."

Jones replied after a beat, not startled, but sounding as though he too had been pulled from deep contemplation.

"Aye, sir."

They banked in tandem, engines growling as they followed the city's edge. From above, the details sharpened—rooftops, streets, people gathering in clusters like ants.

"This isn't Blighty, is it?" Reynolds murmured.

"No, sir," Jones answered. "Feels like we've flown off the edge of the map."

Reynolds's breath caught. "You see the ruins by the river?"

Jones frowned. "Yes... big as a city, isn't it?"

Reynolds didn't reply. The thought was impossible—though no more impossible than anything else unfolding beneath them.

They flew lower, skimming the rim of the phenomenon. The sharp border where London ended and wilderness began curved in a perfect circle, its precision almost obscene. Streets met grass with surgical neatness; buildings stood open like dolls' houses, severed walls revealing parlors, stairwells, and half-cut rooms facing the emptiness beyond.

Reynolds's voice dropped. "God help us."

He banked again, scanning the ground. The plain was uneven, rippled with holes and furrows. "Too rough. Put a wheel wrong and we're for it."

"Hang on," Jones said. "East of the city—there. Look. A road. Straight and flat. Looks old, but it might do."

Reynolds squinted through the canopy. A pale scar of stone cut across the green, almost hidden beneath the grass—straight as a die. "I see it. Hard to tell where the grass begins, but it looks solid enough. Follow me in."

They dropped altitude, the hum of their engines deepening. Wind buffeted the wings, rattling the canopy glass. Reynolds adjusted the trim, the familiar weight of the aircraft alive beneath him.

"Undercarriage down," he said quietly, feeling the clunk of the wheels locking into place. "Flaps full."

The Hurricane descended in a controlled glide. The grass rushed upward—green blurring to gold. The first jolt hit hard; the second held. Tyres bounced against uneven stone before gripping. Dust and seeds burst outward, the tail swinging slightly before he steadied her. The Hurricane skidded, slowed, then rolled out along the ancient track. Reynolds let her run until the engine coughed, then throttled back, easing to idle. He turned gently off the road, bumping through tufts of grass to clear the way for Jones's approach.

Prop wash stirred wildflowers into a whirling cloud as the plane came to rest. Reynolds cut the mixture and the engine shuddered to a halt. The propeller slowed, each rotation lazier than the last, until it stopped altogether. The sudden silence pressed in like a physical thing. Only the ticking of the cooling engine and the whisper of wind through the grass remained.

For a moment he sat still, hands on the controls, breathing in the thick air of the cockpit. Through the canopy he watched the second Hurricane line up on approach, wings dipping as it followed his path.

He drew a slow breath, the sharp tang of fuel mixing with clean air beyond it. His heart still hammered from the landing. He unlatched the canopy and slid it back. Cool wind flooded the cockpit.

Jones's landing was smoother. The second machine touched down with a short hop and a squeal of tyres, bounced once, then rolled out cleanly. The two planes came to rest within fifty feet of each other, engines finally silenced.

The pilots climbed down, boots crunching on unfamiliar soil. Grass brushed their knees—soft, dry, and full of life. Jones crossed from his aircraft, tugging off his leather helmet, hair plastered to his forehead with sweat.

"Well," he said, scanning the horizon, "this isn't Kent."

Reynolds followed his gaze. The city lay a hundred yards away, rooftops gleaming in the low sun. Smoke curled lazily from chimneys. Beyond it stretched an endless plain of wild grass and forest, unbroken and silent.

"No," Reynolds said quietly. "It isn't."

He turned slowly, taking in the view—the dark trees, the far-off river, the distant mountains. The world felt impossibly large.

Jones shaded his eyes. "Feels like we've flown right off the edge of the map."

Reynolds nodded toward the city. "Come on. Someone there must know where we bloody well are."

They began walking, tall grass whispering around them. Behind them, the Hurricanes stood cooling in the light, their painted hides glowing faintly where the sun caught the curves of their wings. Ahead, the wind swept across the strange new world, bearing the thin, uncertain voices of London's bewildered souls.

Preview Chapter 2

As dusk settled over the plains, the sky deepened from bruised orange to soft, velvety violet. The last rays of sunlight brushed the rooftops of London, gilding brick and slate in a fleeting band of gold before surrendering to the cool blue of approaching night. Beyond the city's ruptured boundary, the wild stretched endlessly—tall grass swaying in slow, whispering waves, forests crouched dark against the horizon, their ancient silhouettes printed sharp against the dying light.

Along this strange new edge, buildings damaged by the event leaned precariously over the abrupt fall from pavement to open soil. Chimneys had split. Walls sagged. Windows gaped like broken teeth. Here and there, a structure collapsed entirely, its fall echoing like distant thunder across the plain. Bricks tumbled into the tall grass where the building had once continued, each crash often followed by a cry from someone still inside. Dust rose in soft, ghostly clouds, drifting outward into the twilight like the fading smoke of battle.

People moved through the dimming streets like restless spirits—dazed Londoners wandering between the fractured edge and their darkened homes and businesses, faces pale, steps tentative, as though afraid the world had not yet finished settling into its new shape.

The air itself felt wrong in its purity—fresh and sweet, carrying the scent of grass and damp earth from the wild beyond. Gone was the familiar tang of smoke and oil, soot and damp brick that had clung to London's breath for generations. For the first time in living memory, the city smelled of the countryside. The freshness brought no comfort; it only deepened the sense of dislocation.

Again and again, eyes turned toward the horizon—searching for sense, for explanation—and found none. Only the vastness of the plain, the unbroken wild, and the black line of trees beyond. Those whose homes or shops had stood near the edge could only stare at the grass where familiar streets and neighbours had vanished, swallowed whole by a world that had never known them.

The hum of London's life—its trams rattling, its lorries clattering, its Underground pulsing deep below—was gone. In its place lay a stillness so complete it felt unnatural, a silence that made the ears strain for what had been lost. Radios hissed with static. Telephones carried no sound. The taps ran dry. London had been severed.

They were no strangers to darkness; the wartime blackout had shrouded the city in enforced shadow for years. But this darkness felt different. It was not an imposed dimming, but the vast, unbounded gloom of a land untouched by man—deeper, older, and far more absolute.

People lingered in the streets, unwilling to retreat indoors. They spoke in low, uncertain tones, their voices small in the immensity of the silence. Many stood close to the sharp boundary where their world had been sliced away, peering out into the grass as though expecting the darkness to deliver an answer to what had happened. On one point, all agreed: the sky had shimmered before the world beyond vanished.

And so they waited—staring into the emptiness, listening for a sound they would recognise, a sign that the world they knew still existed somewhere beyond the grass—as the last of the light bled from the sky.

From the roof at the center of the phenomenon, Sarah and Peter watched the people gathered in the streets below.

Sarah glanced at him. "Do you think we can get back?"

Peter didn't answer at once. His eyes stayed fixed on the line where London ended and the wild began. "I don't know, Sarah," he said quietly. "I hope so."

For a while neither spoke. The city stretched silent beneath them, its darkened streets silvered by the rising moon. A stray breeze swept across the rooftops, carrying the scent of grass and cool earth — so out of place it made Sarah's chest tighten.

A low rumble sounded behind them, the scrape of stone against tile. They turned. Behind them, Anselm had shifted, lifting his great head just high enough to peer over the roof's edge. His golden eyes caught the faint light as he surveyed the city.

The dragon blinked once, slowly, then lowered his head again and pressed his jaw against the tiles. A soft, weary sigh escaped him.

Peter nodded. "Aye. Captain Linton was right. Best you stay out of sight for now."

Anselm gave a faint rumble of understanding and folded his wings tight against his sides.

At street level, Captain Linton and Orville moved through the unsettled crowd. The cut of Linton's uniform and the assured calm of his voice lent a fragile order to the confusion. His clipped, upper-class accent carried over the rising anxiety as he directed wardens to begin lists and account for each street, each building, each person they could find.

Orville walked beside him with his hands clasped behind his back, pausing to speak with distressed citizens. He offered what reassurance he could, gently and without pretense.

No one understood what had happened. Some said it was a new German weapon—gas, perhaps, or some ghastly hallucinogen. Others feared that the rest of London itself had been obliterated. A few wondered if they were still in England at all. Most had not seen the city's edge for themselves; distance and darkness kept them clustered near familiar streets, clinging to what little certainty remained.

Orville tried to explain—the stone, the lab, the doorway—but the truth, spoken aloud, sounded no less fantastical than the rumours. He let the words trail off rather than risk doing harm.

He was a wiry man with a prominent moustache and thin mutton chops—the sort that had gone out of fashion years earlier but suited him nonetheless. His brown tweed jacket hung easily from his shoulders, and the Brodie helmet he carried from Dover out of habit and stubborn duty sat slightly askew on his head. He had worn it with pride in the Home Guard, and though it served little purpose here, he had brought it all the same.

At sixty-two, Orville had long carried a quiet wish to do more for the war effort. That chance had come when Captain Linton asked for his help deciphering the amber stone. He had spent long nights hunched over brittle volumes, tracing markings that matched the runes carved into its surface. He remembered the standing stones scattered across the countryside, and the old tales his grandmother had whispered—of fairy folk and doorways hidden in plain sight.

Now, as the strange wind carried the scent of grass and earth through London's streets, those tales stirred not as stories, but as truths. The stone had opened a doorway. This piece of London had stepped through. The old magics had never been fantasy at all.

The thought left him not afraid, but awed.

A knot of civilians surged toward them.

"Oi! Captain! What's happened?"

"You're the Army — do something!"

"You saw 'em too, didn't you? Dragons — bloody dragons!"

"My mum's the other side of Clapham — where's she gone?"

The questions tumbled over each other, fear cracking through the exhaustion. People pushed closer, as though proximity to Linton's uniform might steady them.

Linton raised a gloved hand. He waited until the nearest voices fell quiet.

"Please," he called, firm enough to cut through the noise without shouting.

"One thing at a time. We are assessing the situation."

A voice from the back called, "What are we meant to do?"

"For the moment," Linton said, unflinching, "stay where you are, or with those you came with. Keep together. Listen for the wardens—they will see that everyone is placed as best we can manage. No wandering about. No speculation running wild. We will inform you when there is something to report."

A woman pushed forward, her voice tight. "Those creatures—are they coming back?"

A ripple of murmuring followed.

"We have no indication they will," Linton said at once. "The anti-aircraft gun drove them off wounded. For now, the immediate danger has passed."

"Your task tonight is simple," he continued. "Go home. Stay together. Keep calm. Let the wardens do their work."

The panic did not vanish, but it softened. People exchanged weary looks. Some sagged with exhaustion. The crowd thinned slowly, breaking into smaller clusters that lingered in nearby, whispering in low, uncertain tones.

Orville exhaled. "They'll be wanting answers soon."

Linton inclined his head. "In due course. For the present, Mr. Morris, they require steadiness rather more than truth."

He looked toward the deepening night. Above the rooftops, the stars showed clear and countless.

"Besides, we have other matters presently demanding our attention."

He let the words settle a moment before turning away from the thinning crowd.

They moved on as the wardens continued their work, guiding people homeward with clipped, uncertain authority. Faces appeared briefly in shuttered windows, then vanished again. The night gathered around them. Only the small red glow of cigarettes marked where people still stood awake in the gloom.

"We'll have the wardens keep proper lists," Linton said quietly. "Who's accounted for. What supplies remain—food, fuel, medicine. Anything we cannot replace, we do not waste."

Orville swallowed. "And if there's no one but us to do the organising? Not tonight. Not tomorrow."

Linton turned toward the raw boundary where London

ended — a perfect, unnatural circle carved through street and garden alike. Pavement, stone, brick — all sliced clean, giving way to tall grass swaying in a foreign breeze.

"Then," he said softly, "it falls to us to begin."

He drew a slow breath. "More than a mile across, perhaps. Ten thousand souls, give or take. And among them—wardens, constables, railway men, nurses. People who know how to keep a city on its feet. They'll follow direction if someone provides it."

Orville swallowed. "There's no power. No food beyond what's in the shops. How long can that last?"

His voice cracked. "Ten thousand souls—and we're... we're not meant to run a city, Captain."

Linton's expression softened. "Steady on. We're not alone. We'll organise what we can, and others will step forward. Londoners always do."

Orville let out a trembling breath. "God help us," he whispered.

Linton placed a steadying hand on his shoulder. "He may have to."

A soldier approached then, rifle slung over his shoulder — young, broad-shouldered, with a shock of red hair.

"Begging your pardon, sir," Doyle said, his Irish lilt softening the words, "but we ought to think like soldiers. If we're cut off, best we hold what we've got and work outward."

Linton turned to him. "Doyle, isn't it?"

"Yes, sir. Patrick Doyle."

"Go on."

Doyle straightened. "Start with the nearest streets. Get folk organised, find the wardens, see who's fit to help. Then push out, bit by bit. We'll be more use once we've got our own patch in order."

Linton studied him for a long moment, then allowed the faintest smile. "Quite right, Corporal. Sensible thinking."

Orville gave a quiet grunt of agreement.

Doyle straightened, a touch of colour rising to his cheeks. "Thank you, sir," he said, voice steady, though he couldn't quite keep the pride from his eyes.

Linton adjusted his cap and turned to watch the wardens shepherding people beneath the last sliver of twilight. "Very good," he said. "Not much more to be done tonight. We'll begin here—at first light. For now, we should see to getting some rest." Orville nodded, rubbing his hands together for warmth. The air was cooling fast now.

"Aye," he said. "Is there a place we can settle the young ones?"

And above the darkened streets, atop the laboratory roof, Sarah and Peter watched the stars, their eyes wide with wonder.

Anselm lay flat against the tiles, wings drawn tight, his great body still. The city murmured below—shouts, questions, the confusion of a world uprooted—but up here it came only as a distant hum, softened by height and wind. He listened, unmoving as stone.

He had crossed the Channel to bring warning, wounds throbbing beneath his scales. He had risked everything to escape, to keep more dragons from coming. But now was not the time to be seen. They would not understand. They would take him for one of the monsters that had descended on the city earlier.

So he waited, letting the rooftop hide him.

Sarah looked over at him.

"It isn't fair," she whispered.

Peter nodded, his eyes on the thinning crowd below. "They don't know."

Sarah's thoughts drifted back to the barn—to the moment she had found Anselm broken in the straw. She remembered tending him in secret with Peter and Olivia, the long nights spent whispering so her mother wouldn't hear, and the strange contents of the satchel he had carried from Germany. Inside had been proof of what the Germans were doing—of a program to create dragons. Anselm had escaped it, bringing with him the object they used to forge more of his kind: an amber stone.

She looked toward Peter.

"Do you think this is where they came from?" she asked softly. "Dragons."

He didn't answer at once. His gaze drifted beyond the city's edge toward the darkened horizon.

"Orville thinks so," he said finally.

Peter went quiet again. When he spoke, his voice was low.

"I keep thinking about Olivia. If she found her way home."

Sarah turned to him. "Captain Linton said she got away," she murmured. "She was safe with my mum."

Peter nodded, though he didn't look away. "I know."

Sarah swallowed hard.

"I might never see my mum again," she whispered.

Her voice cracked. Tears welled before she could stop them. She turned away, blinking fiercely, the cool night air sharp in her throat.

For a while neither of them spoke. Below, the last voices of the crowd faded one by one, leaving only the sigh of the wind moving softly across the rooftops.

As the city settled, Captain Linton and Orville crossed the courtyard toward the laboratory building, Doyle and the other two soldiers trailing close behind, their footsteps echoing in the hollow dark. Where the great double doors had once stood, there was now only a jagged opening framed by shattered brick and twisted steel. A red dragon—nearly the length of a railway coach—had forced its way through, tearing the façade apart as though it were paper.

They stepped into the ruined lobby. Splintered timbers lay strewn across the floor, desks crushed, plaster ground to dust. When they had first stumbled through hours earlier, dazed by the impossible fact of another world, Orville had barely registered the destruction.

Now he looked again.

Chairs lay overturned. Sections of ceiling drooped low, held by sagging rebar and frayed cables. The air hung thick with dust and the acrid scent of scorched wood—a brutalised building somehow still standing.

He raised his torch. The beam caught motes in the air, glinting off scattered glass.

"Good Lord," he murmured.

They moved carefully through the wreckage toward the stairwell and the upper floors.

On the roof, Sarah and Peter waited. Anselm lay beside them, wings folded tight.

Linton's voice softened. "Time to turn in. Nothing more to be done tonight."

"What about Anselm?" Sarah asked.

Orville crouched near the dragon's head. "What can we do to make you comfortable, old chap?"

Anselm gave a slow, weary shrug.

"I'll find you something soft," Orville said. "How about that?"

Anselm inclined his head once, a low rumble of thanks deep in his chest.

Inside, the lab's upper floor held a row of dormitory rooms—army cots and thin wool blankets left for overnight staff.

"Not the Ritz," Linton said, "but it ought to do."

Sarah and Peter lay down without undressing. Exhaustion overtook fear. Linton left the door mostly shut, a thin line of torchlight cutting across the floor. The soldiers found their own cots and settled in.

For the first time since the event, the city was still.

Preview Chapter 3

The night held for only a few uneasy hours.

At first there was nothing but the whisper of wind along the eaves. Then, from somewhere on the southern edge of the city, a single shot cracked through the dark. Another followed. Then two more.

The echoes rolled unevenly through the streets, bouncing off the fronts of buildings. A heartbeat later came distant shouting—thin, urgent, frightened—and then the hollow pops of more gunfire.

At the laboratory the sound arrived as a distant rumble, like a storm just beyond the horizon.

Sarah stirred beneath the scratchy wool blanket, unsure what had woken her. She lay motionless, staring at the ceiling above her, the shadows deepening where the moonlight didn't reach. She might have drifted back to sleep had the next sound not come: a brittle, far-off snap that pricked at her nerves like a pin.

She tensed. Held her breath. Listened.

Another. Then two more.

Faint, but clear. Like firecrackers miles away.

"Peter," she whispered, loud enough to reach the next bed.

A soft rustle from the next bed. No answer.

She tried again, more urgent now. "Peter!"

This time, a small grunt. "Mmm?"

"Peter—wake up," she hissed.

She lay there, heart thudding faster now.

"Peter," she tried again, a little firmer this time.

"Mmm... what?" he said quietly from the next bed.

She pushed up on one elbow. The faint glow coming through the window outlined her face. "Are those guns?"

Another shot cracked through the night.

Peter sat up at once, swinging his legs off the bed. He rubbed his face and blinked into the dark.

"Yeah," he said quietly. He looked toward the windows, listening hard.

Sarah swallowed. "Do you think... do you think those terrible dragons are back?"

Peter didn't answer at first. He leaned forward, listening. His face was still shadowed, but the frown was clear in his voice when he finally spoke.

"No," he said slowly. "I don't think it's them."

He rose and moved silently toward the window. Another shot cracked in the distance, two quick reports following the first.

From the hallway came the sharp clatter of boots—Corporal Doyle, along with Privates Hargreaves and Stewart, the three soldiers assigned to guard the building, rushing past.

The dormitory door creaked open. Orville entered first, still tugging his jacket into place, with Captain Linton just behind him, composed even in the half-light.

Peter turned toward them. "What's happening?"

"We're going to find out," Orville said quietly, casting a

glance toward the window. "Most likely animals. Anselm will have heard the racket. He'll want to know what's afoot." He nodded toward the stairwell. "Up to the roof, will you?"

He paused, meeting Sarah's eyes. "And stay with him. Best he isn't seen."

She swung her legs out of bed, the hem of her dress tangling around her knees. "Do be careful," she said, her voice tight.

Linton gave her a reassuring nod, his tone steady. "Nothing to worry about yet. Like Orville said, probably animals."

He turned back into the corridor. "Come along, Mr. Morris."

Orville lingered a moment, offering the children one final, reassuring look before turning to follow Linton, their footsteps fading down the hall.

Sarah and Peter slipped out into the corridor. With the overhead bulbs dark, the passage was lit only by the moonlight that found its way in. Pale light pooled , throwing long shadows that made the floor shimmer like water.

Both children carried their blankets round their shoulders; neither had thought to fetch their shoes. Peter padded along in thick Boy Scout knee-socks, and Sarah in her plain cotton ankle-socks, already gathering dust from the floor.

Peter led the way, socked feet whispering softly as they climbed the narrow stair to the roof. Each step creaked beneath them, every sound magnified by the hush that followed the distant gunfire.

They pushed open the roof door. The night air hit them at once—chill, carrying the sharp scent of dew on concrete.

Anselm crouched near the roof's edge, his massive frame half-shrouded in moonlight. A pair of thin Army mattresses softened the tiles beneath him. His wings stayed drawn tight against his sides, as though making himself smaller might keep him unseen. His head tilted toward the southern horizon, ears pricked to the distant shots, yet every few moments he lifted his gaze just high enough to peer over the parapet before ducking back into shadow. His tail, coiled close to his body, twitched restlessly.

Peter stepped forward. "Anselm?"

The dragon turned slightly, one golden eye glinting in the dark. His gaze returned at once to the distant source of the sound.

Sarah picked her way over the scattered gravel and stood beside him, her hands clenched to keep them from shaking. Peter moved to the dragon's other side.

"Orville said it's likely animals," Peter told him, keeping his voice low. "But they've gone to check it out. He told us to come up here and let you know what's happening."

Anselm shifted, the great muscles along his neck bunching as he peered farther into the dark. He didn't speak, but he dipped his head—slow, deliberate—a signal of acknowledgment.

"And he said—" Peter hesitated, then squared his shoulders, trying to sound more like a soldier than a boy. "He said to stay with you."

Anselm's eye turned to them then—dark, intelligent. He studied Peter for a moment, then Sarah, his gaze lingering on her drawn face and clenched hands.

With a soft rustle of membranes, Anselm lifted one wing, then the other, sweeping them forward in a loose circle around the children. The space he made wasn't tight or smothering, only warm, a sheltered nook he offered as naturally as a parent gathering little ones close.

Sarah blinked and glanced up. The leathery edge of Anselm's wing arched above her, silhouetted against the stars. She stepped closer to his side and leaned into him.

Peter followed. The dragon's wingtip adjusted ever so slightly, curling down enough to block the wind but not the view.

They stood together like that—three figures, two small and one vast—framed in the cold wash of moonlight, staring toward the dark edge of the city where the gunfire echoed once again.

Linton and Orville emerged from the building at a brisk pace, boots crunching softly in the quiet. Even before they reached the street, they saw the shape of a crowd—fifty or more Londoners clustered in an uneasy semicircle, their faces pale in the wandering torchlight. Men still in factory coats, women in office jackets thrown over work blouses, a few in aprons or rolled-up sleeves; none had ventured far from houses and ad hoc lodgings. Curiosity about the gunfire pulled them outside, but the dark beyond held too much unknown for even the bravest to probe further.

The sweep of a torch caught the faces of the three soldiers stationed with the lab.

They had already been questioned—that much was clear. Stewart's jaw was tight from repeating the same uncertain answers. Doyle kept glancing south, as if the night might finally offer something to report. And Hargreaves, normally unflappable, looked openly relieved when he spotted Linton.

"Doyle. Hargreaves. Stewart," Linton said, his voice low but direct.

The soldiers turned as one. Stewart gave a crisp nod. "Ready, sir."

Linton returned it, then looked past them to the crowd, their faces lined with worry and half-sleep.

"Captain! You must know something—"

"Is it the Jerries? Is it fighting?"

"Sir, is the city under attack again?"

"Please— I've family the other side of Brixton Road."

The constable, poor man, had been trying to keep order before Linton arrived; now his voice was nearly lost beneath the rising questions. "Back inside, please! Give the men room—go on now—back with you—"

No one moved.

Another volley cracked somewhere to the south, sharper this time, close enough to make several flinch.

A taut, breathless silence followed.

Linton lifted a hand with quiet authority. "All right. I know it's unsettling—anyone would feel the same. We're going to look into it."

A few voices tried again:

"But is it—?"

"Do we need to take cover?"

"Are we safe here—?"

"You are as safe as can be indoors," Linton replied. "Look in on your neighbours as you go. Let us handle the rest."

Linton's words carried weight. A few backed away. The constable stepped in again, gently urging people toward doorways.

Beside him, an older Home Guard warden shook his head with weary resignation and muttered to the nearest bystander, "They don't know what it is. Could be owt. Could be nothing. Best be inside till they sort it."

Linton's eyes swept the area again, lingering on two unfa-

301

miliar soldiers.

He stepped toward them. Both men straightened automatically as he approached. "You two. Names?"

"Private O'Connell, sir," said the first, a wiry man with a young freckled face.

"Taylor, sir," said the other. He was broader in the shoulders, his voice clipped and professional.

Linton gave a short nod. "Corps?"

"Transport, sir," O'Connell replied.

"Medical," Taylor added.

"Very good," Linton said. He studied them briefly. "You can both handle yourselves?"

"Yes, sir," Taylor answered at once.

O'Connell gave a small nod. "Aye, sir."

"Right. You're with us then," Linton said.

"Yes, sir," both men replied, straightening.

Linton turned slightly. "Corporal Doyle—arm these men."

"Aye, sir."

Doyle didn't hesitate. He broke from the group at once, jogging back toward the laboratory building, torch beam bobbing across the courtyard stones. The crowd parted for him instinctively.

Linton turned back to his small formation, but O'Connell cleared his throat softly.

"Begging your pardon, sir," he said, voice low but earnest. "Do you... do you know what's happened? Where'd the rest of London go?"

The question hung in the cold night air. A few civilians nearest them fell silent, watching Linton with the brittle hope of people who desperately wanted someone to know the truth.

Linton's gaze moved from O'Connell to the anxious faces

beyond, then back to the young private. He drew a slow breath before speaking.

"We'll make sense of it in due course, Private. For the moment, our concern is the present. Let's keep our heads and see our duty done. Understood?"

"Yes, sir," O'Connell murmured.

"Good man."

Linton turned toward Orville. "Are you certain about coming, Mr. Morris?"

Orville's moustache twitched with a tight, resolute frown. He rested a hand against the small canvas bag slung at his hip.

"If there's wounded, Captain, ye'll want me there."

Linton gave a small nod—approval, respect, and worry all at once.

"All right. Anyone armed—regulars and Home Guard alike—you're with us. The rest, stay here."

Several Home Guard stepped forward, older men, some stiff in the joints, some with the unmistakable bearing of those who'd marched in France a generation earlier. A few held their Lee-Enfields with sober familiarity.

A constable raised a hand. "Sir—my partner and I were issued sidearms."

"Very good. Keep to the rear unless called forward."

A murmur rippled through the crowd behind them—fear, expectation.

Then Doyle reappeared, crossing the courtyard at a near-run, a pair of rifles cradled in his arms and two bandoliers slung over his shoulder. As he neared the group, the torchlight caught the gleam of the weapons.

SMLE Mk III rifles. The kind a British soldier could fire in his sleep.

Doyle passed the first to Taylor, who accepted it with the calm familiarity of a man who'd drilled often enough to be confident. Taylor checked the bolt, then rested the rifle at the ready.

O'Connell took the second more carefully, more stiffly, but he held it well. Doyle set a bandolier over each man's shoulder.

"Load on the Captain's word only," Doyle murmured, a soldier's quiet guidance.

"Yes, corporal," Taylor said.

O'Connell nodded too. "Right you are."

At the fringe, two Air Raid Wardens hovered uncertainly, neither trained nor eager for whatever lay beyond the torch-light.

Linton pointed to them. "You two—if there's a flare or fire, you're on it. Otherwise, keep civilians indoors and accounted for. Understood?"

They both nodded, relieved to have a task.

Linton turned back to the men who had stepped forward—regular soldiers first, set and quiet, Home Guard just behind them, older faces tight with resolve, rifles held a little too carefully or a little too well. The two constables lingered at the rear, hands near their coats, eyes alert.

"Listen carefully," Linton said. "Keep close. Keep quiet. Follow the lead of the regulars. No firing unless ordered. Understood?"

A low murmur of assent followed.

"Right, lads," he said. "We move silent."

Stewart led the way, rifle ready, his side cap pulled low over his brow.

Each step was measured, boots whispering against the stone as he scanned the shadows ahead. Behind him, the other soldiers fanned out in a staggered line, rifles held low but ready, eyes moving constantly—windows, doorways, the mouths of alleys.

Linton walked just behind them, close enough to observe and direct, but not so near as to interfere. His jaw was set, his gaze shifting from rooftops to side streets, pausing now and then to guide their course toward the distant reports.

A few paces back, the Home Guard followed—men stiff with nerves, fingers clenched on old Lee-Enfields. They moved less evenly, boots scuffing where the regulars' did not, eyes darting more often, but their grips were steady. Two constables brought up the rear. Orville walked behind them all, deliberate, watchful, a presence rather than a participant.

Then—

CRACK.

A single rifle shot rang out ahead. Close.

Every man flinched, just slightly.

"Easy, gents," Orville said quietly.

The street ahead curved gently, revealing a narrow terrace of houses. A handful of civilians lingered outside, faces pale in the dim light, curiosity battling fear. One man stood in his doorway, arms folded tight. Another hovered near a parked car, shifting his weight.

A voice called out, sharp with nerves. "Oi! You lot—what's happening? What're they shooting at?"

Linton stepped forward. "We're going to find out. Best thing you can do is get inside."

The man by the car edged closer, lowering his voice. "Sir—couple of the lads went to have a look. See what all the racket was about. They've not come back."

Linton nodded once. "Were they armed?"

305

"No, sir."

"We'll keep an eye out for them."

The man hesitated, then backed away, casting one last look down the street before slipping inside.

They moved cautiously up the darkened street. The city had fallen quiet in a way that wasn't natural. No trains, no wireless, no distant lorries, only the soft hush of boots on pavement.

Behind them, the Home Guard followed in a loose cluster, their posture stiff with nerves. They gripped their weapons tightly—some cradling them like lifelines, others holding on as if unsure what to do. The two constables came next, more practiced in their patrol than the rest, though even they walked with a kind of reverent caution, like men who'd stepped into a graveyard.

Orville kept to the rear. He moved with the care of someone who'd seen enough of war to know when to keep out of the way. His hands were empty, his eyes watchful. Every so often, he glanced behind them.

A gunshot cracked in the distance.

The column stopped at once. Linton lifted a hand, listening, and for a moment all sound seemed to draw inward. Then the faint echo came again, bouncing through the narrow lanes.

O'Connell glanced toward Doyle, then forward again, squaring his shoulders as they waited.

Without a word, Linton signaled Stewart to adjust their heading, and the group began moving once more, angling toward the source.

"Check your safeties," Linton reminded the men with him. "Mind your arcs. Don't fire unless you're sure what you're aiming at."

The houses closed in as they advanced, the street narrowing into a corridor of brick and shadow. The moon gave little help. Shadows pooled deep between doorways and cars.

Then something stirred.

It moved low across the street—quick, silent, fluid—and vanished behind a parked car. For an instant, no one breathed. Then a pair of eyes caught the light. They were faint, distant, glimmering like marbles in the dark.

Stewart's hand went up, a clenched fist in the air.

"Contact front," Stewart hissed.

Linton raised two fingers, then closed his hand slowly. "Load," he said, barely more than a breath.

Bolts slid back and forward in near silence. Brass kissed steel, muffled by careful hands. Safeties clicked on.

The regulars dropped to one knee, rifles rising, movements smooth and disciplined, like rehearsed choreography.

Behind them, the Home Guard bunched uncertainly. One man took half a step forward, whispering, "What is it?" before catching himself. A magazine slipped from nervous fingers and struck the stones once. The man froze, then eased it home more carefully. One of the constables, startled by the sudden halt, nearly walked into the man in front of him.

Linton didn't turn. "Hold," he said quietly, but with authority that cut clean through the uncertainty. "Eyes up. No noise."

Even the wind seemed to still. Every man could feel it now, that sense of being seen.

At the back, Orville realised his hands had curled into fists. He forced them open again, slowly.

The eyes ahead didn't blink. They didn't vanish. They just watched.

Then, deliberately, the thing blinked.

For a long moment, no one moved. The eyes in the dark stayed fixed, cold gleaming points in the black. Then another pair appeared farther left, low to the ground but wider apart than any dog's. A third glided behind the shell of a parked car, higher still.

Something heavy brushed the cobblestones—a low scrape, like a hand dragged across slate. From between two rows of houses, a shape unfolded out of the dark. It moved on four legs, massive shoulders rippling beneath fur that swallowed the light. The moon caught the curve of a flank, the wet gleam of a snout. It was as long as a car, taller than a man at the shoulder.

A second followed. Then a third. Their breaths came in deep, hollow gusts.

"Dear God," murmured one of the Home Guard.

"Quiet," Linton said.

Two of the beasts slipped sideways, keeping low, vanishing behind the parked cars. The others lingered in the open, pacing, testing, their yellow eyes fixed on the line of men.

"They're trying to flank," Linton said under his breath. "Doyle—right side. Stewart—cover left. Wait for my mark."

The street was deathly still. The air stank of oil, damp stone, and something ranker—the smell of fur and meat.

Then one of the beasts surged forward.

It came in a blur of black muscle, claws striking sparks from the stones. Stewart fired. The shot cracked through the night, then another. The creature shuddered, one shoulder buckling under the impact, but it did not stop. It ploughed into a lamppost and wrenched it sideways, metal screaming as it bent.

"Back! Fall back!" Linton shouted.

The men began to retreat, firing as they went, shots snapping in tight rhythm. From the left, another warg lunged, jaws closing on the bonnet of a parked car and crushing the metal like foil. Glass burst across the street.

"Into that shop! Move!"

They had barely begun to shift when the first beast came again. A great black shape leapt from behind a battered car and hit the street like falling masonry. Stewart fired twice more. The creature reeled, then closed the distance with lunatic speed, jaws forcing the space between man and rifle.

The young, unseasoned soldier nearest the point went down with a strangled sound. Hands clawed at his throat as the beast twisted him clear off his feet. He struck the cobbles hard.

He did not rise.

The dark gathered at his mouth.

"Back! Back!" Linton roared, and there was no mistaking it for anything but command.

The line broke into motion. Men fell back in fragments, calling fire as they moved, rifle reports stammering unevenly. From the flank, another warg struck, slamming into the edge of the line. A Home Guard man was lifted and thrown aside as if weight meant nothing.

He did not rise.

The street swallowed his cry, and the others did not look at him long—there was no time.

In the chaos, a second regular went down hard. Pain tore through his leg and buckled him to one knee. Blood spread bright and fast across the cloth. Orville was there at once, dragging the man behind a parked car, tearing his scarf into strips, his hands working with deliberate speed—steady hands that had known this work before and would know it again.

The beasts were not mere dogs; their weight was law unto itself. One bounded clean over a parked vehicle and slammed into the far curb, stone and glass exploding outward, and for a moment the world narrowed to grinding paws and the small, terrified screams of men beating at fur and teeth. Bullets struck hide and bone; ribs showed and vanished again as the animals drove on, slowed but not stopped.

"Go for the shop!" Linton ordered.

The men moved like a body learning to obey itself—one, two, three paces—then a curse as a boot slipped on cobbles slick with oil or blood. They ran, some firing as they went, some covering with pistols, some simply throwing themselves forward, eyes fixed on the wooden door that might keep teeth out. A warg struck low and took a man's ankle from beneath him. He went down screaming, the sound curdling courage for a heartbeat. Linton grabbed for him, but the beast's attention snapped; the captain shoved the man aside as yellow eyes narrowed and the animal turned.

They burst into the shop in a tangle—through broken glass, under the twisted frame—the last men spilling over one another's heels. Linton slammed the door and it crashed shut with a sound like an execution.

Inside, the air was wrong.

The room smelled of dust and old varnish, of stale soap and cabbage gone cold—then cordite and wet fur flooded it, sharp and animal, carried in on coats and breath. The space was dim and crowded with shelves and a counter; glass tinkled as it settled. Above the stairs something shifted, voices bunched together, a child making a small, terrified sound before being hushed.

310

"Upstairs—now!" Linton barked. "Two at the front windows. Counter—cover the street. Orville, rear."

Orville did not wait for orders. He was already moving, his instincts older than the war itself. He tore his scarf tighter and pressed where the man's leg bled, the heat shocking under his hands. He half-carried, half-dragged the wounded soldier into a shadow at the back, where others fell to with bandages and knots. He spoke without looking—slow counts, steady words—forcing breath back into order.

A woman clutched Linton's sleeve as she came off the stair, eyes wide. "We were hiding, sir. There's others—Mrs. Hargreaves, and—"

"Stay there," Linton said, quieter now, not unkind. "Keep them quiet and out of sight."

Outside, the shopfront thundered as a warg hit the door and the wood bowed. Dust sifted down. A volley cracked from the counter and a beast wrenched back with a cry, nails scrabbling for purchase. A second smashed through the plate glass and fell half inside, teeth bared. Stewart fired once. The animal spun and collapsed, its weight shaking the floor as if a barge had grounded there.

Not all of them fell. One staggered, shook itself, and slunk away a few yards, limping and bewildered, its flank slick with dark wetness.

Inside, men moved with urgent purpose. Two took the stairs under Linton's hand, rifles ready. Others crouched behind the counter, barrels out, making each shot count. Orville tied what he could, forcing men to breathe in measured counts. The injured were shifted wherever space allowed—an arm over shoulders, a jacket folded under a head.

A man behind the counter leaned back, voice tight.

311

"Captain—last magazine."

Outside, something hit the door again. The wood bowed inward, hinges screaming, dust sifting down from the frame. It would not take many more blows.

The remaining beasts circled outside, snapping at scent trails they could no longer read. One broke for the rear of the shop and was nearly at the door before Orville, with a handful of desperate shots, turned it aside.

Linton looked once toward the stair, then back to the door. There were no good orders left.

Then came the sound of running feet from the street—hurried, disciplined, familiar.

"Hold your fire!" Linton barked, raising a hand.

Voices answered out of the dark. "British! Hold fire! Coming through!"

Men came running down the street in a ragged line, spectators turned soldiers, carrying whatever they had—rifles, shotguns, an old Bren gun roped to a shoulder. They hit the beasts on the flank as Linton's men poured their last rounds into the shadows.

A sergeant among the newcomers, white-faced and breathless, pushed them wider, cutting off the street. Caught in a crossfire they had not expected, the wargs fell like boulders, one after the other, their great bodies collapsing against the curbstones.

When the last rifle fired, the street fell into a hollow, stunned quiet.

Somewhere down the road, a whistle blew—the short, rising note of a signal passed between wardens. Other voices carried faintly now, spreading outward as patrols broke into the side streets.

The smell lingered—cordite sharp in the throat, wet fur and blood heavy on the air. Inside the shop, men sagged against shelves and counters, breathing hard, hands trembling. Linton stood for a long moment, aware of the shake in his own fingers, then moved to check the fallen.

There were dead. Two of the men from the lab. One Home Guard. At least three more grievously wounded. Orville worked beside him, and for a while neither spoke. The silence was not awkward; it was necessary.

At the doorway, a young corporal called, his voice raw. "Captain—more men coming from the edge." His eyes took in the ruined street and the heavy shapes lying there like overturned carriages.

Linton stepped into the doorway. He was not a man given to loud grief; his face was tight, his mouth a line.

"See the wounded tended," he said. "Bar the door. We bury no one here if we can help it. Make a list of the dead and keep watch. Then we gather what we can and move if the orders come."

Orville wiped his hands on a rag and met Linton's eye. "There's no beast on Earth like that.."

Linton crouched, not touching it—only looking. The body was that of a great black dog, but scaled beyond anything he had known — shoulders heavy, chest deep, the pads wider than four handspans. The build was that of a hunting mammal, only larger, made to carry weight that rivalled a horse. The muzzle was long and powerful, deep through the jaw, built to seize and hold.

He rose and met Orville's gaze. For a moment neither spoke. Linton looked past him, out to the black streets.

"No," he said. "There's not."

313

About the Author